One Autu

CW00448836

Work, family life
rugby league in the 1990s

To Peter
From a Saint to a Bull
Happy 70th
Geoff Lee

Geoff Lee

London League Publications Ltd

One Autumn
Work, family life and rugby league in the 1990s

A CIP catalogue record for this book is available from the British Library.

Originally published in October 2007 by:
London League Publications Ltd, P.O. Box 65784, London NW2 9NS

This edition published in February 2014

ISBN: 978-1909885-02-8

Cover design by: Stephen McCarthy Graphic Design,
46, Clarence Road, London N15 5BB

Layout: Peter Lush

Printed and bound in Great Britain by Charlesworth Press, Wakefield

Acknowledgements

As with my first three novels, *One Autumn* is dedicated to the cast of thousands, those many individuals and characters, who it is good to know or to have known in the past or to hear talking in the pub, at the match or when travelling on the bus or train. Unfortunately I no longer hear people talking at work since I have now retired from the engineering world. Fortunately though I can still remember many good conversations and humorous situations from when I was at work. This is why whenever I am stuck for ideas I can always cast my mind back to 40 years of being a draughtsman all along the M62 corridor as well as in Wembley and London.

One Autumn is also dedicated to some of those people who contribute to internet message boards and make information about the world and its history accessible to a wider audience. It is from all these sources that I have found it relatively easy to write *One Autumn*, based as it is, on the old saying about work, "They could write a book about this place. It would be a best seller."

A few people however do deserve a special thanks, firstly those who set up and run the Saints Heritage Society, whose website I always enjoy looking at and to Niel Wood, whose history of Pilkington Recreation RLFC helped me write about things that happened over 100 years ago. Thanks to Steve McCarthy for his drawings and design of the cover; to David Williams for the Great Britain rugby league cover photo, Peter Lush and Dave Farrar at London League Publications Ltd for all their work in publishing this novel and to the staff at Charlesworth Press for their printing work on this edition.

Finally any resemblance between anyone I have ever known or worked with in the past and the characters in this book is purely coincidental.

Geoff Lee
Keighley, January 2014

About the author

Geoff Lee was born in the Lancashire glass town of St Helens in September 1939 on the first full day of the war, but it is believed that this was just a coincidence. He first worked at Prescot for BICC (British Insulated Callenders' Cables), but known locally as the Biggest Individual Collection of Comedians.

He called his first novel *Tales of a Northern Draughtsman*. It took him eight years to write, while he was still working as an electrical draughtsman for the CEGB. It then took him two years to find a publisher. It has a background of romance, rock 'n' roll and rugby league and its title was changed to *One Winter* as it is set during the terrible winter of 1962–63. It was published in 1998 and was followed by *One Spring*, set in the 1970s; *One Summer*, set in the 1980s with a background that now included redundancy; and fourth *One Autumn* set in the 1990s with a background of work, family life and rugby league.

His latest novel, *Two Seasons* is set in 2002 and 2003. By this time Geoff had retired from work, mainly because there was no suitable work around and he was still recovering from quadruple heart bypass surgery.

Much of his content continues to be based on the old saying about work that "They could write a book about this place. It would be a best seller". He still enjoys listening to people talking on the bus and train, in the pub, at the match or wherever else he goes and so frequently bases many of his story lines on what he hears from people. He also draws much of his material from what he finds on the internet and in various local reference libraries that he always enjoys visiting.

He continues to have a great interest in rugby league and the way it is changing and expanding in both this country and worldwide. He still enjoys meeting old school pals, work mates and friends and hearing what had happened to them and telling them about what happed to him since they were last in company together, sometimes over 50 years ago!

He also enjoys giving talks in libraries and once attracted an audience of nearly 40 people to Leigh Library, which so far, apart from having five novels published and selling thousands of copies, is the pinnacle of his career as an author.

Contents

Other books from London League Publications Ltd

If you enjoy One Autumn, we have plenty of other fiction titles:

One Winter by Geoff Lee – the first book about Ashurst
Two Seasons by Geoff Lee – the fifth book about Ashurst

Braver than all the rest – A mother fights for her son by Philip Howard – A story about a mother caring for her son who has Muscular Dystrophy and the importance of rugby league for him.

Rugby Football: A united game by Peter Lush
In 1895 the sport of rugby football split when the Northern Union was formed. But supposing the northern clubs had taken control of the sport. This book is the fictional memoirs of David Peterson, the secretary of the English Rugby Association from 1916 to 1940, and looks at how a united sport could have developed.

We also publish a wide range of titles about rugby league, including:

Soldiers' League – the story of Army Rugby League by Sean Fanning. Fascinating history of the development of the sport in the Army since it was recognised in 1994.

In full Bloem by Andrew Hardcastle – Biography of former Halifax player and current referee Jamie Bloem.

Big Jim by Peter Lush and Maurice Bamford – biography of former Widnes, Wales and Great Britain player Jim Mills.

All our books can be ordered from our website, www.llpshop.co.uk or via www.Amazon.co.uk or from any bookshop. Some are also for sale on E Bay. Many of our titles are also available as E-Books for Kindle readers on www.Amazon.co.uk
A full list of our titles in print is available from London League Publications Ltd, PO Box 65784, London NW2 9NS.

1. "Drop your clothes off in here"

"Benny, come over here and tell us summat funny. We could do with a good laugh to cheer us up."

It was Friday lunch time in the Eagle and Child and six members of Wilkinson's drawing office were sat in their usual spot in the bar.

Benny put his pint on their table as he pushed in between Alan and Colin, sat down and said: "Well, I don't know. I can't think of anything. It's all been a bit quiet this week on the Preston front."

He took a gulp from his glass, looked at them sat there all looking pretty miserable and went on: "I could tell you what I heard on my way home last night if that'll do."

"Aye, go on then."

"There were two old women sat behind me on the bus. I heard one say to the other: 'I'm so lonely at home now. I'm really missing him. We used to go everywhere together. We'd go for a walk every morning no matter how bad the weather was. If I went in a shop, he'd always wait outside for me. When I was watching the telly, he'd cuddle up beside me on the settee. I don't know how I am going to manage. I just don't know what I'm going to do without him.

"It was obvious what had happened to her, her husband had died or so I thought. Then the other one said: 'So when are you going to get another dog?'"

Benny was in charge of the transport department at Wilkinson's Engineering Works in Ashurst. Despite having this top job, he always joined the draughtsmen in the pub on Friday lunch time. And today his talent for making people laugh was much in demand. He wiped his lips with the back of his hand and continued: "You know that empty shop in Manor Street I told you about last week. It's opening soon. It's going to be very popular. It will be if the sign in the window is owt to go by."

They waited for his punch line.

"Roger your local butcher."

He went on to ask if anybody had seen the sign in the window of Green's Laundry in Hindley Street: "Drop your clothes off in here."

"Look lads, no matter how bad things seem, at least you've still got your jobs. Not like my next door neighbour Horace. He's an insurance broker. Well he was an insurance broker. He's not now. He's gone broke."

He emptied his glass and changed the subject: "Do you know who I saw in Dob Lane last night? It was Albert Pierrepoint or somebody who was the dead spitting image of him. He was outside Woolworths, just hanging about."

"I thought you were going to say that he was dressed to kill."

"Do you know what, Greeno? That's the first time I've seen one of you lot smile today."

"You don't have John Cartwright watching you all day."

"What's wrong with him? He's all right. He's never done me any harm. Just because he goes to the cemetery with a spade in the middle of the night, doesn't mean there's owt odd about him."

Benny was now in fine form. He waved to a woman stood at the bar waiting to be served, pointed down to his pint glass and shouted out: "Double whiskey will be all right Joan, thank you."

Then he continued: "Did you hear about that bloke from Clock Face who went to London on the train last Saturday? As he was paying for his ticket, the booking clerk said to him: 'Next train is on platform one. Change at Earlestown.'

"He says, 'why can't I have my change here?'"

"42. 42." It was the fog horn voice of Mavis, shouting out the number of the next meal to emerge from the kitchen.

"Baby's yed, chips, peas, gravy and a barm cake."

It was Benny's lunch and meant for the next five minutes, he wouldn't speak a word. In his world, food was God and after that came the Saints, all 13 of them. As soon as he had finished, he took his plate back to the bar, returned with another pint of mild and with a puzzled look on his face said:

"I don't know what's wrong with Mavis to-day. Somebody must have upset her."

"Why?"

"After she'd pulled this pint, I said to her could she put a whiskey in it. She said she could, so I said well could you fill it up to the top with beer please."

Then he continued: "I suppose you've heard the latest news. Aliens have landed in Yorkshire. Yes, it's true. It was on the wireless. There were four of them in a spaceship. They landed inside Don Valley Stadium, where Sheffield Eagles play. As soon as they stepped outside, they all dropped dead. Well there's never any atmosphere there, is there?"

2

"Do you know who I saw in Dob Lane last night?"

Then Cliff spoke. It was the first thing he had said since he had walked into the place.

"Benny, do you know that Ken Holliday is having his stag do tonight. Do you fancy coming with us? We're starting in Wigan Lane Labour Club at half seven."

"Not tonight, Cliff. The wife's gone to her mother's in Doncaster for the weekend and I've promised to show our new Swedish au pair girl how to play bagatelle."

Always happy to offer advice or help, particularly to someone who might soon need it, he went on: "You can tell Mr Holliday that his holiday is now over. A man is not complete until he is married. And when he is married, then he's finished."

Benny was a man of many talents. He had first achieved fame at the tender age of nine when playing cricket on Mount Everest, the name of what used to be the biggest slag heap in Ashurst. There he had once scored 142 runs, not in an innings but off a single ball. In those days if the ball was lost, you could keep running between the wickets until it was found. He would have scored even more if his mother had not unexpectedly appeared on the scene and shouted to him that it was time for him to do his piano practice, something that had embarrassed him enormously.

Another thing that he had been good at as a kid was building dens. On one occasion, he had built one right in the middle of a bonfire in farmer Fairclough's field. It almost cost him his life and

3

that of his two mates too, when the Pemberton Lane gang who they were at war with, had turned up and set fire to it, not knowing anybody was inside.

A few years later going home from work, he had seen flames coming out of the window of a prefab at Hyde Bank and had dashed inside to rescue an old miner who lived there on his own in a wheelchair. This had occurred during his first week as an apprentice, something which had done much to help his future career both in life generally and at work in particular.

He then started talking about the Saints' recent 17–0 victory over Wigan in the Charity Shield. This was something that had made him both happy and rich as he had put £5 on his team to win by more than 10 points. He then moved on to discuss their first league match of the 1992–1993 season, at Leeds on the following Sunday. But before much could be said about it, they heard the 1.25pm hooter, the signal that they were being summoned back to their dark satanic mill.

He finished his drink with one big gulp and quickly went to the bar as the others drank up, stood up and prepared to leave. As they walked through the factory gates, he caught up with them.

"I just felt like one for the road."

"What, Warrington Road?" laughed Alan.

As soon as they walked back in to the drawing office, their boss John Cartwright was waiting for them. It was only just turned 1.30, but knowing what he had been like all week, they were expecting to get another rollicking, this time for being late. But, much to their surprise, they didn't get one. In fact he almost smiled as he asked them all to come into his office and make themselves comfortable. It sounded ominous.

He proceeded to tell them that he was becoming very concerned about their general lack of enthusiasm and interest in their work. It was a big problem and he had felt for a while that he had to do something about it. As a result he had decided to organise a team bonding session. This was something that had been common practice at the company he had until recently worked for in the centre of London.

"Did he say team bonking?" whispered Scott, the apprentice.

Mr Cartwright mustn't have heard him as he continued to talk with enthusiasm about how useful this would be for everybody, himself included. He almost went as far as to say he hadn't led by example himself and also needed to change the way he behaved.

4

Then he went round the room asking who would be able to come into work the following morning to prepare for this event.

If he had said that they would all be paid for their attendance, they would almost certainly have agreed, but they knew that there was no chance of that happening and so a deathly hush was all that followed his request.

He nodded at Alan first, knowing that he was the oldest in the section and someone who the others might take a lead from.

"Sorry John. I've promised to take a group of lads from Hemsley to play a match at Goose Green in the morning."

He almost went on to say that it was Goose Green in Wigan and not Goose Green in the Falkland Islands, but thought better of it.

The boss then turned to Colin: "I'm finishing wiring the house to-morrow, John. It's the only time I've got left to do it before we get our new washing machine plumbed in."

It was true; and how could some one who knew little about electricity challenge an electrical draughtsman on the matter.

"What about you, Cliff?"

Having just had a couple of pints, there was always the chance that one of them would burst out laughing for they all knew exactly what Cliff was going to say: "I'm sorry John, but I'm going to a funeral tomorrow."

It was an excuse that Cliff regularly used to get out of having to do something that he didn't want to do. However the strange thing about all the funerals that Cliff said he was going to, were always on his wife's side. And they were all held miles away in her home town of Halifax in West Yorkshire.

Mr Cartwright knew that it would be pointless asking Dave, Howard or Scott, so he handed out three sheets of paper and asked them to find time over the weekend to read them. Disappointed by their total lack of interest, he closed the meeting and walked back to his office.

In the past, the position of drawing office manager or chief draughtsman had always been held by a person who had himself once been a draughtsman. Now it was held by a man who had a degree in business studies, who only knew about office budgets, time keeping, percentage job completion rates and checking where a draughtsman had been if he was away from the office for more than quarter of an hour.

"How many funerals have you been to now, Cliff?" laughed Alan as they both sat in front of their computers a few minutes later.

Turning to Scott who seemed a little surprised at the question, he went on: "I bet you didn't know that when Cliff used to work at Jarratt's, he once went to the same funeral twice."

Before Alan could tell him about it, they were interrupted by the arrival of the new works manager, Mr Johnson. Cecil Johnson had not been in the position very long and was still a bit of an unknown quantity.

He spent over half an hour with Mr Cartwright and as soon as he had gone, their boss made a couple of telephone calls and then asked Alan to come into his office. For the last month, Alan had been working on a contract to install around £50,000 worth of electrical switchgear into a power station in Portugal. After working all week to the drawings that Mr Cartwright had given him, he had been informed that very morning that they were incorrect and he would have to start again. But, despite that, Mr Cartwright had shown how little he understood about the job, when he had said: "I hope you are still going to get this job finished on time, Alan. You've been on it long enough already. I need it finished before I go on my holidays because I want you to start on the changes in the meter room at Thorpe Marsh Power Station before I leave."

The reason for Mr Johnson's visit then became clear, because Mr Cartwright went on to say: "Mr Johnson wants you to go to Portugal next week and get everything on this job sorted out. It has to be completed by the end of September. No ifs and buts about it. There is a big penalty clause if we are even one day late in getting it all up and running."

Then reverting back to his old self and virtually having to force his words out, he continued: "I'll get your plane tickets and your hotel accommodation organised. You'll have to fly out on Tuesday and I hope you will only need to be there two days at the most."

This was just what Alan wanted to hear. It was what he had suggested when he had first seen how complicated the job was. But Mr Cartwright did not like any of the draughtsmen being out of his sight. To have someone like Greenall being away for three or four days, and abroad too, was just not on.

How could anybody check how accurately his time sheet would get filled out? Who knows what he would have got involved in, and misbehaving as well no doubt while representing the company. But then Mr Johnson was the boss and if he wanted Greenall to go on site, so be it.

Then a bit of bad news, well it was bad news for Mr Cartwright but it was good news for Alan.

"Your friend Mr Cunningham is already on site. He's been there over a week, although I haven't a clue what he is supposed to be doing. You'll have to get him to give you a hand if you have to do any measuring up."

Ray Cunningham worked for the outside contracts division. A very competent electrician and a grafter when at work and a highly entertaining character away from work was Ray. Their paths had crossed on many occasions, going back years to when both had lived in Chisnall Avenue and gone to the same school, although not in the same year as Ray was three years younger than Alan.

Ray was a keen rugby league man. He had played for Liverpool City for a season and once scored a try at Wilderspool, this being what he reckoned was the pinnacle of his career. Shortly after finishing playing, he had been moved from the copper refinery to the OCD. He now worked on installing equipment across the country and frequently travelled abroad as well. As a result he would not been seen in Ashurst sometimes for weeks, even months on end. Then he would return with a load of prints and spend a great deal of time showing the draughtsmen just how useless they were. For the last month he had been working in the Portuguese capital, Lisbon, but had recently moved a couple of hundred miles north to the city of Porto.

As soon as Alan walked into the house a couple of hours later, his wife Thelma told him that Saturday's match had been cancelled because most of the Goose Green team had gone down with a stomach virus. As they ate their tea, he told her about things that had happened at work that day, how well Benny had entertained them in the pub at lunch time, Cartwright's proposed team bonding session and his first trip abroad for nearly a year.

Before they had started a family, she also worked at Wilkinson's and although many of the people that she knew then had left, she was still interested to hear about the old place. She then went on to say that she had seen four former workmates in town that morning. That was nothing unusual for her because she was always bumping into somebody that she knew.

This time it had been Big Joan, who was once in charge of the print room, with two of her grandchildren in the Post Office, on the fish counter in ASDA she had talked with Ray Smith who told her that his eldest lad was having trials with Widnes and his daughter had joined the Royal Navy. Working on the checkout was the former tracer Anne from Sutton Manor and in the car park she had spent 10 minutes listening to the one time chargehand in the copper rolling mill, Mick Ellison, an executive member of the 'been-everywhere, done-everything, met-everybody' brigade.

"He's working in Warrington and a bit out of touch. He didn't know that Tony had been in hospital or that Charlie had won that bowling competition at Bolton or even that Mick had died. He did tell me though that there was an article in last Saturday's *Guardian* about Les Earnshaw."

After they had eaten, she explained how everything on the table had to be taken into the kitchen and have hot soapy water applied to them and left to dry before being wiped with a tea towel and put in the pantry. She went on to tell him that she needed the car to go to Nook End to see her friend Beryl and wouldn't be back before 10pm at the earliest.

After doing what she had told him, Alan decided to spend the evening watching television. As he sat there drinking a bottle of German beer, his mind went back a few years to when Charlie Eccleston had still been working with them. The office comedian, Saints' number one fan, a legend in his own head and his mother's old house in Emily Street and a big mate of Alex Murphy was Charlie. Unfortunately, they hadn't seen each other for ages even though he lived little more than four miles away. He decided to go up to Thatto Heath to see him after he returned from his trip to Portugal. He ought to have visited him before, but he just hadn't had the time.

Then he thought about Les Earnshaw. Les had packed in being a draughtsman when his first novel *The Draughtsman's Tale* had been published. A year later he had written a sequel called *The Actress goes to Heaven* in which the French actress Bridget Bardot is found having a night out in Wigan with the scaffolder Albert Entwhistle from Abram. Two great books they were and all based on the time Les had worked on the drawing board at a number of firms in Ashurst and Warrington. Then he opened up another bottle of beer and was soon fast asleep. Well, it had been a long week, although much of it had been wasted due to the total inefficiency of their useless boss.

He went down to Ashurst Library on Saturday morning to read the previous week's *Guardian*. The general theme of the article in the book review section was about the way that many new writers were linking their employment with their writing, but none of those featured, had earned their money in anything like the way Les had once done. One was a vet with a double-barrelled name from Bournemouth, a second had been a banker in the City of London who had retired to run a hotel in Margate, a third was still a dentist with premises in West Hampstead and the fourth was a retired vicar who now worked in an Oxfam shop in Barnstaple on the north Devon coast and was an active member of his local branch of Age Concern.

The piece about Les seemed to have been tacked on at the end, almost as if to show there was at least one person from north of Watford who could write about the topic under review.

On Sunday morning, with his brother Paul, Alan travelled over the Pennines to Headingley, the home of the Leeds rugby league team. Although they set off in good time, they soon got held up by all the usual lane closures and roadworks on the M62. As a result they only managed to get through the turnstiles just as the home team were kicking off. No programme to get hold of, not a good spot to stand in and not a particularly warm day for anyone wearing little more than a thin tee shirt. In the end it didn't matter as the Saints stormed to a 27–14 victory in front of more than 15,000 spectators.

As he walked through reception on Monday morning, he was given his flight tickets and details of his hotel accommodation by Alice, who asked him if he would mind bringing back some Portuguese postcards and stamps for her young nephew. As he entered the drawing office, he was informed by a happy smiling Cliff that the team bonding session had been cancelled. On the Saturday morning the ever efficient Mr Cartwright had remembered that a month earlier he had arranged to go to London for a meeting, which he had completely forgotten about.

As a result, in the absence of their boss, the day was both relaxing and enjoyable. Various people called in to inform Alan of their knowledge of Portugal, Portuguese culture, Portuguese food and Portuguese women. The wireman Harold Potter, who always went home for his dinner, returned with a holiday brochure and a

Portuguese phrase book. It was clear that Porto had many attractions including a fine beach, many night clubs, museums, statues and a very hospitable population.

When Shaun, who had been at Fidlers Ferry power station on the previous Friday, discovered where Alan was going, he explained how hospitable he had found the locals to be when he had been sent there by a firm he had once worked for in Leeds. He talked of his experiences with two hotel chambermaids at a place called Familicao, about 20 miles inland from Porto. It wasn't the first time he had told this story and it probably wouldn't be the last either.

The only down side to it all was that while he was away, Alan would miss the second League game of the season, at home to Wakefield Trinity on the Sunday and at Barrow the following week in the first round of the Lancashire Cup.

But surely that was a price worth paying for what could be up to a fortnight away with hopefully everything paid for by the firm. An hour later Ray phoned up, asking him to bring six 240 volt DZZ relays with him and a few back copies of the *Ashurst Star.*

It was the first time Alan had spoken to Ray for ages, but by the sound of his voice Alan knew that they were both in for a good time, one that would with absolute certainty involve saying many times: "Two beers please."

But since they would be in Portugal it would probably be: "Two beers and two brandies, please."

From Harold Potter's phrase book, Alan worked out that that would translate into something like: "Queria dois cerveja preta e dois velha por favor."

And if Portuguese spoken by an Englishman with an Ashurst accent was unintelligible to a waiter who spoke Portuguese with a Porto accent, then there was always:

"Fala Ingles?"

At the end of the night if they could still remember it by that time: "Adeus."

And if any local people that they had been with, had been of a friendly disposition: "Adeus amigo" or "Adeus amigos" if there had been more than one of them.

And as he looked forward to this trip, he made a mental note to take a bottle of aspirins with him.

2. The man from Thatto Heath

Ray met Alan at the airport where they had a couple of drinks. They took a taxi to their hotel, took his luggage up to his room and had a couple of drinks in the bar and then went to have a meal and a few more drinks in the city centre. They arrived back at the hotel around midnight, with Alan refusing Ray's suggestion to have just one more drink.

The following morning Ray introduced Alan to Pedro Delgado, the station electrical engineer, the man who would make his visit both enjoyable and productive. In some ways, as Alan was soon to discover, Pedro was a bit like Ray, one of those people who once you had met them, you would never forget them and would forever be pleased you had known them.

When he was a small boy, Pedro's parents had left Portugal to escape from the repressive regime of the dictator Salazar and had gone to live in Paris where his father had worked as a printer. During those heady days of 1968, Pedro had met and subsequently married Gillian, an arts student from Gateshead who was studying at the Sorbonne. The first few years of their marriage were spent in the North East, when Pedro worked as an electrician at the Swan Hunter shipyard at Wallsend. But redundancies right across Tyneside in the 1980s had led to them returning to Portugal, though with fond memories of their time in England. If you ignored the fact that he sounded just like Jimmy Nail whenever he opened his mouth, it could be said that Pedro spoke very good English.

At their first meeting, Pedro looked at the prints that Alan had brought with him, took them outside, put them carefully in a large metal container and set fire to them. Then he took his visitor into the station drawing office, showed him where all the latest information was and introduced him to the three draughtsmen who worked there. By now it was time to enter the station canteen, a scruffy place that served exquisite food, including wine, beer and locally produced brandy.

They spent the afternoon walking round the station, looking in the meter room, the control room, the coal handling plant and the boiler house. They finished by standing on level three looking down on four large AEI generators that had been built at Trafford Park by a firm that had once been known as Metropolitan Vickers.

11

By Friday morning all that Alan had to do had been done. He now had all the information to complete the necessary drawings for the job. He assumed that would mean that he would have to fly home on the following day. Then Pedro came up with his request for Alan to stay for another week. This would make it easy for him to make a record of all the wiring alterations that Ray was about to make in the control room. Otherwise, Alan would finish up back in Ashurst and forever having to ring up. It suited Ray too because he didn't like having to mark up prints, so with Alan on site, he wouldn't have to and the job would get done much quicker.

It took Alan five minutes and one phone call to agree. Then Pedro came up with his second request. It was for Alan and Ray to spend the following day with Pedro, his wife and other members of his family. He lived 10 miles up the coast at a place called Povoa de Varzim. Pedro fed them on a local delicacy, veal's tripe with sausage and butter washed down with copious amounts of brandy and beer. They still hadn't fully recovered by the time they were back at work on Monday morning and by the time Alan checked in at the airport a week later, he was sure he must have put on a stone in weight.

On his return, the first person he saw in the car park was Cliff who told him that while he had been away, the Saints had beaten Wakefield Trinity in the league and Barrow in the Cup and had drawn Widnes at home in the second round. He went on to tell him some even better news. Cartwright was no longer in charge. Mr Johnson had moved him to project manage a scheme to electrify a railway line in the Indian state of Mysore. He had left on the previous Friday, looking pretty pleased with himself. But he wasn't very happy by the end of the next week when he discovered that he would be spending the next six months based in Kirkby, on the outskirts of Liverpool, organising the material schedules and the timetable for delivery of all the equipment. His replacement would be Mr Taylor from technical sales, who had a reputation of under-achievement and mild-mannered bluster and was currently working in the company's London office.

The first part of the morning was spent with Alan talking about what he had done in Portugal. He then went to tell Mr Johnson a slightly different account of how he had spent his time, one which the boss was clearly pleased to hear. As a result of Alan's visit, another large order had now been placed, one which would require him to make a second visit later in the year.

In the middle of the afternoon, by which time Porto seemed a long time ago, a mechanical draughtsman, Pete Mulholland burst into the office with some great news: "You won't believe this. Do you know who I've just seen in reception? Charlie Eccleston. Whatever is he doing here?"

An hour later they were to find out as the man from Thatto Heath came into their office to tell them that Mr Johnson had just asked him to come back. It was to work on a contract that was almost identical to one that he had worked on just before he had retired. How long it would be for was unclear, but it would certainly be for long enough to bring a little joy to their sad pathetic lives.

He then talked about what he had been doing since he had retired. It had included bowling twice a week, working on his allotment, watching the Saints, visiting Thatto Heath Library and doing the odd bit of housework whenever he failed to get out of the house quick enough. Then he glanced at his watch, informed them that he was meeting a blonde from Rainhill in the Springfield and walked out. Cartwright out, Eccleston in. What could be better; and another trip to Portugal on the cards for Alan as well. Good times ahead it would seem.

The news of Charlie's return was welcomed by everybody who had ever known him. Not for nothing was he known as the office comedian and had been so since 1951 when he had first joined the company, one that over the years had had more than its fair share of characters on the shop floor, in the offices and also among the managers and directors. This was in part due to the fact that it had always been the biggest firm in Ashurst ever since work had first started there in 1808. In 1932 one of the most powerful members of the Wilkinson family, Joshua Albert George Wilkinson DSO had taken control. He had ruled with an iron rod until he had died from a heart attack in 1962. After his death, his eldest son Basil, aided by his two daft brothers – Norman the 'do-gooder' and Cyril the 'meddler' – had taken over and from that point on, things had slowly begun to go downhill.

In 1963, Basil had sold the company in rather mysterious circumstances to the Miller Engineering Company, who had their headquarters in Cleveland, Ohio. In the late 1970s, it had been sold again, this time to a company with an address in the Isle of

Man, whose owner was later found to be Basil Wilkinson. In the early 1980s, this period in the company's history came to a sudden end, when he was found dead in a house in Brighton.

Soon after, Wilkinson's had been divided into two separate companies, with one half becoming Wilco-Allisons Products Ltd and the other half, Wilkinson's PLC (1982). By 1988, much of the firm in its new state had moved into terminal decline. Within the year, Wilco-Allisons had vanished completely and the land on which it had stood, now housed a KwikFit, an ASDA supermarket, a Dixon's and a JJB sports outlet.

One reason for the decline in the company's fortunes was linked to the economic and industrial policies of the government. One of the main customers had for years been the National Coal Board, but not any more, as the government proceeded to close down most of the country's coal mining industry. Many other local firms were also beginning a slow process of decline as well. Wallworks, Mathers Foundry, Jarratt's and Hiltons all began to shed labour, contract work out and become a shadow of their former selves. Some companies had even closed down including Dawson's Chocolate Works and Jackson's Brass Castings. As a result what had once been a town with a very work centred culture and life style began to change. Likewise the nearby towns of Leigh, St Helens, Warrington, Widnes and Wigan suffered similarly as unemployment and factory closures began to rise right across the whole of the north of England.

How Wilkinson's had managed to survive in the way it did was always a bit of a mystery. But clearly the writing was on the wall, as the number of draughtsmen, planners, estimators, production engineers, planners, jig and tool men, technical publicity people and print room staff declined in number. It did not happen overnight though. It happened in different stages over a period of three or four years.

Firstly there was the policy of not replacing those who retired, and allowing others to retire early. At the other end of the age scale, the annual intake of apprentices was reduced by half. This was followed by the first wave of redundancies. Much of this had been handled badly. On more than one occasion, a person would leave with his redundancy cheque in his pocket and within weeks, he would come back on contract. This might even be on higher money than he had been on when he was on the staff and with less responsibility. Needless to say this caused conflict between those who had once been good work mates.

More and more decisions were taken by people who had little experience in the engineering world but who were well qualified in business studies. Then when their incompetence could no longer be hidden, business consultants on high salaries were brought in, often with bonus payments added, to produce systems that could save money, this now being more important than producing finished products on the shop floor.

Soon personal contracts were introduced. Everybody at junior management level and above would be paid according to the performance criteria laid down in his or her contract. Attempts to have issues raised collectively by the union were no longer permitted. All overtime payments were stopped, flexibility with holiday arrangements disappeared and everything associated with various production processes became dominated by accountants.

"How much money is in the budget for it?" was a regular question at office meetings which now took up more and more of the working day. Jobs that had to be finished by a certain day sometimes had to wait until the beginning of the next month when there was 'notional' money available to pay for it.

For those who could put up with it, this situation had a funny side to it. No more so than when a team of technical methodology consultants from Manchester appeared on the scene. After a week's intensive scrutiny, they produced a report that basically concluded that the company only had a future if all the existing management team was removed. Not surprisingly those most directly affected by this report unanimously agreed that it was 'not fit for purpose', another new phrase that had entered the company's vocabulary.

Around the time of that terrible winter of 1962–63, Wilkinson's had employed in excess of 100 draughtsmen, each with his own drawing board, which he would stand behind all day long. Now the number was down to less than 20, for with the aid of computer-aided design, drawing time had been greatly reduced. It was a whole different world at work, a world in which thousands of draughtsmen had disappeared from the face of the earth.

Well not entirely so. Alan Ashcroft was now pushing trolleys on ASDA car park, Dave Harper had emigrated to Australia and John Mellor was driving the number 17 bus every hour from the new bus station to Hemsley Parish Church, which was now a

15

warehouse called Ali Baba's Flying Carpets. This was owned by a man, whose parents came from Bombay, and who spoke English as though he came from Wolverhampton. This was untrue because he had been brought up in West Bromwich, but to most folk in Ashurst, all people from around there sounded the same.

So what had all this to do with the return of Charlie Eccleston, the man who claimed to have discovered the Universal Law of Coincidence? It was as a result of another cost cutting exercise by the management, the failure to train a future generation of technical staff who could take over when the older ones left.

The firm had won an order to refurbish a power station in China. Just before he had retired, Charlie had worked on very similar jobs, and it was to tap his brains that he had been asked to return. It was also because there was nobody else available to do the work as numbers in the drawing office were now down to the bare minimum.

On the following Monday, as soon as Charlie walked into the office, he demonstrated that he was still as daft as ever. He took off his coat and then started walking round the office, looking in all the drawers, behind the filing cabinet and under the reference tables.

"Where is it? What have you done with it? Where have you hidden it?"

"What?"

"My drawing board."

"Charlie, we don't use drawing boards any more. It's all on computer now. Didn't Johnson tell you? We've entered the space age. Your old board went on a bonfire about three months ago."

"Hell, fire and damnation. I'd written the telephone number of that rich widow from Eccleston on it. So am I going to be working on one of these computers? Which one?"

Alan pointed to one in the corner and dragged over a chair for him to use. Charlie stroked the top of it; took a tissue out of his pocket and wiped the screen, then sat down and followed his arms.

"What are you waiting for? It won't switch itself on."

"So what button do you press, Einstein?"

Alan leaned forward and pressed the start button and a whole string of numbers briefly appeared on the screen.

"Bloody hell. How did you do that? You must have been on a course for it."

16

The screen was now still, indicating that it was waiting for a password.

"You'll need a password to get in."

"Where do I get one of those from?"

"You pick it. Choose whatever you want, as long as it has more than five letters and less than 10."

"Can I use my mother's maiden name?"

"Yes, what is it?"

"Critchley."

"Nine letters, that's all right, so tell it."

At this point Charlie looked closely at the screen and in a loud voice said: "Critchley."

"Charlie, you are either taking the piss or you don't know how to use this computer. Are you in any way, shape or form familiar with the functions 'pan', 'zoom' and 'stretch'? Do you know the difference between 'save' and 'save as'?"

"Pan is what you fry food in, zoom is what Batman does, stretch is when you have just got out of bed and you are still tired, like I am with this bloody stupid machine."

"Anyway I won't be using it. They've got a young lass from Ashurst Technical College on work experience coming to do all that for me."

"It will be a bloody experience for her working for you. I hope she's thick skinned."

What Charlie had just said was true. What he had to do was mark up a set of prints and Samantha would put it all onto CAD.

As Charlie began to put things on to his reference table and in to the drawers, Alan asked him if he was back on the staff.

"No, I'm employed by a technical recruitment agency from Manchester. They are called Partial Technology."

Alan knew that the name of the company was Total Technology, but Charlie's subtle misuse of their name was typical of him.

"The other thing that's going to greatly affect you Charlie is that nobody is allowed to smoke in the office now."

Everybody who knew Charlie knew how many he used to smoke every day. And everybody who worked near to him had probably suffered with what was now known as passive smoking.

"That's not a problem now. I gave up after I had been in hospital. I wish I'd never started. The amount of money I've wasted on them, I could have paid my mortgage off years ago. Mind you we all smoked in them days, more fool us."

"One final thing as well."

It was Alan again.

"I am now the boss and I set the rules, whether you like it or not. There is to be no talking in here. If you want to leave the room you have to ask my permission and if I find out that you are in a trade union, then you'll be sent to Australia."

Things had clearly got off to a good start and when Samantha walked in five minutes later, looking distinctively like the American actress Jayne Mansfield, they went up another notch or two, particularly when she started by putting lipstick on and wafting some sweet smelling perfume around her.

At the age of 52, Alan was now the oldest member in the electrical section of the drawing office. He had worked for the company for over 35 years and could look back over his time at Wilkinson's with great pleasure. He had worked on jobs that had required him to go out to power stations and other industrial locations all over Britain. He had also gone abroad on four occasions, Hungary to a cotton mill at Gyelo Marnch, Greece to a small steel works an hour's drive north of Athens, to a print works at Bruges in Belgium and to another cotton mill near Mostar where he had had his photograph taken on the bridge over the River Neretva in Bosnia-Herzegovina.

Being the oldest, he was the unofficial head of the section, not that that was reflected in his pay packet. But by not being part of the management team that meant that he still got paid for overtime, which was particularly good when working on site.

A week after Charlie had settled in he came up against a problem with some of the electrical schematic diagrams that had been sent from China. They had all been marked up in red and green, but unfortunately who ever had done it, had done it all in Chinese!

Charlie's suggestion to deal with this problem was for him to go and consult old Mr Lee who owned a Chinese take away in Thatto Heath and who would surely with the help of his children, be able to translate it into English. Alan agreed it was worth a try, but Mr Johnson was not at all impressed with this very unprofessional approach to the problem and arranged for Charlie to spend a day with a member of the Chinese studies department at Manchester University.

As Charlie began to settle into the old routine, it soon became clear to all those who knew him that he was not in good health. He might have recently given up smoking but years of inhaling vegetable matter in enclosed environments had left its mark on him and he knew it. Despite this, he was still the life and soul of any group he was in and nowhere was he happier than when telling others about things he had seen, done or heard about in the dim and distant past or on the previous night in the Springfield, the Vine Tavern or the York in Thatto Heath.

Whenever he talked about his experiences in life, depending on who was in his audience, he would inevitably throw in some highly exaggerated or slightly untrue stories, particularly if someone like the gullible young apprentice Scott was listening.

"I've started growing all my own food." he said one day as he put an apple on his table and then started eating the sandwich he had brought with him for his lunch.

"I never thought I'd say this but I'm really getting into this organic gardening malarkey now."

He looked at young Scott, nodded to him and went on: "Mind you, it's only on my allotment where I do it. If I did my organic gardening in my own back garden, the neighbours would start complaining about all the noise I make with it. They are a right miserable lot, well some of them."

Scott looked puzzled as Charlie carried on: "I've rigged up this gramophone system and fixed it to the side of the hut where I keep all my tools. As soon as I get down there, I switch it on and play organ music to the spuds all day long. If you like, Scott, I'll bring you a bag of my Reginal Dixon potatoes. You can take them home for your mum. They taste lovely. They're great for chips."

Same old Charlie. And a good job too. They don't make them like him anymore.

3. Graham black pudding

Wednesday 30 September 1992 was a strange day, for it seemed that the gods did not want any outsiders to enter the town. The first hint of trouble occurred under the bridge at St Helens Junction where an accident involving a cyclist and a old age pensioner led to the road being closed, causing a long detour for anyone travelling to Ashurst from Sutton.

What made things worse was that on Bold Lane the Water Board were digging a hole in the road 'assisted' by a pair of stop-go lamps that were not functioning in tandem. On the south side of the town, anyone travelling in from Warrington was held up by a van that had broken down at the junction between Dowson Lane and Cullen Road. For people coming in from Wigan or Leigh, they encountered MANWEB digging a hole in Ashton Lane. Even those who lived in Ashurst and who normally walked to work did not find it that easy. A fire in Hall's shop in Egypt Street needed the attention of two fire engines and the closure of Wagon Lane.

Another person with trouble on the road was a farmer from Garswood delivering potatoes to all the factories on Warrington Road. He finally arrived at Wilkinson's around midday with the result that every lunch served had large portions of carrots, cabbage and peas to compensate for the absence of any chips.

The next unexpected event occurred when an electrician doing routine maintenance in the boiler room plunged all Wilkinson's offices into darkness. The same afternoon, the works cat Rufus disappeared. He had been there for as long as anybody could remember, but this was the day no one saw him. There were many places he could have gone or got trapped in but wherever he did that, would probably be his final resting place.

Two other unusual events also occurred that day. Felicity, who had worked in pensions for years, announced that she was leaving in order to travel round the world. That was totally out of character for her, she used to think that going to Liverpool was a threat to life and limb. What was even more out of character for her was when it was learned that she was going with a 25-year-old bus driver from Widnes.

Equally surprising was the news that the raggy-arsed labourer from the machine shop, Graham Black had joined the Jehovah's Witnesses. From now on he became known as Graham Black

Pudding although always out of hearing as no one knew with certainty if his conversion was going to be permanent.

During the afternoon, most people wondered how long it would take them to get home. Those who were most worried were those who were planning to go to the match. A big crowd was expected as both the Saints and the Chemics had got off to a good start to the season and there was always good rivalry between the two teams and their supporters. But soon the news filtered through that the coast was clear for everybody heading out of the town.

Today was Thelma's birthday, which was to be celebrated by a meal followed by some top class entertainment. The meal would be eaten in the restaurant at Knowsley Road and the entertainment would be the expected annihilation of the men in black and white hooped shirts. She did not know exactly what Alan had planned, but she expected it as that was how they had celebrated her last birthday in similar circumstances, at the same romantic location.

Charlie was also relieved to know that he would be in his usual place well before kick off. It was not often that he ever missed a game home or away. He came from a long line of Saints fans. His father had first gone to Knowsley Road to watch the 1920 Christmas derby game against Wigan on the day that Lord Derby had opened the new club house. His grandfather had grown up in Harris Street and as a boy used to watch the team when they occasionally played or trained at Boundary Road.

On his mother's side, Grandpa Roach was a keen rugby league man, but only watched the Saints twice a year. That was because he worked at Pilkington's and followed St Helens Recs who played at the bottom of City Road at Windle City. Another interesting thing about Charlie was that a distance relative was James Warren, who had been the delegate from the Warrington club at that historic meeting at The George in 1895.

The game was a closely fought affair with the Saints finally winning 10–8. Alan and Thelma stood where they had stood in 1963 when she had watched her first match and when she picked out her favourite player. Despite the presence on the field that night of Tom van Vollenhoven, Alex Murphy, Austin Rhodes and Dick Huddart, it had been the other Saints' half-back Wilf Smith who had caught her eye.

As they were walking out of the ground at the end, jostled by everybody else going home or to the pub, Alan pointed out a man standing about 10 yards away. It was Wilf Smith! Now he was a spectator, and someone that many older Saints fans would remember and respect for how well he had served the club.

The second blast from the past occurred in Doulton Street a few minutes later. As they approached their car, they were hailed by a man on the opposite side of the street, stood in the doorway of a house.

"Nah then Greeno. Have you not been put down yet?"

It was Eric Yates, the one whose trickery on Christmas Eve in 1962 had led to Alan meeting Thelma outside the Co-op Hall. Since then Eric had spent much of his life working at Rolls Royce in Coventry. But he had recently come back to Ashurst, and was living with his sister in Alder Hey Road, while looking for a place to buy in the town which he now wished he had never left.

On their way home they drove through St Helens, past Peasley Cross Hospital, along Robins Lane and under the bridge at the Junction, where there was still evidence of the incident earlier that morning. As they approached the Glass Blowers Arms, Thelma suggested they called in for a drink. But much to their surprise it was closed and looked as though it was for sale. It was the place where they had gone after that Oldham match nearly 30 years ago. But now it had changed, like many other parts of the area, some things for the good, some things for the bad and some things beyond all recognition.

That was also true of much of Ashurst and particularly the area around Warrington Road, Aspinall Street, Mersey Street and Atherton Lane where many of the town's biggest factories had once stood. Wilkinson's was still there of course, but nothing like what it had been in its prime.

That was also true of most of the other factories in the town. What was once Dawson's Chocolate Works was now a health centre and a chemist's. Jackson's Brass Castings was now a block of flats and a mining heritage museum and the land on which Pearson Engineering once stood now housed a car showroom, a carpet warehouse and a Curry's.

It was the same in all the surrounding towns. Slum clearances had robbed them of much of their character and their characters. However, one thing in these towns that hadn't changed was their rugby grounds. Hilton Park, Central Park, Naughton Park,

22

Wilderspool and Knowsley Road all remained pretty much like what they had been like during the 1960s and in some cases even before. Some people said that they should be pulled down and new all-seater stadia built in their place. To that comment, others would ask the question: 'Where would the money come from?' And those who had stood in the same spot for years would ask why or say 'over my dead body'.

Some of those who like to philosophise about the meaning of life would say that your sport helps give you your identity. It helps you relate with others who are just like you, people from the same town, people who work for a living just like you do, people who talk like you do and behave like you do. Maybe it was just a Lancashire thing. Maybe it was now part of a previous life style being overtaken in a rapidly changing world but whatever it was, sport in Ashurst and particularly in the shape of the team its residents followed was important, nay essential for many people.

The following day things started off very quietly, except for Cliff who was busily collecting information to take to Venezuela where the scheme he was working on to install a high voltage transformer in an iron foundry looked like going horribly wrong. The peace was broken around 10.30 by the arrival of Ray Sephton, a commissioning engineer accompanied by a visitor.

Ray introduced him to Alan and told him he was from a firm based in west London. But as soon as John Kenilworth opened his mouth it was obvious that he was a Geordie. When the technical reasons for his visit had been dealt with, their visitor pointed to a photograph on the wall behind Alan's computer and said: "Mal Meninga, Sean Day and one of the Beardmore twins."

"How did you know that?" asked Alan.

"You know the old saying 'Don't judge a book by its covers', well here's another one for you: 'Never judge a man by his accent'."

They waited for him to say more.

"I lived in Newcastle until I was 22 and then got a job in Halifax. A few weeks after I had been there one of the lads I had got pally with took me to Thrum Hall. I suppose you could say I have been hooked on rugby league ever since."

"And do you still follow Halifax?"

"Not since I moved to London. I watch the Crusaders now and again but it's not like going to Thrum Hall. Well I don't think anywhere is as good as that place."

23

"I suppose you were at Wembley in 1987 when they beat us."

"I certainly was."

"I don't remember seeing you" laughed Alan.

"You see when I was living in the North East, rugby meant rugby union and I couldn't stand it. But the thing I love about league is the spekkies almost as much as the players."

Aware that he had an audience to spin some yarns to about his time as a spectator, he carried on: "I remember one of the first games I ever saw at Thrum Hall. They were playing Whitehaven and their prop was having an absolute stinker. There was an old woman stood right near us, just behind the dug out. Anyway after half an hour or so, this lad comes over, to get a bandage put over a cut on his arm. While he's stood there, looking at the crowd, this old woman shouts at him: "Number eight. Call yourself a prop. You're not good enough to prop clothes in our back yard."

"Well this must have inspired the lad. He blew her a kiss, went back on the field, scored a try and then collapsed in agony about five minutes later and got carried off on a stretcher. As he went down the tunnel he shouted out to her: "Go home and wash your knickers, you Yorkshire pudding."

As they laughed he went on to talk about an incident at the old Crown Flatts ground: "Dewsbury were always good for a laugh as well. I was there one time when we were playing them in the Yorkshire Cup. A bloke stood behind us must have been a right long suffering local and was obviously getting right pissed off with them. Anyway just before half-time, he shouts out to everybody's amusement: 'Dewsbury, tha's no good. I'm not coming here again to watch thee.' Anyway when they came out after half-time, they had changed completely. Within minutes they were moving the ball around with great skill and after a passing movement involving all the team, they scored under the sticks. This bloke shouts out after all the cheering had died down: 'Well I might come back. But only for t' second half'."

He was obviously enjoying himself now as he carried on about another visit he had made to the Heavy Woollen district: "I once went to watch Dewsbury play Keighley. My next door neighbour was playing for 'em. It was an awful game. The only bit of entertainment came from the St Johns Ambulance men."

"Just before kick off, an old St Johns ambulance man comes out accompanied by a young lad, both of them dressed immaculately. They had a brand new stretcher with wheels on it.

24

After half an hour, one of the Dewsbury players got knocked out and the referee waved to them to come on with this stretcher.

"It was very muddy that day but that didn't put the young lad off. He wanted to make a big impression on his debut. He was at the front pulling this stretcher to the middle of the field whereas the old guy was just walking, holding onto it at the back. They mustn't have tightened the nuts on it because slowly the front end got detached from the back end and then it collapsed in two and the pair of them finished up falling in the mud. Everybody in the crowd burst out laughing, then the referee did and the players and finally the bloke who was due to get carted off decided it was too dangerous so he got up and walked off."

As soon as he finished, Cliff told a story about a game he had watched his younger brother play in: "I once went to Thrum Hall when our kid played for Widnes. There was mud everywhere and they had been playing about 10 or 15 minutes and must have had about 10 scrums already. Anyway Halifax dropped the ball, yet again and the ref, I think it was John Holdsworth, gave head and feed to Widnes. Bobby Goulding picks up the ball and stands there waiting for the scrum to form.

"Just as he was ready to put the ball in the tunnel, he drops it. He picks it up again, wipes it on his shirt and just as he is about to feed, the Widnes front row collapsed. Holdsworth tells them to part and reform and Goulding decides to wipe the ball on his shorts and would you believe it, he drops it again, it hits his boot and slithers away about 10 yards. So he walks over, picks it up and walks back to the mouth of the scrum and then the Fax forwards wheeled round and the two blindside props start scrapping.

"All this time the crowd had been silent and it must have been going on for nearly five minutes. Just as it looked as though something was going to happen, Goulding scratches the side of his face. Near where I was stood, this bloke shouts out in the loudest voice you've ever heard. It brought the house down, well it made us all laugh, including Goulding and John Holdsworth: 'Whenever you've got a moment, Goulding. All in your own good time'."

"That was really funny" said Alan. "I almost chuckled."

"Well, some things are funny when you see or hear them but not quite so funny when you tell them to folk who haven't got a shred of humour in their body."

"Some things aren't a bit funny but they are always worth telling after the event" replied Alan. "I remember when we played De La Salle Old Boys from Salford. They had some players who were apprentice priests."

"Eh lads, it's been very nice to meet you all but if you are going to start discussing religion I'm off back to London."

And with that he shook hands with them all and left, having made a very good impression on his Lancashire audience.

"Do you know, if he had been interested in any other sport, he would have been half way down the M6 by now."

"Well, we call it the greatest game and it certainly helps break barriers down between people or help you make friends quickly."

"Does anybody know yet if our new boss is a league fan?"

"There's more chance of Ian Paisley drinking a pint of mild in St Theresa's club on Saturday night."

"Or Jeremy Guscott playing centre for Blackbrook."

"Or Scott ever going out with that beautiful blonde."

Scott had for a long time been madly in love with Clare who used to work in wages when he first started in the drawing office. His chances of ever going out with her though were virtually nil, or so everybody thought at the time. However, on his last day in the DO he surprised everybody when he told what he and she had once done in her parent's house on Carlton Lane. And later in life he went on to surprise more than a handful of draughtsmen when he managed to fool some of the greatest brains in the land.

4. Reading and rugby

"What's in this month's issue of *Open Rugby*, Alan?"

It was Cliff wanting to borrow a copy of a magazine that Alan bought faithfully every month.

"I don't know why you don't buy your own copy, Cliff. It only costs £1.50 and with all your wealth, that's peanuts."

"I won't read it. I just don't have any time when I'm at home."

"Well, read it at work. That's what I do."

Their conversation was interrupted by Charlie returning some drawings that he had borrowed from Alan. He and Samantha were now working in the old jig and tool office, although he still seemed to spend most of the day in the main office. As he was leaving the room, Alan called out: "Have you read *Open Rugby* this month yet, Charlie?"

"Yes, another cracking read."

"So there you are Cliff. If an old age pensioner can afford to buy it, so can you."

"I'll start next month. So what's in this issue then?"

"Well there's a big piece on the World Cup Final. There's an article by Dave Hadfield about David Oxley and his 18 year rule as the chief executive of the Rugby Football League, Stuart Duffy has written a piece about this farcical eight team Second Division, there's a two page interview with Mike McLennan, Tony Collins has his regular column which I always like reading and there's an article about Cougarmania at Keighley."

"Do you read it all the way through?"

"That's why I buy it."

"You must have plenty time on your hands."

"I've got a routine. I get up at seven and read for quarter of an hour while I'm having my breakfast and then I always try and read for another quarter of an hour after I've had my tea at night. Over the weekend I always try and get an hour each day in as well. All that is only about five hours, but it's amazing how much you can get through if you stick to it."

"I might try that."

It was when he was at Lane Head School that Alan had first got into the habit of reading to a routine. His week would start when he arrived home from school on Thursday evening. There on the living room table would be his weekly present from auntie

Hilda; the latest issue of *Radio Fun* and a threepenny bit for his spend. On Friday, evening, he would get two books out of the library at the bottom of Kiln Lane, which he would read over the next seven days. On Saturday he would take *Radio Fun* to his friend Ken and swap it for *Film Fun*. On Monday after school, his friend Kevin would call round to swap *Hotspur* for *Film Fun* and on Wednesday, he went down to Geoff's house to swap that for the latest issue of *Rover*. Things became complicated when new neighbours had moved into Chisnall Avenue and Maurice wanted to join in; his contribution to the group was *Adventure*. Still it all seemed to work out except, of course, during the school holidays if one of them was lucky enough to go away for a week.

His interest in the written word as a youngster was widespread because he also collected rugby league and football match programmes. Often he would save up his spend until he had enough to send off a postal order to a distant club. The best one he had acquired this way was from Swansea Town when they played in the Third Division South.

One of his neighbours in Chisnall Avenue was a great help too. Mr Roby drove a coach for Gavin Murray in St Helens. He regularly took a coach load of supporters to Saints away games. From time to time, he would also take Liverpool or Everton fans to places like Middlesbrough, West Bromwich or Fulham and would always return with a programme for Alan. On one occasion he had even driven the coach carrying the Everton team to play Derby County and returned with a page in Alan's autograph book full of the signatures of both teams.

Another of Mr Roby's regular runs was on Monday nights, taking members of the Ashurst branch of the Liverpool Chads supporters club to watch the speedway. If there were any spare places on the coach Alan and his friend Eric used to go for free. A nice man was Mr Roby and his wife too. They would surely have made smashing parents if they had ever had any children.

"I'll tell you what Cliff. If you are going to start reading, I can lend you some of my favourite books. How do you fancy starting off with the 1948 *Beano Annual*?"

"Got it, read it and using it to prop the kitchen table up with."

"Did you ever read comics when you were a child, Scott?"

"Alan, Scott still is a child and the comics he reads are things like *Fiesta*, *Forum* and *Penthouse*."

"Look out, here's Johnson."

He didn't stay long. He asked Alan if he could arrange to return to Porto towards the end of the month to discuss the replacement of unit transformer number one with Mr Delgado.

As soon as he had left, Alan said: "You know what that means don't you, Cliff. I'll not be here when the next issue of *Open Rugby* comes out so you'll have to buy a copy. I'll have to borrow it off you when I get back from my little trip to the seaside."

Then he looked at a copy of the Saints fixture list which he kept in his drawer to see what would be the most convenient time for him to go. He would have to be here for 18 October which was the date for the Lancashire County Cup Final. On Saturday 24 October he was going to the wedding of his cousin Marion in Hull and was not going to miss that either. If he went out on the following Monday, 26 October, that would mean missing the Regal Trophy game against Huddersfield on the day after, but at least he would be back by the weekend in good time for the visit of Bradford Northern. And if he wasn't, then spending time with Pedro, eating and drinking well, and filling out his expense form in a creative way surely would compensate for missing that game.

That would suit him because for the next two weeks he would be kept busy working on a design change to the coal handling plant at Blyth Power Station, which might also require him to spend a couple of nights away.

The following day Cliff told Alan that he had started to read for quarter of an hour twice a day: "Getting into a routine was just the thing I needed. In fact, when I told the wife, she decided she would try it as well, although like me she thought that 15 minutes twice a day was far too long. But then we only went to a secondary modern, not like you grammar school boys."

"So what have you started on then, Cliff? *Trainspotting for the under-nines?*"

"It's a book I've was given at Christmas. It's called *At The George* by Geoffrey Moorhouse. It's all about the history of rugby league and how it started at the George Hotel in Halifax in 1896."

"1895 and the George Hotel is in Huddersfield."

"I know. I was just checking that you were listening."

"How much have you read?"

"Just the first chapter. I'm a slow reader. Have you read it?"

"It's on my list. Maybe we could read it together at the same time and then ask each other questions about it the next day."

"Shouldn't you two be asking questions about electrical schematic diagrams? I thought that was why you came here."

It was Dave Merrick, a mechanical draughtsman with a query about Alan's proposed design change at Blyth.

"Do you ever read at home, Dave?"

"I do. In fact before I came out of the house this morning I read the meter for the gas man and left him a note about it."

A week later, the issue of reading cropped up again when Cliff announced that he had finished *At The George* and thoroughly enjoyed it.

"You've read that quick."

"I know, I surprised myself."

"So what are you going to read next?"

"*Haynes manual for the Ford Fiesta*. I think the car is going to need a new clutch."

The week passed quickly and soon they were in the pub on Friday at lunch time. Benny was there and in fine form as usual. It never took much to get him started and once he had started, he just went on-and-on. But today, after having chosen the team for Saints' next home game against Hull, he took a magazine out of his pocket, gave it to Alan and said: "I bought this in Wainwright's in Boundary Road. Have you ever seen it before?"

It was the latest issue of *The Greatest Game*, a magazine produced by the Rugby League Supporters' Association.

"Here, you can keep it. I've read it."

Alan flicked through its pages but before he could make any immediate comment, Cliff had taken it out of his hands and said: "You can have it back tomorrow. I'll read this to the wife in bed tonight. I've heard a lot about the RLSA. I want to see what they have got to say. I might even join it myself if it's free."

"So what stories have you got for us today, Benny? You've been pretty quiet so far."

"There was a bit of an unusual thing on the bus last night going home. We had a women driver. She's been on before. I thought she was fine, but the bloke in front of me didn't seem to think so."

"Why?"

"When we got to the bottom of Bolton Street, she pulled up at the bus stop and then opened the doors. He looked down at the pavement and the gutter, then turns round to her and said: "That's near enough love. I can walk it from here.""

Then he carried on: "Did you hear about that lad Gary who works in the metal fatigue lab? He was in Astley Labour Club on Monday night, playing snooker and was chatted up by some blonde in there, who he had never seen before. He bought her a couple of drinks and she took him back to her place in her car. She had only just moved into the area and lives on her own. He stayed most of the night. When he left, she said to come round whenever he wanted. The next morning he found a piece of paper in his pocket. On it he had written down Margaret 14, Cul de Sac."

"Where do you get these stories from Benny?"

"I got that one from Astley Labour Club. Anyway what's this I hear about you lot turning the drawing office into a library? I take it you'll only be stocking children's books."

"Do you ever read much, Benny?"

"I used to read a lot when I was a teenager; war, history, sport, keep fit, they were my favourite subjects. One day I read that drinking was bad for your health, so I stopped reading."

"That's not true, is it? You told us before that you had read that *TGG* magazine."

"No, I just looked at the pictures. Though I have to say that whenever I go on holiday, I always find time to read the cardigan."

"Is that just when you go to Jersey?" laughed Alan.

"You're not trying to pull over one on me are you?"

At that point Scott burst out laughing. It wasn't anything that Benny or any of the others had said, but a sticker that he had just seen stuck on the back of George Case, a machine shop foreman.

Their conversation moved on to the visit of Hull FC on Sunday afternoon. Benny was going to take his daughter and her new boyfriend. She was a nurse at the Alder Hey Hospital in Liverpool; he was on the staff at the Liverpool School of Tropical Medicine and was an expert in the treatment of malaria. He was from New York, had played American Football and talked about it at great length. Since he had been living on Merseyside, he had already watched Liverpool FC and been to Blundellsands to watch a fellow doctor play rugby union for Waterloo. Now it was time for him to live dangerously and watch rugby league at Knowsley Road. Benny wondered if his heart would stand it. Miles had already commented on the absence of protective gear, as used in American Football in both games. What would he make of rugby league?

31

As they walked back into work, an ambulance raced past. It was a long time since they had seen that. Years ago, accidents at work were fairly common. But over the years safety had improved and rightly so.

The accident had involved a ladder; though not someone falling to the ground. A painter was carrying one and holding it in the middle. As he had crossed the yard, someone had called out to him. He turned through 90 degrees to see who it was. The ladder had turned with him and clouted a labourer on the head, knocked him over and caused him to drop a large tin of red paint. It looked awful, but once the paint was washed away the only thing left was the labourer's sore head.

On Monday morning, within 10 minutes of starting work, Mr Johnson arrived on the scene and asked everybody to gather round. He told them that their boss, Mr Taylor, had died at the weekend. He had been in charge of the drawing office for a few weeks and made little – if any – impression. Mr Johnson went on to say that Alan would be acting section leader for the next few weeks. He said that he would tell them date for the funeral later.

Five minutes later Alan came out of his office and bawled out: "Platt, in my office immediately."

Cliff slowly walked towards him, muttering loudly something along the lines that power had already rushed to Greeno's head.

"Cliff, this is the first executive decision of my reign." He coughed importantly and went on: "Would you represent the electrical section at Mr Taylor's funeral. I am asking you because I know you are well accustomed to going to funerals."

"That's alright boss. Will there to be a job number for it?"

Cliff carried on: "When I worked at Jarratt's, if someone was promoted, it was the tradition for him to buy his section a pint."

"Well, we aren't at Jarratt's or living in the past and as I am now a member of the management team, I am going to give up cavorting with the common herd on Friday lunchtimes."

"And start watching rugby union, drinking Pimms Number Six, and reading the *Daily Telegraph* as well, I presume."

"Yes, something like that. I've got my principles. Go and draw something. Two lines joined at the same point would be nice. And I would also like to be called Mr Greenall from now on"

"Yes, boss."

As he reached the door, Cliff turned round and said: "Eh boss, your flies are undone."

5. Drinking in the Crimea

As the end of the year approached, the issue of whether to have a Christmas party arose. In the past every department had held one, usually in the form of a meal in a pub in Ashurst, St Helens or Warrington. But due to the declining numbers at work and because many people no longer lived near work, they were going out of fashion. Now the wages department was the only one left that still carried on with this old tradition.

In the past the long-serving, tennis-playing Penelope would start things off by suggesting a date to a few of her friends. If that date was acceptable to her 'inner circle' it would be circulated round by word of mouth and unless there were any objections that would be the date on which the 'do' would be held.

The evening started with a Christmas meal, after which the entertainment would begin. Penelope sang three songs, always the same ones and all Bing Crosby favourites. She was followed by Michael from pensions, who did his impersonations and Janet who read a poem she had spent the last three months writing. The rest of those present were then asked to perform, some of whom did, most of whom didn't. After that came the raffle, and finally, the oldest person present gave a vote of thanks to Penelope who would then be presented with a bunch of flowers and a book token by the youngest person present. It was all a little dull, though still enjoyable for those who went.

Unfortunately, Penelope was not able to organise it this year. She had been in hospital a few weeks earlier and had only just returned to work. As a result, her boss Mr Swann told her that he would take over the responsibility for organising everything. He sent a circular round in early November firstly to those who worked in his department and then to those in pensions, sales, transport, planning and finally the drawing office.

Mr Swann's intervention had not been to help Penelope. It was more related to his desire to promote himself. He was a very self-centred and career orientated individual. Previously he had worked in Mayfair in London where he had sought fit to advance his career by becoming the office 'social' secretary. Why he had moved from Mayfair to Ashurst was unclear for the two places had little in common, other than they were both in England. He didn't think organising a little party like this would be a problem; not after some of the social occasions that he had been responsible for in the city where the Queen of England, the Prime Minister and he all resided.

As soon as Alan saw the circular, he burst out laughing: "Cliff, are you by any chance going to a funeral on 17 December? Well you are now and I'm coming with you."

The venue had been changed from The Crimea to a posh restaurant on the far side of Warrington and the cost had doubled. Entertainment would be provided by a lady with a Welsh harp and there was a £2 a ticket raffle with proceeds going to a hospice in Hampshire. By the time the circular had left the drawing office, everybody who worked there had indicated that they had something else on that evening. By the time it had been returned to Mr Swann, only two managers and three others had indicated that they would be attending, all rather embarrassing for Mr Swann as he had put down a non-returnable £50 deposit.

A few days later, Alan had a phone call from Dave Edgeworth, a former draughtsmen. He had been made redundant a few months ago and little had been heard of him since. He had intended to emigrate to Australia but, as it turned out, all he did was sell his house in Gillarsfield and buy another one in Haydock where his wife was a schoolteacher.

"Alan, how do you fancy coming to a do."

"Sure. What's it for and who's going?"

"It's the Draughtsmen's Christmas Reunion at the Crimea. There's a load of the old gang going, Ray Brown, John Turner. Billy Hooper, Geoff Shaw to name but four, who all think you're a pillock."

All were former mechanical draughtsmen who had once graced the drawing office with their presence.

"When?"

"Sometime next month. Roy Orbison is sorting it out."

Roy Orbison, well that was how Ernie Smith was always referred to, due to his looks and the music he used to whistle for most of the day. Good at drawing brackets and his wages. Good at drawing a crowd too whenever he played his guitar in the Wigan Arms at one of their Thursday night rock spectaculars.

The Crimea hadn't changed much since most of them had last been in there, but it was eminently suitable for what could be described as something of a rumbustuous affair. A lot of people who hadn't seen each other for a long time turned up. Everybody

34

had a story to tell about what they had been doing since they left Wilkinson's. Some hadn't changed a bit, some had aged a lot, one or two out of all recognition. And as could be expected, quite a few of the old gang were no longer around.

The evening began with Dave standing up, and banging the table with his hand to quieten things down. Most of those present were surprised to see him in charge. In the past he had never been one of the most prominent members of the office: dependable, likeable, honest and trustworthy, but always in the background, never one to speak at union meetings for example, but always there to support what the office committee were proposing. He ran his hand through his thick mop of hair and began.

"Friends, Rumanians, countrymen and Greeno. It gives me great pleasure to see so many old faces here tonight. It brings a little sadness to my heart though to know that some of our old mates are not here with us to enjoy this do. Some have just disappeared to who knows where, some were otherwise engaged or too ill to come and sadly a few have passed on to that great drawing office in the sky. They are probably now looking down on us and having a laugh. Despite what differences we may have had with any of them or any differences any of us here have had with each other, I trust and hope that we are all good friends now."

"You wouldn't have said that if Lurch was here" shouted out John Tunstall.

Lurch or Arthur 'You can't do enough for a good firm' Wood had once been in charge of the mechanical section of the drawing office and had been hated by all those who had worked for him.

"Point taken" said Dave. "When I include him among our friends, you can take it I've gone senile."

"Excuse me, madam chairman."

It was Benny, the master of flattery, who always managed to get himself invited to any Christmas celebrations.

"Lurch is bringing a lot of happiness as we speak to everybody who still works at Wilkinson's."

They all waited for his punch line. He had already had two pints so they all knew what to expect.

"Yes, it's true. He's gone on his holidays to New Brighton for a fortnight."

Once Benny was on his feet, it was never that easy to get him to stop or sit down.

35

"Can I just utter a few other words of wisdom while the kitchen staff are out looking for a turkey?

"In a word, Benny, no. But thanks for your input."

Dave carried on: "As far as everybody else is concerned, I would now like you all to raise your glasses and drink to absent friends and then to stand for a minute's silence in the memory of those who have passed away."

There were around 60 people in the room. If all the others who were now being remembered had been there, the number would easily have been doubled. How long they were all stood up was unclear; maybe it would have gone on even longer if they had not been interrupted by the doors being opened and the rather raucous voice of one of the bar staff saying to the girl behind her: "Don't forget to bring the beetroot up."

Although it was a Christmas party, the food was not Christmas food. It was the pub's speciality, steak pudding, known locally as baby's yed, chips, peas and gravy, a solid Lancashire dish. It was followed by Christmas pudding with custard, an honest attempt by the landlord to stick at least in part to tradition.

The reason for the minute's silence was uppermost in everyone's mind as they sat down and prepared to eat. People remembered old friends; some were now dead; and some had moved away and had never kept in touch.

First there was Mick Henderson, their favourite Wiganer, who they would never forget. In the war he had been a gunner in the Royal Navy and in 1942 had taken part in the hunt for the Bismarck. He was a keen rugby league fan, had followed Wigan since the 1930s and while he had worked at Wilkinson's, spent much of the day, every day, arguing about it with his mate Charlie Eccleston. One of his great disappointments in life was that his son neither shared his love of the club nor lived in the town, but in Amsterdam with his Dutch wife. Mick doted on his grandson who spoke Dutch, Flemish, French and English with a Wigan accent. Sadly, Mick had recently passed away, probably from a combination of too much exertion from his new hobby of gardening, plus more than 50 years of smoking cheap cigarettes.

Len Turner was another person who had left his mark. He was the one who had organised the union. He had spent ages trying to convince everybody that they should all sign up and so be able to do something about what they were for ever complaining about.

Stan Pearson had been the office war hero. He had joined up

in October 1939, been injured at Dunkirk and later served in North Africa. In 1945 he had taken part in the liberation of the Belsen concentration camp, something which he rarely spoke about. A few weeks after retiring, he had run to catch a bus, struggled breathless up the stairs, sat down and died from a heart attack.

John Rigby came from Prescot and first worked at the town's largest factory, British Insulated Callenders Cables. In his teenage years he had been friendly with John Lennon through playing in a rock 'n' roll band, the Rainmen. He arrived at Wilkinson's in the early 1970s and although he hadn't stayed long, was fondly remembered, not for his drawing skills, but for his stories about the Beatles. Rumour had it that he was now living in London.

Les Earnshaw was once a sheet metal draughtsman and had worked at most of the factories in Ashurst; the last was Wilkinson's. Now he was an author and lived in London. His novels were based on his time in industry. His main character was called Albert Entwistle, a scaffolder from Wigan. From time-to-time they saw his name in the paper or on television. His most notable appearance had been a hilarious interview with David Frost.

Alan Groves had been the electrical section leader and really an OK guy. He lived in Grappenhall on the far side of Warrington; well he did until he surprised everybody by running off to Malaga with a woman who used to work in the gas showrooms.

In charge of them all had been John Battersby, the chief draughtsman until he retired and went to live at Bridlington. He had one great love in life, sailing. This had come from his experiences on a destroyer in the Royal Navy in the war. He could talk about that all day if anybody would listen. No-one had heard from him for ages; clearly he was now living under the radar.

Others who would be remembered may not have worked in the drawing office, but had still made their mark. They included people like Roy Garner – the engineer who had retired to a life of permanent golf; Billy Tunstall, the former rolling mill foreman and a good friend of Sam Holroyd who surprisingly was not present; Harold Potter the wireman and Big Joan who had been in charge of the print room, along with her assistant Rita.

Others remembered were three tea ladies who served them before vending machines had been introduced. Joan the tea lady from Leigh, Nancy 'the never', so called because she never had any change and never stayed long, and Hazel Hutton from Earlestown who had left to become a teacher.

The following morning little was said in the office by those who had gone to Lymm the previous evening. Not much was said by those who had been in the Crimea either, but that was because they all had huge hangovers. It had been a real good do, many old acquaintances had been renewed and a few important deals done. Ken Finney was persuaded to leave Gillarsfield Conservative Club and play for Hemsley Parish Church in the Ashurst Crown Green Bowls League. Ron Hall, whose brother was the landlord at the Collier's Arms, had told John Shields, who had been barred since last Christmas, that he could come back again if he behaved. Frank Fenton, having told everyone that he was now a landscape gardener, had some orders to mow a few lawns.

One thing that everybody was conscious of was the fact that every year after a 'do' like this, within the month, one of them would have died. As expected it happened, and on this occasion, it had been Arthur Fryer whose widow had opted for a cremation in keeping with his surname.

The only sad thing about the two parties had been that Penelope had been cut out of both. Well not quite. There had been a whip round at the Crimea, one which was sufficient to buy her a bunch of flowers, a box of chocolates and a book token.

For Mr Swann, the attitude of the staff towards his efforts was the last straw. He had never enjoyed his stay in Ashurst, somehow things had not worked out as he had intended. He had once described Ashurst to one of his London friends as a cultural desert inhabited by morons, maniacs and monkeys. But then compared to Mayfair, Ashurst did have its own distinctive features, which Mr Swann had never really fully enjoyed or understood.

When everyone returned to work after Christmas, they were told that Mr Swann had left the company. Normally, there would be a vacancy to be filled. However, Mr Johnson had made it clear before Christmas that there was no money for new staff. Then Penelope came to his rescue. She told him that she was now well enough to return to work full-time; and said that she could handle everything Mr Swann had done, and even do it in a morning. In her opinion, Mr Swann had been a waste of space. Mr Johnson said nothing. Her offer would save money, but how dare she say this about his relative. It later transpired that Mr Swann was his brother-in-law, something both had kept quiet, but by then, Mr Johnson as well was no longer working in Ashurst.

38

6. Christmas Day 1992

The last few days before Christmas trundled slowly along. In the past, they were a time of great anticipation and excitement and the younger you were, the greater the anticipation and excitement. But when you have passed your 40th and then your 50th birthday and no longer believed in Father Christmas, then things are just not the same.

Back in the 1960s, the period before Christmas had a certain magical element to it. At work, it all came to a climax on the morning of Christmas Eve. The first half of the morning had always been spent in the drawing office, taking long lost drawings back to the print room, clearing out the drawers, putting a new backing sheet on your drawing board, throwing out any out of date reminders and taking down the calendar for the current year and replacing it with next year's. However all this would come to an end when the tea lady Joan appeared.

At this point, it was time to start on the mid-morning feast and the hour long tea break, during which time the chief draughtsman John Battersby would give his usual speech. As 12.30pm approached, it was time to get to the pub – before the works were let out – for the Christmas dinner and a few pints of Greenall's best bitter. Then it was back into work to try and find some other section's office party to con your way into. That was what generally happened and went on until the earlier finishing time of 4pm, though for some members of the staff, it was even earlier if they could find a good excuse to leave or noticed that their own boss had already left.

This was also a time when tricks were played on workmates, usually aided or fuelled by alcohol. There was nothing like that now; mainly because of the ban on drinking at work for good health and safety reasons.

The world was a whole different place now, not only at work, but everywhere else. This year the last day that had been worked was Wednesday the 23rd. This meant that the whole of Christmas Eve could be spent in the Greenall household preparing for the family gathering on the following day. When Alan was a small child, in the period just after the war had ended, that was one of the most exciting days in the whole year. All the family would gather at his grandparents' house in Silkstone Street. It would begin with the Christmas dinner, a long drawn out affair. This always finished before three o'clock just in time to listen to King George give his five minute speech on the Home Service. Then a few games would be played, after which uncle Jack would hand out the presents. They would then eat their tea, usually turkey sandwiches and cake, which was followed by the horse race game. Finally, all the visitors would have to struggle through the snow back to their homes. It was a day when his granny and granddad were in charge of everything and how well they had always done it. Sadly, now they were both dead and the house that granny had been born in and lived in since 1891 was owned by Alan and Thelma who continued this old family tradition.

For Thelma though, things had been quite different when she was a small girl growing up in South Wales. Her mother had died in 1944, when she was less than a year old, and so she had been brought up in a children's home in Cardiff. In those days, she had never enjoyed the last week before school broke up. All the other girls in her class would be talking to each other about what they were going to do over Christmas, what presents they were hoping to get and which of their relatives they would be visiting or would be coming to their house. At the home, Christmas Day would be pretty much like any other day except that all those who lived there would be given a paper hat to wear. They would pull a few crackers, and listen to a little story about baby Jesus from one of the most unchristian and unfriendly of people, before eating their Christmas dinner.

The first family Christmas dinner that Thelma had enjoyed was in 1962, something that she would never forget, because that was the day she had first met Alan's granny. It was also the day she had fallen ill, so ill that Doctor Jackson had considered sending her to the hospital, but didn't because he knew that she could really have received no better treatment and loving care than Alan's grandmother could give. Then two months later and by which time she was well enough to return to work at Wilkinson's, she had been virtually adopted by Alan's granny and granddad.

In 1968, she and Alan got married and bought a terraced house in Beswick Street, where they had lived until granny was finally convinced that at nearly 80 years old, she would be better off living in the Greenfield Old Peoples' Home in Dob Lane. And within five minutes of her leaving the house that she had lived in for so long, four other members of the Greenall-Holding-Tabern-Pickavance dynasty had moved in.

The people who would be present this year would include their daughter Rebecca with her boyfriend Jason with whom she shared a flat in London and their son Robert, probably with his latest girlfriend who would almost certainly be a student like him at Birmingham University. There might also be Alan's older sister Joan, who had moved to Rainford and was never easy to contact or get a decision from, after the sad death of her husband Roy.

Alan's brother Paul and his wife Dorothy would also be there, possibly with some of their grandchildren. An invitation had also been extended to their good neighbour Phil. During the summer his wife Cynthia had died and he had spent quite a lot of time since then with his eldest daughter Jenny who lived in Southport. But she had gone to Spain for Christmas, so it was only right he shouldn't have to spend the day on his own. So how the day would turn out would really be based on who came, how long they stayed and how much they had to drink.

However, things did not exactly go to plan. First Robert had turned up a fortnight earlier and apologised for the fact that he would not be home at Christmas because he was going with two of his friends from university to Milan, where they would be staying with Maria, another student friend and two of her friends as well, and almost certainly girls. Then Rebecca had rung to say that her boyfriend Jason had surprised her by telling her that he had arranged for the two of them to spend Christmas week at a hotel at Zermatt in Switzerland.

Despite this, and the absence of anybody under the age of 40 in the house, it was an enjoyable day. Everybody arrived on time, by 1pm all the food was on the table and they were ready to eat. Before they started, Alan stood up and asked everyone present to drink a toast to absent friends and relatives, and as everyone stood up, Thelma added: "And especially to granny and granddad."

As they began to eat, the parents talked about what their various offspring were doing. Paul and Dorothy had two children; Michael, who worked in local government in Warrington and had two children and Peter, who worked for the National Grid at Penwortham near Preston and whose wife was expecting their third child.

41

Joan had had three children, the first of whom had gone to live in Canada and kept only the barest contact with his mother, the second one lived in Rainhill, worked on the railways and was married to his job and the third who had made up for her two brothers, having brought six children into the world, one of whom had played rugby league for Hull Kingston Rovers for a while and now lived at a place called Sunk Island which was not far from Spurn Point on the banks of the River Humber.

Then Joan asked Phil about his four sons. From him she learned that one was a consultant at Alder Hey Hospital in Liverpool, one owned a newsagent's shop in Warrington, a third taught sociology at Bradford University and the fourth who had hardly ever done a decent day's work in his life, made a living out of drugs and petty crime, that is when he was not resident in one of Her Majesty's guest houses.

"Don't ask me how he turned out like that, Joan. I don't know. We brought them all up exactly the same."

Then he asked her what she was doing now that she was living on her own in Rainford "After Roy died, I decided to come out of his shadow. He was a good man in his own way and a good father too, but I suppose people would now call him a male chauvinist. He was always trying to put the world right, I just wish he had had a bit of success with it. He was out nearly every night at meetings of one sort or another. But when the miners got defeated, it sort of finished him off. The day he walked out of Sutton Manor was terrible. After that he just went downhill. Tragic really but then Thatcher and her lot never cared one bit about people like Roy." They all remained silent as she carried on talking about her new life: "After his funeral, Roy's sister came to see me and stayed for a few days. Then she invited me to go and stay with her for a bit. She lives up in the north of Scotland, a few miles from Aberdeen. While I was there we talked a lot and she got me interested in her politics. It was not the sort of politics that Roy had been involved in, more about the state of the planet and how it is slowly being destroyed. I got quite interested and since then with plenty time on my hands, I've been doing a load of reading about it. It's frightening what's happening and nobody wants to know anything about it. Global warming, that's what she calls it and one of the worst culprits is big business in America."

Alan had never heard his sister talk like this before. It was clear she had had her eyes opened and now that she was on her own maybe she was going to get involved in something that she had obviously come to believe in.

Then Phil chipped in. He was similar to what her husband Roy had been like, a shop steward at work, a long time member of the Labour Party and frequently out at meetings two or three nights a week. More recently he had had a lot of discussions with his third eldest lad, the one who taught sociology and who was convinced that his dad was wasting his time being a member of the Labour Party. Phil wasn't sure about green politics though, but surely that was better that than another wishy-washy Labour government and their politics of compromise with the capitalist system and subservience to whoever was in charge in America.

The wine and the beer continued to flow, the discussions carried on, there were no children present to want them to stop talking and play pass the parcel or the horse race game. Before they knew it, it was time to leave and a very enjoyable evening had been enjoyed by all. It would probably have been different if Robert had been there though. During his time as a student he was developing some pretty strong ideas about the nature of society. If Rebecca's boyfriend had been there, they would probably have come to blows for Jason was a firm admirer of the Iron Lady, someone who, in the view of their auntie Joan, had put into operation policies that had led to the death of her husband.

Boxing Day started off rather badly as Alan and Thelma both woke up with terrible hangovers. They ate their breakfast late in silence and declared, in different ways, never again. A couple of aspirins followed by black coffee and a walk round the garden cleared their heads, a little if not totally, and by lunch time they were ready to focus on the next part of the Christmas holiday, which involved the visit of the men from the other side of Billinge to Knowsley Road.

They set off in good time, or so they thought. There was bound to be a big crowd and there was. They drove into St Helens, inched slowly down Duke Street, turned into Boundary Road and inched even more slowly as far as the baths. It was clear they would not get much farther so Thelma turned into Horace Street, drove past the library and finally parked at the top of Dilloway Street. They now had just over half an hour, but they still didn't make it in time. By the time they had found a spot on the terraces, Frano Botica had already put the visitors in the lead with a converted try after only four minutes. But that was to be the only try the visitors scored that afternoon.

Despite being without their powerful prop, Kevin Ward, the Saints ran riot. The pack were outstanding, tough as teak against an equally strong Wigan six. Alan Hunte scored first, then Sonny Nickle and Hunte again, followed by one from Chris Joynt and with Paul Loughlin slotting them over with ease, by half-time the Saints were in the lead 24–6 with Martin Offiah having gone off and been replaced by a young Jason Robinson. Early in the second half, Dave Lyon went over and then the composure of the visitors began to fall apart as Kelvin Skerrett clobbered the young Kiwi winger Jarrod McCracken and was sent off. Soon after two more men went in the sin bin for 10 minutes, one from each side, Andy Platt and Sonny Nickle. But soon after they returned, Nickle scored again and before the final whistle went Tea Ropati had gone over the whitewash leaving the Saints coasting to an incredible and unbelievable 41–6 victory.

By the time they had walked back to the car, avoiding two gangs of lads having a right set to at the top of Rivington Road, all memories of their hangover had gone and they were ready to have a couple of drinks to celebrate the afternoon's performance. But it still took them quite a long time to get home. It took them over 20 minutes just to get onto Dentons Green Lane.

As soon as they arrived back home, they had a cup of tea, changed, and went down to his brother Paul's house for the evening. When they arrived, Paul's eldest son Michael was there along with his wife Monica, their two young sons Kevin and Keith and his sister Joan. It was going to be one of those minority rule nights, when whatever the two lads wanted, they would get. There wasn't going to be much time for Alan to tell Paul about what they had witnessed that afternoon. After they had eaten, all attention was focussed on Ludo and then Monopoly. But by eight o'clock, little Kevin was fast asleep.

At this point Monica mouthed some words to Keith: "Uncle Alan, can you tell us about our family tree?"

"He's been going on about it all week, Alan. They've been doing history at school and his teacher has asked them all to find out what they can about their family over the holidays."

Alan had started work on the family tree back in 1963 and had carried on with it from time-to-time, whenever he could find the time. Quite recently, he had put all the details into his computer and printed it off onto a large A0 size sheet and given a copy to Monica and thought no more about. Keith left the room, ran upstairs as though his life depended on it and returned with the sheet and from then on the evening was spent with Alan explaining who everybody was. Surprisingly his sister Joan not only showed great interest, she even had a few scraps of information for him as well.

Young Keith was over the moon: "Can I take this to school, uncle Alan? It's belting."

His response made Alan feel just how worthwhile his efforts, now some 25 years ago, had been. It didn't make him feel quite as good as he had felt at Knowsley Road about four hours earlier, but not far off. From what Joan proceeded to tell them, he learnt that two of their distant relatives had been born on the other side of Billinge, which technically meant there was Wigan blood in the family. He also knew about granny's great grandmother who had arrived in the town from somewhere in Wales over 100 years ago. And of course his own two children Rebecca and Robert were half-Welsh because of their mother's background.

The following day should have been devoted to doing as little as possible in the Greenall house. Too much alcohol on Christmas Day and Boxing Day, standing freezing on the terraces at Knowsley Road for over two hours and Keith's 101 questions to answer about the Holding-Tabern-Pickavance family had tired his brain. But then his neighbour Phil wanted five minutes of Alan's time to help him repair his shed that had collapsed in the previous night's gale force wind. The five minutes lasted nearly an hour.

It was turned three when the pair of them were able to settle down to an afternoon's entertainment to be provided by the Marx brothers, Morecambe and Wise and *The Wizard of Oz*. But they were soon interrupted by a knock on the front door. Thelma went to answer it and a couple of minutes later returned with a young woman who Alan had never seen before, or so he thought.

Thelma indicated for their visitor to sit down and then said to her husband: "Alan, do you know who this is?"

He didn't, how could he?

In a strong American drawl, the woman said: "I'll give you a clue. I stayed here for a couple of nights in 1972 with my mother."

The amount of alcohol he had consumed had slowed Alan's thinking capacity, but even if he hadn't touched a drop for over a week, how could he know what she was referring to. 1972. That was over 20 years ago. It was up to Thelma to remind him.

"Alan, remember that young girl Allison who we heard crying in Mrs Pilkington's yard with that little baby. They stayed here for a couple of days and then went to Blackpool in that old Mini van. Well this is that little girl."

Yes, he did remember now.

The young girl Allison was only 16 when she had a baby and had run away from her home in Chorley to come and find a distant aunt who she thought lived next door in Ashurst. But she was wrong and had come to the wrong house and the wrong street. She had stayed for a couple of days with the Greenalls and then made contact with her auntie Marlene who was the younger sister of her mother who had recently died. After she had left and gone to live in Blackpool, Allison had kept in touch for a couple of years and then contact had been lost, as often is the case. Suddenly out of the blue that young baby and now a bubbling American teenager had returned to Silkstone Street.

"My mum asked me to call and to send you her best wishes. We went to America when I was five years old and now we live in New York with my stepfather. My mum works in the theatre and dad is in a rock band, so thanks to you, things have worked out really well for us."

"And what are you doing over here in England?"

"I'm in a young peoples' theatre group, we're touring for a couple of weeks. We're playing at Liverpool tomorrow night, so I just had to come and see you. You see, my mum always tells me that you saved our lives."

Hilary stayed for over an hour, she really was a nice kid although her snappy Bronx accent made it hard for Alan and Thelma to understand what she was on about half the time.

"My mum is quite famous now, she's appeared in a couple of films with Richard Gere and Madonna and she's got her own band as well. She'll be over the moon to know you are still here and keeping well. And if you are ever in New York you must come and stay with us. We'd love to have you."

Finally it was time for Hilary to leave; but not before she took a few photographs of Alan and Thelma and of the house and left a video of a concert in a Brooklyn night club in New York, one that featured her mum, Allison, playing bass guitar alongside one Cheryl Sarkisian La Pierre, better known as Cher.

7. Hugo van Dijk

On the first day back after Christmas, the draughtsmen had hardly had chance to switch on their computers when Mr Johnson appeared and told them to go to the meeting room. One might have expected him to say good morning or Happy New Year or something else of a sociable nature but true to form they heard nothing like that from him.

Maybe it wasn't going to be a happy new year, as they were soon to discover. What he had to say was for a wider audience also for all the department heads, salesmen, junior managers, section leaders and other important members of the staff had been summoned as well.

"I have brought you all here because I have something very important to tell you. On 1 January, Wilkinson's PLC (1982) ceased to exist. It has been taken over in its entirety by an engineering company called Koen Koevermanns who are based in Holland with headquarters in Amsterdam. The financial situation that we found ourselves at the end of the year was drastic. On the other hand, Koen Koevermanns have a large number of orders for the Middle East. What they do not have is the capacity to meet those orders in their two factories in Holland.

"As a result all the existing work that is currently going through the factory will continue, but will have to be completed by the end of March. Beginning in April, we will be working on these new contracts. It is work that we can and must do successfully in order to ensure a long term future for all our jobs in the UK. It includes design, detailing, construction and installation. It is both a challenge and an opportunity for us all.

"As far as the employment of everybody who was on the books at the end of December is concerned, little will change until the end of April. Any changes after that will be the subject of negotiations which will conform to standard European employment legislation. It is not envisaged that there will be any redundancies, certainly not during 1993.

"Various changes will be brought in over the next few weeks, one being the introduction of flexi-time. This will bring us into line with the people in Holland. The transition to a leaner and fitter organisation will ensure a healthier future for us all. I am sorry that this news is not the best way to start the New Year, but all I can say is that if things had not been carried through as quickly as it was, it would not have gone through at all. Quite frankly gentlemen, we would have had to close down within the month. The financial position was so bad, although not the fault of anyone in this room."

He then declared the meeting closed, said now was not a good time for discussion and asked everyone to leave, except for the draughtsmen. As the last one left the room, he closed the door.

"As far as the drawing office is concerned from now on, you will have a much more important role to play. One immediate change is that all drawing and design work will be done on a computer aided design basis. All the drawing boards will be removed as soon as is possible. CAD training will be provided for anybody who needs it. This may be done here or at Ashurst Technical College.

"As part of the new arrangement, four draughtsmen from the Amsterdam office will be joining us. They will be in a position to help implement a smooth transition to what we hope will be a bright future. There will be much work for you all to do. It will also be necessary for you to get used to travelling to Saudi where most of the work is bound for. Please make sure you all have an up-to-date passport.

"I have already explained the reasons for the urgency of it all. If it had not gone through last week, I would now be telling you when and where to collect your P45s. I will have more to say to you later in the week as I have to go back to Amsterdam for a meeting this afternoon."

And with that, he looked at his watch, picked up his papers and without saying any more, left the room.

"Well that's a turn up for the book. What do you think of that, Cliff?" said Alan as they walked back to the drawing office.

"It all sounded double Dutch to me."

"I had expected him to say we were closing down" said Colin.

"No doubt there will be a catch in it somewhere."

"I liked it when he said how bad the situation was at the end of the year, although that was not the fault of anyone in the room."

Then Cliff put everything into perspective when he asked if anybody knew what the Dutch for bullshit was or was it bulbshit?

"That could even have been Basil Wilkinson giving that speech."

48

True to his word, Mr Johnson returned later in the week to give more details of the changes to drawing office procedures. The most noticeable change would be that the old wages office would be redecorated and turned into the new drawing office.

By the end of the week, it had begun to sink in that standing in front of a drawing board for 37 hours a week would soon be a thing of the past. For the last 18 months, Alan had been doing both, working on his board on jobs that required modifying existing paper drawings and on the computer on new jobs. Doing the two had helped break up the day, but he now realised that soon he would be sat in front of a computer monitor all day, every day. But then, Mr Johnson said there would be scope for travelling abroad, so the future looked interesting and with now working for a Dutch company, perhaps the future was orange.

There was one other significant change. The new drawing office would house all the draughtsmen together, electrical, mechanical, sheet metal and jig and tool. But how well would Charlie fit into the new arrangements? If he was going to stay longer would he still have Samantha to do all his CAD work?

By the end of the week they learned that as soon as they were installed in the new office, they would be joined by the four new draughtsmen: two were English and two were Dutch. Interesting times ahead it appeared.

At present the electrical section was made up of Alan, continuing as acting section leader, Cliff, Colin, Shaun, Howard and Dave along with the apprentice Scott. It was still almost as large as when Alan had first started there in 1961. Then in addition to their old section leader Alan Groves, there had eight draughtsmen: Charlie, Mick, Yorky, Len, Stan, Alan, Dickie with his bad back and Tony who later moved to Halifax to help his dad run a pub and become the masseur of a women's rugby team. Now Alan was the oldest and the 'boss' of sorts. Soon they might be joined in their new office by four new draughtsmen, well that was if they were all electrical. But it was not quite clear at this stage what their discipline was. They might be mechanical, sheet metal or jig and tool. They were soon to find out.

When Mr Johnson said they were coming from Amsterdam, it was assumed that they were coming to work here and no doubt settle or at least lodge in the town, but that was not quite how it worked out. The first one to arrive entered the building for the first and last time on a Thursday morning. He brought a load of drawings, showed them to Alan, went out at lunch time, came back, said goodbye and never returned. He was known as 'the Flying Dutchman', for he had literally flown in and flown out.

The second was an Englishman who originally came from Northampton. He arrived on Monday morning and worked for a week. He checked all the drawings that his colleague had brought, explained everything to Alan and left on the Friday afternoon, totally unaware that he had been expected to stay any longer.

On the following Wednesday, the third one arrived. As soon as he opened his mouth it was obvious where he came from. John was clearly a Wiganer, and a rugby league man as well. But two days after he had arrived and settled in with his mother at her house in Whelley, he had to return to Amsterdam to finish off a job that he was certain he had already completed.

The fourth one to make an appearance was Hugo. He was going to be here for three months so there would be a close link with the new company. He was very friendly, not the sort of person that you would want to fall out with though, for he was six feet two, weighed around 15 stones and included Thai boxing as one of his hobbies. He would be well remembered for his time in Ashurst for he must have been the first draughtsman for over 50 years to wears clogs at work. He was also famous for some of the things he had said in all innocence.

The first was at the end of his first week when, in all seriousness he had asked in the pub at lunch time: "Alan, where is the nearest brothel?"

His second occurred the following Friday evening. Alan had taken him to Knowsley Road to watch the Saints play Halifax. They had arrived at the ground early enough to watch a curtain-raiser that featured two under-11 teams, one from Newton-le-Willows and one from Haresfinch. Hugo had watched the action with great interest. He was a big soccer fan and had never seen any form of rugby before, though he was clearly impressed. As the teams changed ends at half-time, he had turned to Alan and said: "It is great. I enjoyed it, but why are the players so small?"

He spoke perfect English, although with a pleasing Dutch lilt or twang, spoke French, Italian and Spanish as well as a language used in Indonesia, having learnt it while working in Jakarta for over a year. He was always happy to demonstrate his skills on the computer, in particular to Scott, who was keen to learn from him. He also had many interesting stories about the war, not about his own direct experiences as he was only born in 1956 but more about those of his father and grandmother who had both been in the Dutch resistance and also of one of his wife's relatives, who had been strung up to a lamp post for his collaboration with the Nazis. What was also interesting about him was the fact that during the time he spent in the drawing office, he managed to interest his new workmates in the history of Ashurst.

On his first Saturday morning, he had gone into Ashurst library and started chatting with the lady who was in charge of the local history section. Whenever Hugo spent time in a place he liked to look into its background, history and culture. As a result, he was quite knowledgeable about Jakarta, Paris, Madrid and Naples. He was soon to add Ashurst to his list. It was coal mining that most grabbed his interest, something that had dominated and influenced the town for around 300 years.

But if there was one thing that Hugo couldn't grasp, it was Ashurst humour and particularly punning and the deliberate mis-use of words. One lunch time he had gone out for a walk with Alan who had taken him to see the 'Stinky Brook'. To get there they had walked along Canal Street and then returned along Sprint Lane. That afternoon Hugo had made some reference to the Roman influence on the town and Colin had asked him if he knew how Canal Street and Sprint Lane had got their names. The first one was obvious, Hugo had said, but he didn't know about the second.

"It was when the first Roman centurions were marching from Chester to Wigan on their way up north to build a wall for Hadrian. They came over a bridge near where the River Mersey gets quite narrow at Warrington and then headed towards Wigan. As they approached Ashurst, the Stinky Brook smelt most foul. It was always bad, but on that particular day it was terrible. So the leading centurion told his men to put two fingers over their nose and then sprint for a mile, hence Sprint Lane."

Hugo stayed nearly three months and certainly made his mark. On his last day he took them all to the pub and bought them two pints and their lunch as well. As they were enjoying his last few hours with them, Cliff said: "Hugo, can I just ask you one question. Did you ever find a brothel in Ashurst?"

His reply showed that he had also learned about Lancashire humour for his answer had them in stitches: "Yes, I did. It was at

Hemsley. It was at the top of Well Lane, number 24 I think it was. I went there every Friday night. She was a lovely little blonde."

Everybody except Colin burst out laughing. It was where he lived and everybody knew that Colin always went out on a Friday night for a few drinks with his brother-in-law and never came back before midnight.

Over the course of his stay in Ashurst, Hugo heard quite a few stories about Basil Wilkinson. At first he seemed quite sympathetic towards their old boss, which led him to mistakenly say that the man seemed to have had a raw deal from his staff.

"I wouldn't say that" said Cliff. "You won't know that he once sacked Greeno for fighting in the office."

"What was that for, fighting off a butterfly?" laughed Scott, who was now joining in with all the humour and the back chat.

"No, it was for thumping an apprentice who had upset him, so be careful. Greeno has a dark side to him."

"Are you going to tell us then, Alan" asked Hugo. "I didn't think you were that sort of person."

"In those days, the firm used to take on half-a-dozen graduate apprentices, young men who had been to university and got a degree and wanted some experience in industry before getting a job in top management. They were nearly always right arrogant bastards, well most of them, a couple were all right."

"One of them was in here with us when Charlie told us about a coach load of football fans from North Wales going to watch Bangor City play St Helens Town in the FA Cup. By mistake, they finished up at Knowsley Road watching the Saints. When he'd finished and we'd all had a laugh at it, this graduate said something like: "Typical Welsh. All they are fit for is shagging sheep."

"Well I shot across the room, pushed this bloke up against the wall and shook him and called him a little fascist bastard, a bit strange really because he was bigger than me. Unfortunately the whole thing was witnessed by Basil who was in the top half of the office at the time. He came straight down, told me to get off the premises for good and told the graduate to go and get checked out at the surgery."

"So what happened then?"

"There was a quick meeting of the office committee, Len, our shop steward, went down to see Basil to try and sort things out and get him to change his mind. Basil told him that as far as he was concerned the draughtsmen could go and have a meeting about it in Boundary Lane Park. So that is what Len decided we would do.

"As we walked out, Basil rang the security office and told them to lock the car park gate which meant we couldn't get our cars out, neither could the six-two shift get out or the two-ten shift get in so there was chaos on Warrington Road. The police came down, went up to see Basil and bollocked him. He then had to Len to tell all his members to come back into work.

"Len took that to mean it included me and that was the end of it. Well it was until the Transport and General shop steward went in to see Basil to negotiate an extra hour's pay for the lads on the six to two shift being locked in the car park and unable to get home to their wives who were all worrying themselves sick at not knowing where their husbands were."

8. Dietra van Poofen

A month after Hugo arrived, he had to return home for the funeral of an aged relative. While he was away, the place went very quiet. It was amazing what an impact he had made in such a short time. Their computer skills had risen as had their knowledge of life in Holland, both of the city of Looperskapelle in the province of Zeeland, where Hugo had been brought up and much more of Amsterdam, where he now lived. It was during his absence that Alan remembered an incident there, one which had involved Basil Wilkinson: "I must ask Hugo if he knows a lady called Dietra van Poofen when he gets back" he said to Cliff later that day.

"Who's she?" said Cliff, who had never heard of her.

"She used to work in the entertainment industry over there."

"You dirty old man" laughed Scott. "Tell us some more."

"I never went with her, but Basil did."

Alan laughed and continued: "Basil used to go all over the world to get orders. But no matter where he went, he always managed to come back through Schipol Airport and spend a couple of nights in Amsterdam, because there was somebody there who he always liked to visit. It was this lady, if you can call her that, Dietra van Poofen. She was a rather large lady with a face eminently suitable for the radio although she clearly turned him on.

"Anyway he arrived at Schipol one afternoon, rings her up and arranges to meet her in their usual bar. They probably had a couple of drinks and as they are getting ready to go up to her room, a load of lads from Ashurst on a dirty weekend pile into the place. One of them was Gordon Mather who works in the machine shop. As soon as Basil sees him he tells Dietra he has to get away, so she puts her jacket over his head and hurries him past these lads and up the stairs to her room. As they go past, one of these lads shouts out: 'Bloody hell, love. If he's got that over his head, he must be even uglier than you are.'

"Now Gordon doesn't say anything to anybody but a few weeks later, he goes again on another stag weekend. He takes a couple of photograph of Basil with him. He'd got them out of the company year book. They go back to the same bar, and lo and behold, Dietra is there sat in the window, smiling at anybody who was walking past. He shows her the photographs, she tells him that she has had him a few times and says that she'll tell them more about him if they pay her. So they all chip in a few guilders.

She tells them what Basil likes to do and then says that if they pay her some more, they can take rude photographs of her. When she sees how much they had collected, she even told Gordon that if he made it up to 100 guilder, she would take him upstairs and give him a poofen von de plonk for free, though he hadn't a clue what that might be, or so he said. Anyway when the lads come back to work, all these photos of Dietra get passed round the factory. Some bright soul even sent one to Basil's wife."

"Is that true?" asked Scott, for it was a story that appealed very much to his sense of humour.

"Go and ask Gordon. He still works here."

The arrival of Hugo, and his continual asking about the history of the town and what else existed in the town, made people begin to look at the place in a different way. In fact for such a small town there was actually a large number of what could be called cultural or social organisations.

Among them were Hemsley Train Spotters, Ashurst Ramblers, Weight Watchers, Ashurst Astronomers, The Town Hall Opera Society, Gillarsfield Child Poverty Action Group, Dob Lane Cycle Club, Ashurst Local History Group, Astley Pensioners' Club, Wigan Lane Allotment Holders, The Friends of Victoria Hospital, Nook End Oxfam Group, Carlton Lane Language Club and Ashurst College Retired Members Indian Cookery Group.

Not quite as public was the Victoria Wife Swapping Club whose members usually gravitated to the back room of the Victoria pub in Nook End on a Saturday evening, the Crimea Card School and Dob Lane Anarchists. All this was in addition to the many sporting organisations, football, rugby league, cricket, crown green bowls, table tennis and snooker clubs being the main ones.

The church groups held their activities on their own premises, but most of the other organisations met in Carlton Lane Conservative Club, Hemsley Liberal Club, West Central Labour Club and the Ashurst Mechanics Institute. What these last three buildings had in common was that years ago, each had looked onto Sheep City. This had once been a grazing place for sheep on land owned by Lord Billinge. After his death in 1900, it was found that his family had illegally acquired the land during the period of the Enclosure Acts.

55

As a result it was taken over by the Council who proceeded to build Ashurst Market, one of the most spectacular pieces of architecture found in the whole of south Lancashire. Now these buildings were in the busiest and most traffic congested part of the town. Savoy House occupied the fourth corner, with a DIY store on its ground floor, a restaurant on the first floor and a night club on the second.

Unfortunately, with the progress of time and great changes in public and private transport, the Market Hall and the streets and buildings around it, were now in the wrong place. This came to light when the Ministry of Transport decided, that in order to improve the traffic flow through the town, a bypass was needed, which would cut right through this well-loved part of town. As a result, things began to happen, none of which on their own was that much significant, but seen together made conspiracy theorists out of many local residents.

The first item of significance was a speech made by Councillor Owen in Astley Labour Club, marking the 100th anniversary of the Beswick Colliery massacre, when police had charged striking miners, killing three and injuring many others. Not having much grasp of labour movement history, he had used the opportunity to outline plans to modernise many of the Council's facilities. A new library would be built on the site of the old pit which would provide free access to computers and free use of meeting rooms for the growing number of local organisations. It would also house a permanent exhibition about the massacre and details of other events involving the local mining community.

When asked where the money would come from, he hinted vaguely that it would be from the Common Market, when asked why, he said it was because Lancashire generally and Ashurst in particular deserved it. Asked when it would start, he replied as soon as certain financial deals had been finalised. The *Ashurst Star* ran a series on what the town might look like in 10 years time with futuristic drawings that meant nothing. Soon afterwards, Councillor Owen – along with three other prominent members of the Council – disappeared to Brussels, Strasbourg, a new housing development in Milan and back to Brussels for a few more days. There he met a reporter from the *Sun* and rather foolishly told him that he had never ever eaten so well in his life. He even made matters worse by saying he would have to join Weight Watchers as well or no-one would recognise him when he got back home.

A few days after he and his partners in crime had returned, the Council voted to close down the Mechanics Institute on grounds that it failed to comply with basic health and safety rules and regulations. Money was made available to enable the Liberal Club to relocate to the top of Wigan Lane, soon after a fire destroyed much of West Central Labour Club.

It was rather ironic that one of the last meetings to be held there had been the Annual General Meeting of the Ashurst branch of the Fire Brigades Union. In fact if their meeting had gone on an hour longer, they could have dealt with the fire under Any Other Business.

The new link road was but the latest in a long line of changes that the town had seen, or maybe truer to say had suffered. Its introduction, and the chaos caused by its construction and all the attendant destruction of houses and other buildings brought little joy to most people who lived there. Some said that it brought employment into the town, but the main beneficiaries were really the construction companies who had won the contracts. As a result many more streets and well-loved buildings were demolished. Luckily though, much of that which had been gone had been photographed by Harold Atherton.

Harold was a leading authority on the history of the town and the founder of the Ashurst Local History Group. His interest in the subject had started when he was a small child and his great grandfather had lived next door. Maurice Atherton was born in 1868 and had been a bricklayer for much of his working life. All the things that had happened in his lifetime, he had remembered. Some he had even witnessed, including the Beswick massacre.

As a bricklayer Maurice had helped build many of Ashurst's most popular buildings. He had taken great pleasure working on the town hall and Ashurst railway station. Now his great grandson was going round taking photographs of them before they were pulled down. Good with his camera, though not quite so good with words.

"If he had still been alive today, he would have turned in his grave" was something that Harold had once said to a reporter from the *Liverpool Daily Post*. Most recently, he had acquired a camcorder and had moved into making videos as well, something that his grandson Jason was busily helping him promote as an indirect way of accumulating enough capital for him to start making films of a more dubious nature.

57

It wasn't long before the idea of taking photographs of the most interesting parts of what was left of Wilkinson's factory surfaced. Some thought it was a stupid idea, taking photographs of being at work, but others thought quite the opposite. It certainly found favour among another of Ashurst's organisations, Wilkinson's Ex-Foremens' Guild. This was made up of former foremen who on retiring had continued to meet, mainly for a game of bowls and a drink in the summer and a game of cards and a drink in the winter.

Among the various things they also did was to swap books, jigsaws, help each other with DIY and visit old pals in hospital. The former iron foundry foreman Cecil not only visited his counterpart Fred from the brass foundry in Peasley Cross Hospital in St Helens every week for six months, he also visited Fred's wife at least once a week as well. Fred had asked Cecil to keep his lawn mowed and his garden tidy. Cecil just extended the task to looking after the aspidistra that was growing old gracefully in her front room and her busy Lizzie that was spreading out all over her bedroom, just like he did quite frequently.

As time went on, foremen who had retired from other factories were allowed to join in its events. These included trips to Blackpool illuminations, the Rugby League Challenge Cup Final, Chester Zoo, the Granada Studios in Manchester and an afternoon tea dance at the Floral Gardens at Southport on the first Friday of the month. Soon there was a need for a committee and a treasurer and a bank account. Within a year they had enough members, expertise and financial clout to start organising trips abroad.

This quickly became very popular and the sight of around 30 old age pensioners waiting on the town hall steps for one of Turner's coaches to take them to Hull for the ferry to Zeebruggge, received a few ribald comments from younger men and women passing by on their way home from work. There would have been more if it was known that the 'lads' were planning a trip to northern France, starting off with a few nights in Paris. Sadly, fewer members returned than had set off because two had heart attacks through over-exertion in the middle of the night and came home in a coffin.

While Hugo was away, the rest of the office talked a lot about him and his stories of the night life of Amsterdam. On one occasion Harold Potter, the wireman, was present with a few queries about one of Scott's drawing. He chipped in with a story about when he had first visited the city. It was with a group of young people made up of a dozen apprentices from firms on Trafford Park and a dozen or so members of the South Manchester Christian Fellowship. The common link between the two groups was Mr Hollins, the personnel manager at an engineering company during the week and Sunday school teacher at the weekend.

The group had spent the first two days in Rotterdam and then travelled by coach to Amsterdam where they had stayed at a young peoples' hostel on Marnixstraat. During this time and for no apparent reason, Mr Hollins had taken a great dislike to Harold. On the third night, before everybody had set off to look at what the city had to offer, Mr Hollins had called them all together and reminded them they might all be God fearing Christians, which wasn't exactly true of the apprentices, but the city was full of temptation, sin and wickedness. He didn't exactly explain what form that might take, but even the dumbest of them knew. Then off they all went out to enjoy themselves.

The following morning after breakfast Mr Hollins and his assistant, the aptly named Mr Grey, stood in front of the group and told them off for the fact that over half of them had not returned to the hostel before midnight, some had not arrived before three or four in the morning, two had only arrived back in time for breakfast and one had just walked into the room. Then he told them he had warned them all about the sin and temptation to be found on every street corner and said he was now going to make an example of one of the worst offenders. Not surprisingly, he eyeballed young Harold, who looked as though he hadn't slept a wink all night.

"You, young man. Did you go with a woman last night? I want a true and honest answer. One bit of untruth and you will be back in Manchester before nightfall. Well did you?"

"No sir."

"Potter or whatever your name is. Did you go with a woman off the street last night?"

"No sir".

"This is your very last chance. Answer this question honestly. Did you go with one of those tarts off the street?"

"No sir."

"You are lying. You are lying. I saw you with my own eyes."

"Sir, I did not go with one woman at all last night. I actually went with two women. It was a 20-year-old blonde and her mother and I must say they made me feel very welcome."

At this point everybody burst out laughing and from the back of the room, someone shouted "Apologise", then joined by another and another.

Mr Hollins really was a strange man. You don't take someone to the pictures if you don't want them to see the film. You don't take them to a restaurant if you don't want them to eat the food. So why do you take someone to Amsterdam if you don't want them to have the chance to experience at first hand, Dutch family life in a wholesome and loving way?

"We'll have to tell Hugo about that," said Alan, but on his return the Dutchman was something of a changed man. He had obviously been affected by the death of the person who he had seen buried. He later told them that it had been his aunt, the person who had helped bring him up after his own mother had died when he was 12 years old.

At her funeral he had discovered that she had been a member of the Dutch Resistance during the war and had been tortured by the Gestapo before being sent to the Sorbibor concentration camp, something that she had never told him about.

9. "Ravenhead went years ago"

Wilkinson's had always fed its employees well. Its canteen was situated on Warrington Road, about 100 yards from the main gates of the factory. It was built in 1932 and later extended twice so that by 1960 it comprised two kitchens, four offices and five rooms for the main purpose of eating. These were the Rose Room, the Bluebell Room, the Hyacinth Room, the Main Hall and the Small Hall, with each used by different sections of the workforce. The Main Hall was also used for dances, the occasional large meeting and back in 1945 for the biggest ever children's' party to celebrate the end of the Second World War.

When visitors were taken to the canteen for their lunch, it was how important they were that determined which room they would eat in. But with all the reductions in the size of the workforce, the building had been sold to a property developer in 1986. He divided it up into a number of industrial units and offices and renamed it the Ashurst Enterprise Zone. As a result the management turned what had previously been the paint shop into a much smaller canteen, although none of them ever saw fit to venture in there. To a man they decided that it was inappropriate for them or their visitors to eat in, but obviously all right for everybody else.

In order to cater for the senior management and their important visitors, the practice of providing a buffet service was started. The contract for this was placed with a company called Gillarsfield Gastronomics. This was run by the suitably named John Cook, who had been the former canteen manager. He was a very friendly person and was particularly friendly with John Kay who was in charge of the general contracts department, something which gave even greater meaning and substance to them maintaining their friendship.

One person who was very impressed by the quality and amount of food that was provided by what became known as The Two G's, was Dave Shuttleworth, a mechanical draughtsman who had only recently arrived at Wilkinson's.

"It's a long time since I've been to a do like that" he commented one afternoon after he and Alan had spent the morning with three engineers from Eggborough power station and been invited to join them for lunch.

"I think it must have been on my wedding day."

This was the cue for Shaun to chip in with another story from the time he worked on the dark side of the hill: "We used to have a buffet at least once a week when I was at that firm in Leeds."

As soon as he said that, the others knew that they were in for a laugh, which was always the case when Shaun started talking about his old firm.

"They would normally have meetings in the morning and so usually the food was brought in about 11.30am and left in a room that was next door to the drawing office. After those who had been in the meeting had finished eating and left, us lot would be in there to finish off what they had left. If we hadn't eaten it, it would only have got thrown away.

"Now one of the draffies was a lad called Billy Warner, who we called Billy Buffet because he just loved to eat. One day the food appeared very early. About 10.30am, I told Billy that the meeting had been cancelled and we would be in for a right royal treat that lunch time. Now, Billy never liked being the first to go in there so he asked if anybody else fancied having a bite now, but we all said we were too busy. But Billy was like a man possessed. Finally, he can't stop himself, so he said he was going on to the shop floor, picks up a couple of prints and disappears. We all knew where he was going so we just left him to it.

"He was only in there a minute when he sees the bosses coming along the corridor with three visitors. They had literally just flown in from Germany and been met at Leeds/Bradford Airport. Instead of having the meeting first and eating later, they decided they would eat first so to get out of the way, Billy left his glass of orange juice and half-eaten butty on the table and dived under it.

"He then has to sit there, hidden by the table cover for over half an hour while the visitors had something to eat. When they'd gone, Billy climbs from under the table, drinks his orange juice, puts a couple of pies in his pocket and just as he goes to leave, the boss came back looking for some papers he thought he had left there.

"'Bloody hell, Billy, you are quick. We've only been gone two minutes and you are scoffing already.' If only he had known.

"When Billy comes back into the office, his section leader wants to know where he had been and where the prints he had taken with him were. After saying that he had been on the shop floor all this time, Billy says he must have left them on the bench downstairs. By this time all the other draughtsmen had gone to the buffet so instead of going downstairs to 'look' for the prints, the daft bugger goes back into the room, nips under the table and picked up them and his notebook, much to the amusement of everybody there.

"He was such a gullible person was Billy. One day I left a note on his desk to say that there had been a telephone call for him while he had been out of the office and he had to ring up a Mr Lyon. When he rang the number, it was London Zoo!"

"An old favourite," laughed Alan.

"One time my mate Mick got hold of some Leeds City Council headed note paper, typed a letter out and posted it to him at home, informing Billy that because his back garden was such a tip, they were going to turn it into an allotment for all those tenants who didn't have a garden. We convinced him that the council had the right to do this and that he had to do something about it, otherwise there would be no end of people working there. So he spent a whole weekend tidying the place up and digging the soil over. Then Mick sends him another letter which said that the council were pleased with what he had done and would be delivering a lorry load of horse manure for it. The letter gave a telephone number in the town hall for Billy to ring to say when he would be in to receive it. Unfortunately, it could only be delivered to the front of the house so he would have to be there to take it through to the garden. It was hilarious listening to him on the phone asking if it could be delivered in the evening after he got home from work."

The conversation stopped for a while with the arrival of Mr Johnson's secretary with a bundle of drawings for Alan. After she had left, Shaun carried on: "The best one though was when Mick lent him a porn video. Billy had to wait until his mam and dad had gone to bed before he could watch it. It had only been on a few minutes when he heard his mother coming down the stairs. He switched the TV off quick and stood on the window ledge behind the curtains in the front room, hiding. She rummaged around looking for her pills, turned out the light she thought he had left on and went back to bed. The daft thing was, anybody walking past their house would have seen him stood there."

"How do you know all this?"

"He used to tell us. No matter how daft the things he'd done were, he just couldn't keep it to himself."

"Mind you, madness ran in his family. He had a brother called Frank. Billy told us he worked in waste management. We found out later that he was a bin man. And then there was his cousin. He worked for the Ministry of Transport. One day he did a traffic survey in the middle of Dewsbury and parked his car in such a position that it caused a great long traffic hold up."

"I think you're making it up now Shaun."

"I'm not, it's all true" he replied in a way that clearly indicated that it wasn't.

Then Dave chipped in. It was the first time he had talked about the previous place he had worked at in Rochdale: "We used to have a boss who was very religious, but the way he treated people was atrocious. He was also a health freak and went out for a run every lunch time. When he came back, he had a shower downstairs, then come up the back way and into his office and had his lunch. One day this electrician, who hated his guts, waited until he had set off and then goes into the showers and hides his towel. When Connors comes back, he strips off and goes straight into the shower and then can't find his towel so he has to cover himself with some old sacking. But what made things worse for him was that the electrician had locked the back door so he had to come through reception and the main office, with a face like thunder as you might expect. And of course the tale went round the factory that he had got the sack."

Telling stories like this was part of the culture not just at Wilkinson's, but at most factories in the town. Inevitably the teller might add a bit on to make it funnier, but that didn't really matter. There was, however, one exception. It was Davis Pumps, whose factory had been based in the most unsuitably named Rose Petal Lane until it was closed down. Its contribution to the cultural legacy or economic well-being of the town was nil. It might have been higher in the 19th century, a period of time which the firm had never left for, of all the people who had ever worked there, not one had ever come up with some interesting story or humorous tale about the place.

In fact when people who had worked elsewhere went there, they changed too. It was a bit like the film *Invasion of the Body Snatchers* although it usually took around a month before a normal person would exhibit symptoms that warranted concern by

64

relatives, friends or neighbours. When the building was finally demolished, the land was taken over by the Council and turned into allotments. Strangely those who now tended their vegetables there also began to experience personality disorders. One man who had been an atheist all his life started going to Gillarsfield Methodist Chapel, a second man put up a six feet high wooden fence to stop his neighbours looking in his front window while another painted his house, the first time it had seen paint since the end of the war. But the weirdest thing was when a man who for years had complained about the very presence of his mother-in-law on the same planet, invited her to come and live with him and his wife.

Other unusual things happened around that time as well. There was quite a scandal among the hoi polloi when the manager of Ashurst marriage guidance council ran off to Spain with the wife of the town clerk. In addition, three murders occurred in the town along with a failed bank raid, and a major corruption case was uncovered in the town hall. Some said that they were just events that do occur from time to time in any small town and there was nothing to link all these events together. However, two members of Ashurst Astronomy society did record the sighting of UFOs all in the Nook End district of the town around the same period.

But then, Ashurst had always had a bit of a reputation as a rum place. Various strange things had happened there in the past. Many years ago it was believed that a giant had once lived in a cave where the Hemsley Shopping Centre was now located. According to the records, he was seven foot tall and weighed over 20 stone. His legend and his existence lived on and mothers in the area would still say to their children when they had been naughty "You behave yourself or Big Harry will come and get you".

Another distinctive thing about Ashurst was its accent. The word 'the', was always dropped where ever possible, but then that was fairly common around South Lancashire as in "I'll go t' top of our street". It was different from the accent in St Helens, although that could be explained by the fact that large numbers of Irish people had come to the glass town in the 19th century; whereas there were few instances of any having settled in Ashurst.

The accent was closer to the Wigan or Leigh accent, as in the letter 'o' sounding more like an 'e' as in the words down, round and out sounding more like dewn, rewnd and ewt. That was truer of those who lived in Nook End and Hyde Bank, which often seemed to have a language of its own. All this had been true up to the late 1970s, but with the movement of people away from where they had grown up, the old dialect words were falling into disuse and accents merging, particularly among the younger generation.

One person who had left the town a long time ago and had moved in to high circles in London but who had not lost his accent was Les Earnshaw. He was now living in a flat in Islington and knocking round with some right arty types, but still behaved like a man from Gillarsfield, which is what he was. So the news that he was coming back to Ashurst to research material for his next novel was greeted with joy by his old workmates for he would surely call in to see them on Friday lunch time in the Eagle and Child.

As expected there he was the following week, stood at the bar supping a pint of mild. As soon as they all sat down and he opened his mouth, those who had known him from the old days knew he hadn't changed one bit.

"Tha'll never guess who I was clarting with last week."

'Clarting' was a real old Ashurst word. It meant having a few drinks with.

"David Frost. He sent his regards to you all."

"I bet he doesn't drink mild," laughed Cliff.

"Maybe he doesn't, but he always gets the ale in whenever we go for a night out together."

Then Colin said, with a very straight face, that he had read in his paper the previous day about David Frost currently being in New York.

"One thing I've learned since I've been down there is don't believe anything you read in the paper" replied Les.

"I mean all this business about Lord Lucan having disappeared. I saw him last week in Harrods."

"What were you doing in there?"

"I can't say. I was on a secret mission."

"What, like when you worked here and getting a drawing right first time was mission impossible" laughed Alan.

"Have you met anybody else interesting?"

"I met Sandie Shaw last Saturday. She was in Clarks on Kilburn High Road buying a pair of shoes. Anyway never mind about her, how's my old mate Charlie? Has anybody seen him recently?"

"Have you not heard?" Alan said.

Les's face dropped. He obviously feared the worst.

"He's back here working on contract."

"I don't believe that."

"We don't believe half of what you tell us about what you do in London."

"There's always an element of truth in what I tell you."

"Like there was always an element of truth in your drawings; like the scale was right even though the dimensions were wrong."

"So why isn't he here or has he gone teetotal in his old age?"

"He's gone to Fiddlers Ferry. He wasn't sure how long he'd be there. He's fine. Anyway, how long are you staying up here? We can organise a night out if you like. We can have it in the Brown Edge."

The Brown Edge was a pub in Thatto Heath and the scene of some memorable social events, one of the best being when Mal Meninga had turned up with a couple of Aussie rugby league players and with a jersey signed by all the Kangaroos touring party to be used as a prize for a raffle to help pay for a little girl from Ackers Lane receive expensive medical treatment in America.

"Well, if we're going to have it there, I'll tell Tom Jones and see if he fancies a night out. With him being an old miner I can go and show him where Ravenhead Colliery is."

"Was."

"Why has somebody pinched it?"

"It went years ago."

"Where to?"

Typical Les one liners; which boded well for the following week.

67

10. The Pretoria Pit disaster

Unfortunately, the get-together did not take place because the weather went strictly Siberian for a week and by the time things were back to normal, Les had returned to London. They had all been pleased to see him and particularly young Scott who had never met an author before.

On the following Monday, Alan brought a copy of *The Draughtsman's Tale* into work for him. By the end of the week Scott was proud to announce that he had read the first chapter. Some people might have thought there was nothing brilliant about that, but in Scott's case it was good. It was the first book he had ever willingly chosen to read. By the end of the month, he had given it back to Alan and asked if he could borrow the sequel *The Actress goes to Heaven*.

The books made a big impression on the young apprentice, for whom a whole new world was slowly beginning to open up. It was around this time that he moved from being a lad to taking the first steps towards manhood, as he began to learn some very important lessons about life. The first one he had finally learned was to always think about what you are going to say before you actually say it.

It happened on Friday afternoon after Colin had said that he was going to spend the weekend at Abergele where his mother now lived.

"Wales would be all right if it wasn't full of the Welsh."

"I think Greeno has just removed your name from his Christmas card list" laughed Colin a little while later.

"Why, what have I done wrong now?"

"I thought you knew that his wife Thelma comes from Wales."

Alan laughed when Scott walked into his office and apologised for his comment soon after.

"Always engage your brain before opening your mouth and you'll go a long way in life" was Alan's response.

He had been a young apprentice himself a long time ago and had done a few daft things in his time, so why not pass things he had learned to the young lad?

As Scott spent time with the draughtsmen he quickly began to grow up and show more interest in what was going on in the world around him. After he had read the two books by Les, he began to develop an interest in local history. It had started when Alan had asked Colin: "Where are you off to to-night Colin, is the opera or the ballet?"

"Dob Lane Old Peoples' Home. Why? Do you want to come?" Colin had replied in a rather uninterested way.

"Let me guess. It's to see one of your aged relatives and make sure that your name is still in her will."

"We're going to see my great auntie Alice. It's her birthday. She's 93 today."

"A bit of a special day then."

"I suppose it is. I know that we'll get another little history story from her, the same one we get every year."

Scott looked up as Colin continued: "Every time it's her birthday she tells us in great detail about happened when she was 10 years old. It was the Pretoria Pit disaster, the worst one we have ever had in Lancashire. Have you ever heard about it?"

Alan had vaguely, but none of the others had and certainly not Scott. He had never had much interest in learning about history, certainly not about 1066 and all that, a view he had obviously got from the monotonous lessons given by a very dull history teacher.

On the other hand, Colin often like to tell tales about what had happened to his relatives over the years and they were always worth listening to, although often quite sad, like the one they were about to hear. But this was the first one that Scott had ever shown any interest in and clearly he was quite moved by it.

"She was brought up in Westhoughton. Her dad was a collier, just like his father and grandfather had been. There was nothing unusual about that. Her mother took in washing in order to help bring her up and all her brothers and sisters. Nothing unusual about all that either. It was her 10th birthday and she had been looking forward to it all week. She knew that when she got to school all her friends would pull her hair 10 times and throw her up in the air, it was the usual sort of thing they used to do. But as they were having their breakfast they heard an enormous explosion. Everybody knew what must have happened.

"The noise had come from the Pretoria pit, which was only half a mile away. The fathers, uncles and older brothers of most, if not all, the children in her class, in fact in her school, worked at the pit, so everybody was worried as you might expect. I don't know if anybody went to school that morning. What would have happened is that all the women would have gone down to the gates of the pit to wait for some news. They were soon to find out.

"The roof had fallen in and it had led to a huge explosion. There was not much anybody could do about it, her father was killed, her eldest brother was killed and the little lad next door was killed as well. He was the youngest there and, would you believe it, it was his first day at work and also his last. And tonight she'll tell us about it yet again. It's strange really, she'll not be able to remember what she had for breakfast this morning, but she'll be able to reel off everything that happened on that day in 1910."

The other listened quietly and with respect as he went on: "It's always the same. We'll all sit or stand in round the bed. We'll give her her birthday cards and presents. There'll be a bit of small talk, the great grandchildren will tell her what they are doing at school and then at some point she'll burst into tears and tell us about what a terrible day it was for her and all her family, the start of more poverty and sadness for everybody in Westhoughton."

"Why don't you record it? It surely would be a fine bit of oral history."

"I keep thinking I might do."

Then he carried on: "Can you imagine what the funerals must have been like? There were 844 men and boys killed that day. Only three survived. The other strange thing about it was that it happened just before Christmas, 21 December. But her birthday is today, that's six weeks later so she's obviously got it wrong, not that I will ever tell her. Anyway it wouldn't make any difference, would it?"

Then he carried on tell them more what he knew about the incident. This obviously made a big impression on Scott. With the closures of all the Lancashire pits, it was hard for a young lad like him to appreciate what life must have been like in the days when there were seven working pits in Ashurst alone and when at least once a month, sometimes once a week, a family would be deprived of a bread winner due to an explosion of methane gas or an accident in the bowels of the earth.

That night Scott told his mother about what he had learned that day about the events at Westhoughton.

"If you are interested in stuff like that, you should go and talk to Mr Ratcliffe. He used to work at the Beswick a few weeks before the great disaster there. That was about the same time as well."

From now on, he grew increasingly interested in the history of the town and particularly its mining history. Then Alan told him that with his new found interest, he should have a go at constructing his family tree. It was another new thing for him to take up and one which had a couple of bizarre twists to it. Scott lived in Waterdale Crescent in Sutton in St Helens and had always been led to believe by his mother that they had originally come from Billinge. But as he did what Alan had suggested, which was to talk to as many of his older relatives as he could, he discovered that his dad's side of the family had originated from Wrexham in North Wales.

The other interesting thing was that on his mother's side, he had a distant relative called John Pickavance who had been born at Gillarsfield on 29 March 1837. Was this the same John Pickavance that Alan had found to be one of his relatives as well? Did this mean that Scott and Alan were related? Did this mean Scott had to start calling his section leader uncle Alan?

There was, however, no chance of anyone being related to the next apprentice to spend time in the drawing office. It was another of the dwindling number of graduate apprentices, in this case Michael from London University. Unlike Scott, who had spent two months with them, Michael only needed to spend a week there to learn what a draughtsman did.

It was clear from his attitude and general demeanour that he already knew more about electrical engineering than the rest of the draughtsmen put together and the only thing that they learned about his family was that his father had narrowly missed being elected to Parliament at the last general election.

But those MPs who had been elected were continuing to wreak havoc across the north of England, with engineering companies closing down all over the place. Among the firms in Ashurst that had been closed within the last year had been Dawson's Chocolate Works, Jackson's Brass Castings, Pearson Engineering and Davis Pumps.

Fortunately Harold Atherton had managed to take photographs of the outside of each building. He had also been inside both Jackson's and Dawson's; but Pearson's didn't really have anything worth photographing. But for some strange reason, he was not allowed into what had been Davis Pumps by its former owners. Maybe they had something to hide, but by the end of March no one would ever know.

71

One firm that did not need anybody to enter its premises and take photographs though was Wilkinson's. Until his death in 1962, old man Wilkinson had himself been a keen photographer and had a fascinating collection of every part of the firm when it had been in its prime. These were all safely stored in Ashurst Museum under lock and key.

When Basil had died in 1982, the main link between the Wilkinson family and the firm went. However, it was with the death of his wife Cynthia and then a few weeks later his younger brother Norman, that the final link was severed, although neither of these two had ever been known to do anything productive.

Norman Wilkinson was always known as the 'meddler'. He was a complete waste of space. He would do little useful for weeks on end and then suddenly come up with some hare-brained idea. Then he would rush into the machine shop usually to get his idea worked on. He would often do this on a Saturday morning when he knew Basil was not around. On one occasion he had collared a man working on a rush job on his lathe, pulled rank and got the man to stop what he was doing and work on what Norman wanted. As a result on the Monday morning, the man had to explain to his foreman why the bracket that he had come in to make had not been left on the goods outward table by lunch time on the Saturday.

"It'll only take me an hour to finish it" he replied in his defence.

That wasn't good enough. It had been arranged for the bracket to be collected first thing on Sunday morning by an assembly man, who would have spent an hour fitting it to a large casting which would then have been crated up and loaded onto a lorry on Sunday evening and taken down to Tilbury Docks, ready for loading onto a boat heading to a steel works in Brazil.

On hearing of what had happened, Basil had gone ballistic and virtually had him barred from ever going on the shop floor again. Fortunately, there was a positive end to this because on entering the English Channel in very foggy conditions en route to Rio de Janeiro, the boat had been in a collision with an oil tanker and had suffered severe damage. If the casting had been on board, the boat would probably have sunk, so maybe all's well that end's well. Not surprisingly, Wilkinson's used this as the excuse for why the delivery was late and even managed to get it loaded onto a ship leaving Liverpool docks on the following Monday.

The factory was still known locally as Wilkinson's despite the fact that all of the original Wilkinson family were now dead. Sometimes those who did not work there, but lived nearby would complain about its smells and the way its smoke and pollution attacked what was pegged on their washing lines. But with the division of the factory into two, and then the demise of Wilco Allison Products and the demolition of such pieces of outstanding architectural beauty as the copper refinery, the iron and brass foundries and the three rolling mills, all was fading into the past.

Alan was steadily becoming one of the oldest employees on the staff. He knew the layout of the factory better than most people. In the past Wilkinson's had been divided into four separate divisions. Not only were you not allowed to go into any of the three divisions you did not work for, you even had to get permission from your foreman or section leader to visit a different part of your own division. However, the works maintenance department serviced all four divisions and one of their main responsibilities was lighting and heating. During his apprenticeship, Alan had spent six months on what was usually referred to as light duties. As a result he had been all over the factory during the day and on night turn as well. It was a job that kept him pretty fit as well, because not only did he have to carry fluorescent lights up many flights of stairs, or levels as they were known. From one extremity of the factory, the pattern shop in the brass foundry, to the mineral insulated cable division at the other, it was well over a mile long.

Plenty of scope here for a young fit apprentice making social visits around the place to see various mates or have a dekko at the new filing clerk in the telephone cables test lab or Boadiccea and her gang of rude girls who worked in the foundry pattern shop. There were also some locations where it was possible to hide, places where bosses would never go, the best one being on level 26 in the copper refinery. This could only be reached with the aid of a steel ladder and clambering across duckboards, not that any ducks were ever seen there.

Another good place to hide from the bosses was the sun lounge, so called because it was an ideal place to sun bathe unobserved, as well as unclothed, in working hours. It was the roof above the second floor of the metal fatigue lab and the only way to get to it was up the stairs at the far end of the lab. As a result anyone on the roof could always be warned about the

73

approach of somebody important. The four lads who worked there were careful not to spend too much time up there, because the evidence would be immediately noticed by their newly acquired sun tan. However, things began to get a little out of hand when they had been joined by the metal analyst Stephanie who within a month of starting had acquired an all-over tan.

In the past, a job at Wilkinson's was a job for life; but now that was no longer true. Stephanie was typical of many of the younger ones who just worked there for a few months or maybe a couple of years and then moved on or were moved on. It might have been the time spent getting a fine tan at work that influenced her future career path. A few months after being made redundant, she had become a business woman and opened up a Sun Tanning Lounge on Dob Lane.

11. Springfield tales

Alan always liked to get into work early. Most weeks he managed to do it, at least once, twice if he really tried hard. Timekeeping had never been one of his strong points. Today, though, he was in his office at the unearthly hour of 7.40am. He had a very good reason for this, because the previous night he had been rung up by one of the outside contracts division men telling him he had better get to Eggborough power station as soon as possible to sort out a major problem.

In Alan's estimation it was something that might take 10 minutes over the phone, but in the view of the messenger it was something that might need a gang of six men a week to resolve. In the absence of Mr Johnson, and in view of a recent circular that had gone round the drawing office, allowing draughtsmen some degree of freedom when deciding whether to go out on site, Alan decided to go. He also decided to take another draughtsman with him and who better to spend all day with than Charlie. Hence the reason to get hold of Benny, among whose responsibilities, was the allocation of company cars, or in this case the company van.

By 8am, he'd signed for it, got hold of the keys and was sitting on Charlie's chair as the man from Thatto Heath breezed in.

"Sorry I'm half a minute late, boss. The butler was a bit slow running my bath. It won't happen again."

"Charlie do you ever remember a comedian from Leigh called Ken Platt?"

"Yes sir, certainly sir, he was quite a humorous chap, I do recall."

"What was his famous saying?"

"I won't take my coat off. I'm not stopping."

"Indeed you won't. Today you are coming with me to Eggborough. We may just have a slight problem with that new cubicle we've designed for the control room."

"There is no 'we' about it. It's the new cubicle that you've designed for the control room. I've had no say in the matter."

"Well, be that as it may, we might just have to do a lot of measuring up which is why I have chosen you to hold the tape."

"If you've got a job number for it, I'm your man."

As is usual with company vans, it was in a right state; but by quarter past eight they had managed to remove enough rubbish

75

to enable them to sit down and put the various bits and pieces they were taking with them, on the floor behind them.

"Do you want me to act as your guide and read the map, knowing that you aren't very good at doing two things at once?"

"I suppose so" replied Alan as he adjusted the seat, switched on the engine and wiped some oil off the windscreen.

"Right then. Just back up about five yards, turn right, then left past that motor bike, head straight for those gates and turn right into Mersey Street and then keep a look out for the nearest motorway cafe."

It looked like being a good day, unless work got in the way.

"So what made you late this morning?"

"I went in the Springfield early and came out rather late."

"Oh, that's all right then. I'll only knock 15 minutes off your timesheet."

"Could I make a suggestion? Instead of us having about two hours for us dinner and saying that we only had half an hour, can we just make it an hour and threequarters?"

"'For us dinner': you're beginning to talk like a Yorkshireman already and we haven't even got onto Warrington Road."

"Just getting in the mood."

"For what?"

"Me dinner."

Alan then explained the technical reason for the visit as a result of the conversation he had had with the electrician, Jack Bradbury.

"Hell, that name's a blast from the past."

"Why?"

"Have you never heard of him? He came from Thatto Heath, he was a brickie at Ravenhead and he was one of the best players we had at Knowsley Road just before and just after the war."

Obviously the man who had rung Alan was not the same man. If it was he would have been turned 80 by now.

Alan said nothing for he knew Charlie would soon be regaling him with another story from the good old days.

"I can still remember the first time I ever watched him play. It was against the Australians. We had a combined St Helens and St Helens Recs team. 1937 it was. They just beat us, I think it was something like 15–7 but it was a great game."

"Charlie, that was over 50 years ago. How can you remember stuff that far back?"

"I remember that game because it was played in midweek in December and they didn't have any floodlights, so they kicked off at half two. I was on six to two that week, but we weren't very busy so they let us finish early. A big gang of us walked it there from work. I reckon half the crowd that was on the ground that day had clocked off early. We got in just as the teams were coming out. Then just as they kicked off, this bloke behind me starts pushing me in the back. I didn't do anything at first, it was a big crowd; then he did it again and then again. So I turned round and was going to give him a right mouthful and saw his face. Do you know who it was? It was my dad with a big group of his workmates from UGB."

Quite often when Charlie got started on some event or incident from the past he would go on-and-on about it. Sometimes it might be from an incident from the war, another time it might be about something that happened when he was still at school. Often it was about incidents that had taken place at a match, or on the way to or from a match. Then it might be about things that his relatives had told him about and particularly his granddad. He was now somewhat oblivious to his surroundings and so, sat in the works van, which by this time was approaching the M62, with Alan's eyes set firmly on the road concentrating on his driving and keeping an eye on everybody else who was heading east, it would be like having the radio on. All you had to do was tune in and then sit back and listen, learn and laugh.

Today it was the link and the rivalry between the two sets of supporters from the same town that Charlie wanted to talk about.

"It used to be really strange working at Pilks before the war. It would be a bit like working at a firm in Billinge or Ashton, with half the folk who worked there being Saints fans and the other half being Pie Eaters. It was like that in the electricians' shop. There must have been about 40 of us worked in there then. Most were Saints fans, well we nearly all lived within walking distance of work and the ground. But there were probably about a dozen who followed the Recs. The foreman did and three of his chargehands as well as the woman who worked in his office and did his paper work.

"It was great there with all the regular banter and joking. Sometimes a bloke might get married to a girl from the other side. That sometimes caused a bit of trouble. Then there was the thing about where you lived. My mate lived in Dodd Avenue and married a girl from Mulberry Avenue. They didn't have enough money to put a deposit down on a house, so his auntie said they could go and live with her while they saved up. That was very nice of her, the only thing was she lived in Seddon Street at the bottom of City Road. He said it was like living abroad."

He paused as a group of about a dozen motor bikes roared past and said: "Must be practising for the TT. A bit early for it" and then carried on: "I remember the day the news got out that the firm decided they were not going to carry on with running the team. You could see who were the Recs fans then, just by the look on their face and their hunched shoulders as they walked round. It was a good thing that the war started soon after, if only to take their minds of it."

"You know that the Recs reformed after the war. 1947 it was and exactly 100 years after the firm had first set up the works social club."

"What sports did they first play then?"

"It started off with a cricket team, and then they introduced bowls a bit later on. It was in 1879 that they started playing rugby. I know that because my great grandfather played for them. He worked at Plate Works at Cowley Hill and lived in Spray Street which was handy for him because in the early days, they used to play at Boundary Road."

"They weren't founder members of the Northern Union, were they?"

"Not at first, but they applied to join the following April."

"You sound like a professor."

"Well I don't profess to be one."

"Carry on."

"Their first game was a friendly against Crompton and a few weeks later they played their first proper match against Walkden in the Lancashire Second Competition. A bit later they played in the Challenge Cup. They got through the first round dead easy."

Charlie paused for breath but more so for Alan to respond.

"Why. Who did they play?"

"Nobody, they got a bye. And then they got beat in the second round in a quite high scoring game by Rochdale Hornets."

Again he paused, like he always did when his audience would be waiting for his punch line.

"8–3."

"The following season the interest in rugby declined and more of the workers wanted the social club to have a soccer team so the Recs withdrew from the Northern Union for a bit but by 1913, just before the war started, they had had enough of it and rugby became the number one game at Pilks again. There was no agreement at first which code, but what swung it for us was the fact that lots of people who worked at Pilks wanted the competition between the Recs and Saints to come back. So they reformed and played the various 'A' teams for a season and then everything was disrupted by the war.

At this point Charlie got out a sandwich from his carrier bag, put the bag back on the floor opened up the sandwich and muttered: "Oh no, turkey again." and asked Alan if he wanted to swap.

"I've brought nothing. It's a good canteen at Eggborough. I can wait until we get there, although that doesn't mean we can't claim something for eating at Birch Service Station. Carry on with your lecture."

"My next bit of history comes from my next door neighbour. Last week I told him that the wife's name before she got married was Bacon and she had been brought up in Duncan Street. He took me into his house and gets out this box where he keeps all his old programmes. He's a right hoarder. He shows me a piece of paper that had the names of all the players registered to play for the Recs at the start of the 1913–14 season along with the name of their previous club.

"On it there was a William Bacon and he used to play for Westfield Amateurs, which probably meant he lived near Westfield Street. I reckon she could be related to him but I haven't had chance to look into it yet."

"I've never heard of Westfield Amateurs."

"You won't have heard of Parr Recreation or Sherdley Athletic or St Helens White Star or Eccleston Rovers either, will you? They were all on his list."

He readjusted his seat, wound the window down a bit and carried on: "I'll tell you the names of a few other clubs as well. That's if you want me to or should we just spend us time spotting BRS lorries?"

"Carry on."

"Well, from what I can remember there was Leigh Shamrock, Pemberton, Warrington, Dentons Green, Runcorn and Wigan Islanders."

"Nobody from Ashurst then?"

"There was one lad called Berlin Barnes and he used to play for a team called Chisnall Avenue Bluebottles."

"You're joking."

"I am about the club, but not about the bloke's name. Whatever was his mother thinking about calling him that?"

The journey seemed to take no time at all and soon the cooling towers of Eggborough power station were in full view.

They signed in at reception, chatted to the girl on the desk who by the way she pronounced such words as fine, time and mile clearly indicated that she came from city of Hull. They walked down to where Jack had his little office cum store room, chatted for five minutes and then went up to the intended location for the new control cubicle. They looked at the layout drawing that Jack reckoned was wrong and convinced him that he needed to get to Spec Savers as soon as possible. They then decided that if they moved sharply they could be at the front of the queue for lunch in the canteen before any members of staff arrived.

As soon as they had finished eating, Alan said with all seriousness: "Well there is only one thing now left to do."

"What's that?"

"Find an excuse for coming here."

"I suppose we could have a look in the meter room. The last time I was here there were no labels on the voltmeters."

"I thought you said you had never been here before."

"Well I haven't, but let's face it, most power stations are the same aren't they. Maybe it was when I went to Agecroft or was it Kearsley."

"Both knocked down. It must have been your drawings again. I know what we'll do. We'll go and see if Frank Griffiths is in the control room."

"Who's he?"

"He's one of the station engineers. I worked on that AVR system with him about six months ago. He's a good lad."

Frank was a big Featherstone Rovers fan, always ready for a discussion about rugby league and fishing, his other great interest in life. He was sitting there eating his sandwiches and by the way his face lit up, very pleased to see two visitors from over the hill.

80

Alan explained why they had travelled all the way over from Ashurst on what proved to be something of a fool's errand and wondered whether Frank might find something they could look at or give advice on that might lead to some more work for Wilkinson's; and so make the whole day not a complete waste of time.

"Well, maybe you lads can help me on something. It concerns the black start facility we have. It's when we use the gas turbine on generator number two to get things running when the whole grid system has gone down."

A black start was something that both Alan and Charlie had heard about, but had never experienced. It sounded interesting.

"Tell us a bit more. As you know we are from Lancashire and as a result we are of course pretty clever."

"And modest too" smiled Frank.

"The problem we've got with the way things have been designed at this station is that when we start the system up again and get the first generator turning, but before we can start exporting power from the unit transformer back onto the station transformer and then onto the grid, the lights in the ladies toilet keep going out."

12. "He'll be a typical manager"

Everybody in the electrical section of the drawing office was very busy. Part of the reason for this was because they were two men down. Cliff had been away for a week and it looked like he would be off for at least another week too. He was on jury service, not that he wanted to be.

Earlier in the year when he had been informed about this requirement for him to fulfil his civic duty in two month's time, he had realised that he couldn't get out of it by using the excuse about going to a funeral in two months time. So now he was involved in listening to a case that involved a man from Nook End carrying out criminal activity that had resulted in an old lady from Astley going to her own funeral.

The other absent draughtsman was Howard. He was in a cotton mill in Morocco. It was his first trip abroad and he was struggling. Most of the problems that he was dealing with had nothing to do with the electrics, but they still needed sorting out. He was spending a lot of time on the phone talking to the mechanical draughtsman, who should have been the one to make the trip.

Another reason why they were rushed off their feet was due to the fact that one of the graduate apprentices had been 'working' in the office. Leonard Worthington had recently spent a month in the mechanical section. He appeared to be quite capable of working on his own. He spent three weeks drawing brackets, flanges and auto-leveller back cover plates. At the start of his final week, he had been given the job of drawing two very similar assembly box lids. One was for a cotton mill in Iran and another was for three identical box lids to go to Indonesia.

The job required a little more knowledge than the work he had been engaged on earlier. He was quite capable at using the computer, but he had not quite fully understood the difference between the functions of 'save' and 'save as'. Neither had he fully understood the office drawing numbering system. If the office checker had not been off sick; or if another draughtsman had cast his eye over the drawings, his basic error would have come to light immediately.

Because of the need to get his drawings to the shop floor as soon as possible, because the quality control man was in a meeting and because the lorry that was due to collect a large casting to take to Liverpool Docks, arrived early, then prints of Leonard's drawings were sent to the shop floor unchecked.

What Leonard did was alter a master template drawing. But it wasn't until three days and four jobs later that this was noticed. As a result, a number of drawings for equipment currently being manufactured on the shop floor had to be double-checked and where necessary corrected.

Before long, into the office came Benny. He wanted to know why his transport schedule for the month had to be altered. After a discussion, he informed Alan of his solution to the problem. He would delay the delivery of four assembly boxes due to go to Turkey, send one to Iran and three to Indonesia. The order for Turkey could still be completed on time, although his paperwork would still have to be done first and Leonard's changes removed. It was an easy enough way to get round what might have been an expensive mistake.

"I think those little efforts on my part deserve a couple of pints on Friday, Mr Greenall."

"Well, I have to say Benny, of all the transport managers that work here you are undoubtedly the best."

That was not much of a compliment because there was only one transport manager in the place, but it was hardly the time or place to make that comment, not it would have bothered Benny.

"So what's new in the funny farm here today?"

"Well for a start there's today's paper. That's brand new. Then there's Scott's explanation of how he managed to get 38 wires in a 37 core cable, that's new, as was Colin's excuse for being late this morning."

"Well, all that I can say is that I must congratulate you on the way you approached this problem and came straight to me. You obviously know that I am the most important person in this place. You didn't waste time trying to sort out something which is beyond your comprehension and ability."

"It would appear that for once you were right, Benny."

"Alan, it was just mind over matter. I don't mind and you lot don't matter. In fact, I often wonder how some folk learn to walk. Tell me again, who was the clever pillock who cocked this up?"

When he learned that it was the graduate apprentice Leonard Worthington, he grimaced: "Another idiot destined for a job in high management, no doubt."

The phone rang. It was for Benny. They listened to him as he began quoting dates, times, order numbers, delivery note numbers and quantity schedules. Suddenly he started to sound like Peter Sellers. They knew what had happened. Whoever was on the other end of the line had hung up and Benny was doing his usual trick of pretending to talk in some obscure language. Then he moved the phone a couple of feet away from his mouth, wafted the air in front of it and said: "Bloody hell, he must have had some curry for his breakfast."

"Who was it?"

"Haven't a clue. It's pitch black over there. I couldn't see."

Then he carried on with his observations about someone else he regularly came into contact with: "You know, my daughter's boyfriend is a bit like you lot. He never ceases to amaze me. They went out for a walk on Sunday along Garswood Lane. As they were going past the orchard, the one that's next to the Winwick, they stopped to talk the farmer who was working there. Lover boy says to him: 'How much are you selling your apples for?'

The farmer says: 'You can have as many as you can carry for five pounds.'

So the lad says: 'I'll have 10 quid's worth then.'

"Actually he is quite a nice lad, he teaches history at St Bede's although I think he's got a bit of an attitude problem to his work. He really believes that school is just a place to go to between your holidays."

Then he told them something he had clearly made up in the last hour or so: "I was reading an interesting book about football last night. Did you know how soccer became more popular than rugby? It was invented by the Druids. Yes, it's true. They were going to play it at Stonehenge. It was going to be rugby they played but they wasted far too much time trying to stand two stone pillars on top of each other for the goal posts.

And with that he walked out whistling away, as happy as Larry and much happier than Leonard whose name was now mud.

Ten minutes later he was back.

"Alan, are those leveller boxes for Indonesia left hand or right hand?"

Alan looked worryingly in the contract schedule.

"Left handed."

"Left, that's right. Good job too."

"You had me worried there, Benny."

"Has anybody seen a ten bob note?"

"It's all right really. I knew they were left handed. I only came back to pick up something I must have left here. I just thought I'd give you a little shock."

"What have you left?"

"A ten bob note. Has anybody borrowed it? Anyway, while you are emptying your pockets and looking in your drawers, can I just check a couple of other things about that PX699 job that's due to go to Turkey next Thursday."

And with that he went serious while he made sure that everything on his delivery note for the Adana mill near to Istanbul tallied with what was on his amended schedule list.

Halfway through the afternoon, he reappeared yet again.

"What have you lost this time, Benny? Is it a pound note?"

"No, it's about that delivery to Adana. You know it's in two parts, the chute feed system now and four control cubicles and the auto-levellers in two months' time. What are the chances of delivering them two weeks earlier?"

"Why?"

"It's Hermann von de Plonk and his new system. He doesn't like the way I have done this job for 20 years. If the cubicles and levellers can go earlier, I can put some other stuff that is due out there by the end of the month in the same container."

"Are you trying to impress him, then?"

"No. I'm just trying to get him off my back. It will all be different at the end of next week."

"Why?"

"I daren't tell you, but you'll love it."

He had his own distinctive ideas on what made a good manager. If his department had not had such a good record in handling all the company's transport needs, he would no doubt have been sacked, or at least demoted, years ago. But he also had a devious side to his make up and possibly changing the delivery to Adana might have some other reason for it. Maybe like when he had arranged matters so that he had to personally deliver a small pack of spares to the Rossi Ferbaro mill in Italy a couple of years earlier. It was a pure coincidence that on the same day Liverpool were playing Juventus at a stadium about three kilometres away from the mill.

With the factory now being part of the Koen Koevermanns group some aspects of the place's culture and traditions had begun to change. One difference was the way in which newcomers were treated during their first weeks. In the past, anybody who came from nearby places like Earlestown, Newton-le-Willows, Derbyshire Hill or Sutton, was considered as an outsider until he or she had worked in Ashurst for at least a year.

But now that people travelled from much further afield to get to work, this ridiculous practice had gone and a good job too. Now in the jig and tool section were four design draughtsmen, Joe who travelled every day from Jericho, that is Jericho near Bury of course, John who lived at Port Sunlight, Tony who could see Blackpool Tower from his bedroom window and Terry who came from Eccles. Among the new managers was one who lived in deepest Cheshire and another who lodged at Hoylake on the Wirral and went home to Withernsea, on the far side of Hull, every Friday lunchtime.

Conscious of the need to respect local culture and traditions and to make the employees feel at home while working for a Dutch company, various new practices were introduced. One was to let everybody out half-an-hour early on Queen Juliana's birthday, as happened in the Netherlands. This hadn't gone down too well with those who travelled by bus though, because nobody had told the local Arriva transport people and so a lot of employees had stood waiting in the pouring rain for half-an-hour until the usual fleet of buses arrived at the normal finishing time.

Generally, the new bosses seemed to behave in a much more civilised way than any of those who had been in charge before ever had. But then, as some of the more cynical observed, they would still have to obey the economic laws of the system which had always been to make maximum profit by making products cheaper than your competitors. And if that meant making people redundant, or worsening conditions, or doing away with the annual pay increase, then tough.

All over town, redundancies, unemployment, short-term contracts and part-time working were still the order of the day. But it still came as a great shock when the manager of Barkers' Plant Hire committed suicide one Sunday evening on Lowton Bank. He obviously could not bring himself to tell his staff on the following morning that the firm had ceased trading the previous Friday.

Another victim of the worsening economic climate was a young man from Nook End who had spent months doing up an old miner's cottage, only to have it repossessed a week before he got married because he had been unable to keep up the payments on his mortgage. It was also a sad day for Mrs Kitchener from Glebe Street, who had to sell her father's war medals for his service to his country at Dunkirk in the Second World War, a country whose leaders would appear to have forgotten about the likes of him.

There seemed no end to all the gloom and doom. Nine months earlier, the Conservative government under John Major had been re-elected, albeit with a reduced majority. Things seemed bleak, with little future in sight for many of the residents of Ashurst. One outcome of this was the way many young ones started turning to drugs. Shady characters, who had never been seen in Ashurst before, were observed hanging around outside schools talking to pupils and offering them small packets of what looked like washing powder.

Outbreak of mindless vandalism continued with growing frequency. Bus stops were regularly smashed, and Saturday night on Dob Lane and in the town centre was more like the wild west than a so-called civilised society. Buses no longer ran on various routes after nine o'clock and pubs began to employ men of large proportions to restrict who could enter and drink in them.

87

It was against this background, and partly as a result of this decline in civic standards, that the emergence of people with a message of hope for the future began. Jehovah's Witnesses were seen and heard knocking on doors with their fundamentalist message based on a book written nearly 2,000 years ago. They were followed by members of the Church of the Latter Day Saints – Mormons from America and then the Unified Church of the All Fearful re-emerged.

All seemed to be convincing enough to recruit people, though few of them ever seemed to work for a living and certainly not at Wilkinson's, except for Graham Black Pudding and now his wife Helen. Then on to the scene burst someone with his own set of ideas about the future, someone who was Ashurst born and bred and who had in his time worked at Davis Pumps, Mather's Foundry and Wilkinson's. It was Clive Parker who was becoming known as the global warming man.

He wasn't a freak, or a weirdo, a bookish intellectual or a university graduate. He wasn't associated with any political group or party and had stopped going to church the week he had started work. He drank in The Lamb, played pool there a couple of nights a week and at the weekend he would be seen out-and-about town with his mates.

Although not an aggressive person, he did have the ability to look after himself and on a couple of occasions had been arrested for brawling in a pub and on one occasion at a music festival in Leeds after somebody had called him a 'Lancashire twat'.

Clive was becoming increasingly convinced that the atmosphere of the earth was warming up because of the presence of what he called greenhouse gases. These were released into the air through the burning of gas, coal, oil, wood and other similar fuels. Among the biggest culprits were the motor car, coal fired power stations and aeroplanes. If not checked, in 20 or 30 years' time this would lead to the Arctic and Antarctic melting, the level of the oceans rising, massive flooding on all the major coastlines and the possible change of course of the Gulf Stream that might easily bring back the Ice Age to Britain.

At first most people ignored him, but as time went on some began to think there might just be an inkling of truth in his views. But most of those that he knocked around with just poured scorn on his meanderings. Then one evening, a lecturer at Ashurst College invited him to speak at a meeting organised by a group of environmentalists from Liverpool University. The meeting got a lot of publicity and quite a few of those who knew him decided to go along to listen to what he had to say. As always reporters from the *Ashurst Star* and the *Ashurst Reporter* were in attendance as was someone from the Press Association.

Also in the audience were about half a dozen of the regulars from The Lamb who had clearly been in that pub for the last hour or so. Clive had spoken for nearly half an hour and then in questions and comments from the floor, others had joined in. Finally the chairman of the meeting declared that in his view, it had been a very interesting meeting, he personally had been made to look at the issue afresh and would very much like to ask Clive to return maybe in a couple of month's time, hopefully with new evidence.

Then, up jumped Clive's best mate Jake to ask a question. Both he and his four companions might have been expected to pass some comment during the course of the evening, but all had been relatively quiet. Maybe Clive's message had made an impact on them. Maybe pigs would be seen circling round Queen Victoria's statue in its new resting place as well.

"Can I just make a suggestion? Why don't we do something positive about these greenhouse gases? Why not start a campaign to get Heinz to close down their factory?"

It seemed an odd suggestion, there were no chimneys belching out smoke from the factory and in addition Jake's cousin worked there as a quality control inspector. Jake carried on: "You said that the worst greenhouse gases come from the car, the plane and from burning oil, wood and coal, but you missed one of the worst emitters of noxious gases and much of that is due to that Heinz factory."

What could he be getting at? If he had had a go at Wilkinson's it would have made a lot more sense but surely not Heinz, whose factory was about five miles away at Kitt Green in Wigan.

"Yes, what Heinz produce is making things worse and it's the one thing that our professor friend Mr Parker has ignored because he is one of the worst culprits."

They all waited for his explanation and as they waited they heard his mates chuckling among themselves.

"It's farting and eating their baked beans makes it even worse."

89

And then with perfect timing he demonstrated loudly as if to make his point in a most graphic manner. Then he looked at his mate sat next to him and said out loud: "Billy. You shouldn't have done that, not in here. Have you no manners?"

At this point Billy stood up and asked if he could speak. Was he now going to have a go at his mate? Were things going to end in farce? Surprisingly though they didn't, far from it. His contribution to the meeting was short and to the point but then Billy never was one to waste words.

"Never mind about what my so called buddy here has just said about baked beans. From what I've heard tonight, if we don't do something about what Clive has told us, with this global warming malarkey, us lot will soon finish up as has beens."

It was probably the first time he had ever spoken at a public meeting, and probably the first time he had ever been to a public meeting. It was a good start for him though, because a few years later he was elected to the Council as the Green Party candidate for West Central ward.

13. "Do you still drink shandy?"

It had just finished raining as Alan set off to walk to Whitaker's Brewery Social Club to meet up with three people who he had once been big mates with when they were all teenagers.

Alan, Ronnie, Ken and Jack were now in their 50s, but only Alan still lived in Ashurst. Ronnie had been one of his class mates at Lane Head Junior School as had Dorothy Pilkington, who was now his wife. Ronnie had worked at Wilkinson's before moving to BICC at Prescot. Then he had gone to work in the oil industry in the Middle East as a quality control inspector. He lived there for 20 years and made a fortune. On returning to England, he put his money into a garden centre at Ormskirk where the two of them now lived.

Ken had served his time as a fitter at Jarratt's machine tool factory. It was there, at the age of 23, that he had his stroke of luck. His foreman had asked him to make a bracket and then go and fit it to a machine that had been installed incorrectly in a cotton mill at Strasbourg in eastern France. After he had done that, he then had to make an identical bracket and do the same thing to a similar machine that had just been installed in a cotton mill in Milan. When that was done he had to return to Strasbourg to make a few minor adjustments, before going back to Milan to do the same.

This has led to him becoming the company's number one installation engineer, going round Europe, modifying various older machines. But no matter which part of the world he found himself working, he always managed to find time to come back home to Platt Avenue where his dad still lived. As a result Alan always had a good idea what he was doing; if not from him directly, then from his dad who Alan frequently saw around town.

Little was known about Jack. He had served his apprenticeship at Hiltons, but after being made redundant from there he worked for a short time in Wigan and then had disappeared. Whatever had he been doing for the last 40 odd years? They were soon to discover. He had made contact on his way to visit his daughter who lived in Southport. Driving through Ormskirk, Jack had called in a garden centre to buy her a bunch of flowers and who had served him there, but Ronnie. It was as a result of this short encounter that the grand reunion was organised.

91

Ronnie had arranged for them to meet in Whitaker's Social Club in Birch Lane, because it was a place that attracted an older type of drinker; didn't have a juke box blaring out and so was an ideal place for a good chin wag between old friends.

As Alan walked into the place, he saw plenty of people sat around who he knew. The first person was a man who lived at the top of Beswick Street. He passed the time of day with him and his wife and discovered that they were intending to move south to be near to their son and grandchildren. He walked over to the bar, bought a pint of bitter and as he put the change in his pocket, he heard a deep seated laugh from the corner annex. That was Jack. He just knew it. That bit of him clearly hadn't changed.

He walked over to the three of them and shook hands before sitting down. The first one to greet him was Ronnie: "We've got a 10 bob kitty, Greeno. Are you going to join us or do you still drink shandies?"

Well he hadn't changed much.

"How long has she let you out for, old lad?"

Same old Ken.

"You've left your Zimmer at the bar".

And now Jack.

It is always difficult or maybe awkward in situations like this to get started. Does one person talk for maybe half an hour and then the others follow or does everybody just have five minutes or is it better to ask questions of the others or what? Well, it was a bit of everything, the conversation flowed easily as did the ale and before they knew it, it was turned nine and the evening's entertainment was about to start with a comedian from Widnes followed by a singer from Newton-le-Willows. By that time Alan had heard enough from the others to realise, just like him, they all had a tale to tell, although his life had always been in Ashurst whereas the other three had travelled far and wide.

Before they had started telling their stories though, they had been interrupted, firstly by a man working his way clockwise round the room, selling the *War Cry*. By the time they had got shut of him, they had been confronted by Big Al, going the other way and wanting to sell them tickets for the bingo. Finally they had each others' undivided attention. Nothing was planned. It doesn't happen like that. How could it? But before it did start, another old blast from the past suddenly stood before them, Malcolm Freeman, who they had all once known. He was there because he lived at the top of Birch Lane and this was his local, just another coincidence of which life is full of if you know how and where to look for them.

Before they did get started, Jack apologised for having to leave them for a few minutes to make a phone call. While he was away Mal told them briefly about another old friend who had just died and two others who still lived nearby. But it was Jack's past that they were most interested in. They just didn't have a clue what he had done. As a young man he had had all sorts of ideas for his life. Had he realised any of them? They were soon to find out.

Around the time Alan had met Thelma during the winter of 1962–63, Jack had been going out with a girl called Maureen who used to work in the warehouse at Jackson's Brass Castings. She was a member of Ashurst Harriers and was one of the fastest girls in the club in more ways than one. Jack was pretty fast too. He played rugby for Leigh Miners and had had trials with Warrington, but without success. Later that year they broke up. She ran off to London and to make a complete fresh start. Jack had gone in the opposite direction and headed north to Aberdeen. He had chosen there because he knew that if the drilling for oil in the North Sea, was successful, it would transform Aberdeen into a boom city.

"A mate of mine was already up there and so he helped me get fixed up with a job and some digs. They were a bit rough, I had to share a room with three other lads, but it was dirt cheap and I was getting plenty of overtime. I didn't have any long-term plan. If it worked out well, I would have stayed. If it didn't, I was going to go to Australia. I'd always fancied going there and I suppose I was trying to get as far away as I could from where Maureen had gone.

"The bloke who ran this lodging house was originally from Bolton. We got on really well, but he was too old for it. One day he told me that he was thinking of packing it all in. What did I think, he asked me. So I came up with a brainwave. I told him I would buy the house off him, I'd run the lodging side of it and he could carry on living there rent free until he found somewhere else to live. He was really pleased with that.

"Then I told the others what I was going to do and if any of them wanted to help me get the place modernised, they could live there on a reduced rent until we had done it. By the end of the year, we had got it rewired, new floorboards in, new kitchen, painted and decorated, new carpets, the works.

"Next door there was a widow called Janet. When she saw what I was doing, and how I had treated the old man, she suggested that I could employ her to do the cooking, washing and housework for us all. There were about 10 of us in there. She was up to her eyes in debt, and couldn't afford to carry living there much longer without some income. So I took her on. She cooked a breakfast and an evening meal for us all, did all the washing and kept the place decent and I put everybody's rent up to pay her. Then me and her sort of got into a new situation."

"You mean you started shagging her."

"It all started innocently. My room was having new floorboards done, so she suggested I get a camp bed and sleep in her room."

"And did you?"

"I bought a camp bed and I slept in her room, but the two statements while true were not directly related."

"That's a nice way to put it."

"She had lost her husband at sea five years earlier and had become a bit of a recluse until I turned up and turned her on."

"Lucky her."

"Lucky me, she had five years to catch up on. I suppose that you could say that it wasn't love, but it was certainly very good.

"Then she suggested knocking a doorway in between the two houses. We did that and used two of her rooms for more lodgers, Texans with money to burn. By this time, money was pouring in because I was still working, five, six or sometimes seven days a week. The value of property in Aberdeen was rocketing and the two houses had probably gone up 300 per cent. But all the time I kept thinking it couldn't last. Unfortunately it didn't.

"Janet and I were getting on all right. She was nice, but there was just one thing that I couldn't stand about her. She was a heavy smoker and as time went on, it got on my nerves. They call it passive smoking now; well I had a bellyful of it with her. I kept trying to get her to stop, but she wouldn't. Then one day she came back from the doctor's to tell me she had got cancer in her throat. Two months later she was dead.

"So I decided it might be a good time to leave. I sold the whole business and went travelling. One of the Texans was going back so I flew over there with him. I stayed a few days in New York in his apartment and then the pair of us bought a car and drove to California. That was one hell of an experience. It took us nearly two months. We rented a place and started living the high

94

life. He then got involved in the drug scene, upset somebody he shouldn't have, got caught in an armed robbery and was sent to prison for seven years. So I decided it was time to get away from the place."

As a kid, Jack had always been fascinated, even obsessed by American gangster films, but when he began to observe it at close quarters through the things his friend Miles was getting into, he knew he wanted no part of it. And so the prospect of coming back to England appealed, particularly as he still had plenty of money from his time in Aberdeen. So back he had come.

"On the plane I started talking to a woman from Ohio. She was an author and was heading for Europe to research material for her next novel, her sixth as it turned out. It was partly based in pre-war Warsaw, where her family had lived, then in California where she now lived and partly in post-war England, which was why she was going to spend a month travelling round this country.

"So I thought I'd pull a fast one on her. I told that I was also an author and had had two books published."

The other three smiled; another one of Jack's far-fetched stories no doubt, either for them or for her.

"I told her I didn't use my own name and wrote under a pseudonym."

"What, William Shakespeare?" laughed Alan.

"No, Les Earnshaw."

"You cheeky bugger, you can't use Les's name."

"Actually I knew Les very well. In fact, some of his stories were based on things I had told him about when I worked at Mather's. When we got to London, she told me she was staying in her friend's flat in Hampstead for a month and would I like to stay there with her. I accepted her offer, we hired a car and spent the next four weeks driving round and generally having a good time at her expense, or so I thought. Then one evening she told me that she was waiting for money to be transferred from her bank in Ohio to one in London, but there was some stupid hold up. She asked me to lend her a couple of grand, which was no great problem. Unfortunately, that was the last I saw of her."

As they all laughed at his misfortune, he went on to tell them that the next day he got a demand for the rent. She had had a scam going with an estate agent and so he had done the same thing and got out of London quick.

"So where are you living now?"

95

"I'm staying at the Griffin in Eccleston, but I've just put an offer in for a two bedroom apartment on that new housing development down Bentley Lane in Gillarsfield."

"Will you be on your own there?"

"Not quite sure at this moment in time."

"What do you mean?"

"Do you remember Maureen?"

"How could anybody forget her?"

"Well the last time I saw her was just before I went to Aberdeen and she went to London. Now her surname was Brighouse, a bit unusual for some one who had been brought up in Whitehaven. So last week I had a look in the telephone directory for Cumberland and found someone called Brighouse at Egremont. I rang up and do you know what, the guy who answered was her brother. I told him who I was and he told me that she had lived in London for a long time, but had just moved to Southport after her husband had died. He gave me her number and I went to see her last Monday."

"And?"

"She made me a nice breakfast."

"Are you going to see her again?"

"What do you think?"

"Lucky you. I always fancied her, but could never catch her."

"You would now if you chased her."

"Has she changed much?"

"Well I wouldn't say that she was overweight, just under tall. She's got three kids, one lives in London, one in Darwen and one in Sydney."

"Are you still working?"

"Yes, I'm driving a van for Turners, three mornings a week, I've got an arrangement with a firm in Bootle to do their welding work when they need it and at the weekend I have a large part working for an outfit in Wilmslow making hard core porn movies."

He just hadn't changed one bit.

"I bet you'll be surprised to know that Greeno does a bit of media work now Jack."

"Yes, he delivers the *Ashurst Star* round Astley and Nook End on a Thursday night. I've seen him doing it."

"Are you still at Wilkinson's then?"

So Alan told them briefly, well as briefly as you can talk about 30 odd years of your life, working at the same place although for a number of different bosses.

Then Ken talked about working as an installation engineer all over Europe and Ronnie followed with his account of what it had been like working in the Middle East. Before they knew it, Big Al was calling last orders; the time had flown by. When they were a lot younger they would have then decided to go clubbing or for a curry. But each had a good excuse why they couldn't do that.

Dorothy had told Ronnie she would be outside in the car at 10.30, but would not be there five minutes later, to take him home to Ormskirk. Jack had arranged for a taxi to take him back to Eccleston, Alan had to be up at six the following morning because he was going to Drax Power Station in North Yorkshire and Ken had the weakest excuse of all. He had promised his wife that he would take the dog out for its late night walk. Still they all left with the intention to keep in touch, just like you always do in these situations. But unfortunately the next time they were all in the same place, one of them was lying motionless in a wooden box.

97

14. My name was Sandra Watts

As Thelma placed his evening meal on the table, she told him that she had had a visitor that afternoon. It was someone that they both knew well, the former mechanical draughtsman Ray Hewitt. He was often known as Ronnie Hilton, partly because he used to work at Hilton's and because he was good at impersonating the 1950s crooner with the same name. All the time he had worked at Wilkinson's he had been a well respected and well liked man, with some pretty powerful ideas about how society should be organised and in whose interests.

In the 1960s he had been one of those who had helped to get the union started. The main man though had been Len Turner. It was Len who frequently put his neck on the line in his position as chairman of the office committee, having to meet and negotiate with Basil Wilkinson. But it had usually been Ray who had come up with the best ideas on how to tackle Basil.

Basil often said some of the most stupid things. Ray's method of fighting Basil was to get the members to do exactly what Basil said. It was something that nearly always paid off. Like the time Basil had told Len that if all the draughtsmen wanted to be in a union, they could go home now. He had said that at around 3pm one sunny afternoon and by four o'clock they were all on their way out of the factory. It was that little incident that made them realise that even though Wilkinson's was not a member of the Engineering Employers Federation, they were still a powerful force to deal with the firm if they all acted in a united way.

It was after he had retired five years ago that Ray had begun to interest himself in matters of wider international importance. He had exposed a whole viper's nest around the time of Basil Wilkinson's death. He had become even more involved following the suspicious death of their former workmate Joe Platt on the highway between Wellington and Clarksfield in Ohio. And it was he who had begun to investigate some of the dubious activities that the company's former managing director, Stephen Williams, was involved in on the other side of the Atlantic Ocean.

Ray was also well-known and respected for other more ordinary activities and pastimes. His home made beer was a pleasure, as was his own special version of Ashurst lasagne con onione and his Lancashire hot pot mit sauerkraut. He was a fine bowler, being the star man in the Victoria Park bowling club and a good snooker player too.

So his reappearance on the scene was very welcome. What international scheming and governmental double-dealing had he discovered now? Was there more corruption in the committee rooms of Ashurst Council to be exposed or had he discovered who killed John Kennedy. But maybe he was just trying to find somewhere to hide away from his good lady friend Theresa, now growing increasingly aware that the pair of them would never get into Heaven together, if he continued with all his ungodly materialist views.

"So how is he and what does he want?" asked Alan.

"You'll soon find out," she replied. "He's coming round here at seven."

"I hope he brings a few bottles of his latest brew with him."

"He said that he's coming here because he thinks there are some bugs in the house."

"Well he should hoover the place a bit more," said Alan, although he knew Ray would mean that someone in authority maybe in Whitehall or in the offices of MI5 or MI6 was listening in to what he was doing or saying on the phone.

Ray arrived an hour later, carrying four bottles of his latest offering, his Black Brook Brew. Alan began by telling him about the firm now being part of the Koen Korvermanns empire, who was still working there and about a couple of old timers, one of whom had just died and another who at the age of 72 had just married his neighbour's 30-year-old daughter.

He could tell though that Ray wasn't really listening, he was clearly just itching to move onto more important matters.

"Alan, do you remember when Joe Platt from Hyde Bank who used to work in the chemistry laboratory, was working in America trying to find out what Stephen Williams was getting involved in?"

"Yes."

"And do you remember that we had that arrangement whereby Joe posted his coded letters to my sister at Billinge Hospital, just in case they were being opened up before the GPO delivered them to me."

"Yes."

"Well my sister finished work up there about 18 months ago. Last week she called in to see an old friend. Just for old times sake almost, she looked in what used to be the mail room and

99

found this letter in her old pigeon hole. It must have been there for ages."

He gave an envelope to Alan who opened it and took out a sheet of paper, unfolded it and read the contents:

"Dear Ray,

My name was Sandra Watts. I say this because by the time you read this letter I expect that I will be dead because my doctor has just told me that I have but a few weeks left. I was a friend of your colleague, Joe Platt. They said that he was driving over 100 miles an hour on the highway between Wellington and Clarksfield when his car went off the road and that there were drugs and a gun in the car. I know that morning he was at a place called Lorain about 20 miles north from here, but the police told me to keep quiet when I told them they were wrong. Nobody would have believed me anyway and they said they would take my little girl away from me. I know what they can do if they want to and I had a bad record, so I said nothing. I know I should have done something, but I was on drugs, Joe was dead and my little girl needed me and I needed her.

As I get near the end of my life on earth I have started going to church. I met the policeman there who had threatened me before. He also does not have long to live. It is strange, but we have almost become friends. He told me never to believe bad of Joe. I think he was trying to say sorry for what he did or maybe that Joe had been set up.

Joe always spoke well of you. You are a nice man, I am sure but there are some very bad people in this world and in our police. May God be in your heart.
Sandra."

"Look at the date on the envelope Alan."

It was 4 December 1991. The letter must have been in Billinge Hospital for over a year.

"There's not much we can do with that, is there? Sandra is probably dead by now and even if she wasn't, how could you get hold of her and how much use would she be?"

Ray then produced another envelope.

"Look at this. It came last week. One of the women on reception is a friend of my sister and she kept hold of it for her, because she knew she was coming."

It was a much more relevant note and much more recent for it was dated 17 January 1993:

"Dear Ray,
You don't know me and you never will, but I knew Sandra Watts and I also knew Joe Platt. I don't think he knew what he was getting himself into and he paid for it with his life. Since then the situation has got worse. Things he was looking into have become a lot clearer now. Stephen Williams is not now around that much. They have given him a number, that's why. There are bigger people involved on the scene now. These are the names of the some of the people who he was involved with.

O'Neill, Wilton, McKenna, Reagan, Finlayson, O'Hagan. They are all front men for other more powerful figures and have connections in the CIA and the Pentagon. They also have people in high places in London, including some close to your government. If they get their way there will be war in the Middle East. It is all to do with oil.

From The Silent One."

"I suppose that you are now going to tell me that you have started to investigate these characters."
"I've started to, but it's not that easy. I wish he'd given me their first names. I mean the name McKenna, there were the McKenna brothers who Joe said even the Mafia didn't dare cross, but then there is a McKenna on the board of three large corporations in America. There are a lot of people called O'Hagan as well. Some names are fairly obvious, but looking into what they are doing is going to take a lot of time.
"The other thing of interest that I have discovered concerns this new Dutch company Koen Koevermanns. I looked up details of their board and directors. They have interests all over the place, including a small company in Sacramento, making ball bearings for the American space industry and among their directors is Sandra Czerny. Do you remember her?"
"Vaguely."
"She was on the board of that company in Brighton called Southern Power Design, the one that Basil Wilkinson had some dealings with. She also has a sister who works for the CIA and her

husband was based in the American Embassy in Santiago when Pinochet crushed Allende's Government.

"The whole thing is a bit like chasing your tail and, to be honest Alan, I'm still as interested and enthusiastic as I ever was; but somehow I haven't the energy."

"How old are you now?"

"I'm only 69, but I sometimes feel like 79."

"So what do you want me to do?"

"Nothing. I don't really know what I am going to do, but I just wanted to let a couple of other people know. I'm going to tell Charlie and Sam as well, but haven't got round to it yet."

"So what else are you doing with all your spare time?"

"What spare time? My eldest daughter has just gone back to work, so I pick her little lad up every night from school and go for a walk with him or we play football. I'm painting the house, still doing a lot of cooking at home and I've just started reading science fiction stuff. It's different from what I normally read."

"Do you still play snooker at the Conservative Club?"

"No. I'm barred. They got a new steward in there. He knew me when I was at Hilton's. Nasty piece of work he was. He told the committee what I was like then and I have had my membership suspended while they look into it. Me and the brother-in-law play at Whitaker's Social Club in Birch Lane. Mind you I might get barred from there as well if they find out that I brew my own ale."

Then he carried on in a much more sombre mood: "I don't know about you Alan, but once you reach my age you start wondering about life and whether there is going to be another one. Well I do, and I've been an atheist ever since I was 16. The way I look at it is to believe that it is as likely there is a life after this one as there was life before this one. But I can't remember anything of it."

"Les Earnshaw could. He once told me that he could vividly remember being a French peasant and marching to Moscow with Napoleon in 1802."

"Well he always did have a vivid imagination did Les. Do you ever see anything of him?"

"He was intending to come in to see us when he was at Leigh for that writers' festival, but never made it."

"Has he been on television again?"

"I don't think so. Somebody would have said if he had been."

102

"That programme he was on with David Frost was one of the funniest things I ever saw."

"I know he's been for a drink with David Frost. I think he said Tom Jones and Englebert Humperdink were there too."

"Aye, and they were all drinking mild as well, I suppose."

"Well say what you will about Les. I'm glad to be able to say that I've known him."

"Aye, and me too."

"You know Charlie has been working here as well, don't you?"

"Yes, Mick Ellison told me. I often see him in ASDA."

"He's nearly 70 now, but you'd never think it."

Then Ray asked about his two children, Rebecca and Robert. After that the conversation roamed over a few other former workmates and friends, some of whom had died, some of whom were ill or rarely seen out and about, and others who seemed to have settled into playing golf every day.

It had been good to talk to Ray, although he didn't seem to have the same zest about him as he once did. He had always been very mentally alert, full of ideas about how to fight a good fight, but a bit less so now. Maybe his home made beer was so good that he was drinking too much of it. Maybe his home made cooking was also so good that he was eating too much of it. He had certainly put on weight, although he was still playing bowls, walking into town every day and tending his allotment in Hemsley.

Normally his discussion with Ray would have been the first thing he would have mentioned to the others the following morning in work. But now there was no one in the electrical section who knew him. He told a couple of the mechanical lads at lunch time, but neither had been that close to Ray. Neither could he tell Charlie. He was down with the flu, brought on no doubt with having spent the previous Sunday afternoon stood in the rain at Knowsley Road for the game against Castleford.

On Friday night he watched Saints beat Hull Kingston Rovers 34–14 in front of less than 5,000 spectators. Alan still enjoyed going to the game, still shouted at the referee and still jumped up-and-down and waved his fist in the air when they scored along with all the other speccies. But somehow it just didn't seem as good as it used to. As he walked back to his car in Gladstone Street, his mind wandered back to the spring of 1966 and two games he had watched between the same two teams.

First there had been the third round of the Challenge Cup when Saints had won 12–10. Five weeks later, the Humbersiders had returned looking for revenge, this time in the Championship semi-final. Again Saints had won, this time by the slightly wider margin of 14–6. What a back line the Saints had had that night with von Vollenhoven, Murphy, Benyon and Len Killeen wearing the numbers two, three, four and five.

Then his mind went back even further, to the days when he first started going to the match. That was when his favourite players had been the likes of Duggie Greenall, Joe Ball, George Parsons, Jimmy Stott and Alan Prescott. Yes he must be getting older he thought, well he was, but so was everybody else. He also thought about his son Robert and daughter Rebecca; the many times he had taken them onto Mount Everest and built dens, played hide and seek and thrown stones at tin cans, not the sort of thing they would enjoy doing now.

The following Friday he made a rare visit into Yorkshire, to Halifax and the famous ground at Thrum Hall. It was his favourite away ground, with its sloping pitch, knowledgeable and ever-friendly supporters. He always enjoyed watching the way the players came out of the pavilion and had to push through the crowd to get onto the pitch. When he had been there in the past it had always been packed, not so much tonight though, with only 5,500 to watch a close game finishing with an 18–12 win for the men in red and white.

Normally he would have discussed the game with Cliff on the Monday morning, but he was currently working on a job in Belgium. When he returned he would wonder what had hit the town while he had been away. The evening he had flown out from Manchester Airport, a fire had destroyed the Fleece Hotel.

It had always been a special place for the people of Ashurst to visit and drink in. It wasn't a pub; it was more like a hotel with a large open area where drinks were served. It was where a bloke would have taken a girl to really impress her. Often local dignitaries would grace the place, famous rugby league players would be in there, Frankie Lane had once stayed there, Bill Hayley and the Comets too. Within a week of what some people honestly believed a bit of council inspired arson, the whole of the land on which the building had once stood had been cordoned off. Within a month it had been flattened and by the time Cliff had returned, the place was unrecognisable.

As a result, the council took the inevitable decision to knock down the adjacent buildings, which included a pie shop, a bike shop, the Ivan Novello music shop and The Picture House cinema, which actually was on the other side of the street. This was something that resulted in a lot of opposition from local people.

In the period after the end of the war, Ashurst had eight cinemas, the Savoy, the Capitol, the Hippodrome, the Scala, the Oxford, the Electric House, the Showboat and the Roxy. These were all within half a mile of the town centre. In addition there was the Hemsley Dog, the Nook End Pavilion and Dob Lane Music House. But with the growth of television in the 1950s, the appeal of the silver screen began to decline. By 1970 only The Picture House, Capitol and the Roxy were still in business. Now the only original one left in the town seemed destined for demolition.

The whole issue of the slum clearances and knocking down older parts of the town was controversial and often split both communities and even families. In one case it had even led to a death. That happened in the Sullivan family, who had lived for years in Judd Street. Mr Sullivan wanted to leave, his wife didn't. One morning, after the postman had delivered a letter about the issue, there had been another big row. Before long, Mr Sullivan needed to go upstairs. She followed him and stood at the bottom of the stairs, still telling him she was staying put. At the top, he stopped, paused to get his breath back, pointed to the banister rail that was slowly coming away from the wall and shouted out:

"Look at this bloody thing. It's dangerous. It's like the rest of this bloody house. It's not safe to live in."

He pulled at it to make his point. It came away from the wall, he fell back and tumbled down the stairs. By the time the ambulance had arrived to rush him to hospital he was dead.

A couple of weeks later, for no apparent reason, the council reversed the decision to knock down The Picture House cinema.

This received big support in the town, even among those who rarely went there, but for whom it was a fond link with their youth.

By now much of the town centre had been pedestrianised, but most Ashursters thought that keeping The Picture House standing was too little too late. They felt that the town was losing much of its character. Typical of this was the soulless bus station, with a layout which even confused the bus drivers.

"More vandalism by Ashurst Council."

It was around this time the Gillarsfield Freedom Party came into being. Their solution to every problem that the people of Gillarsfield faced was independence from Ashurst Council. The small group who ran the party did not really live in Gillarsfield; most of them it seemed lived in cloud cuckoo land. After one of their committee meetings, which usually started in the Queen Victoria at six o'clock and went on until closing time, they decided that once Gillarsfield was free and independent, they would send a delegate to the United Nations and seek to join the International Monetary Fund.

How politically serious they were, or how mentally stable, was never quite clear but all their aspirations for Gillarsfield disappeared when John Telford, the party chairman and his wife Jill Telford, the membership organiser and the hub around which everything was democratically decided, had a bust up over the Common Market.

For the short time they existed, they provided entertainment for the people of Ashurst. But they also provided a smokescreen behind which the Council carried on as before, until everything was thrown into turmoil by a financial scandal in the housing department.

15. Sam the writer

It is amazing how fast word gets round or how quickly a rumour can start. It only needs the sight of a person in a place he or she should not be, or with someone he or she is not normally with, to start it. A bit like the time one of the foremen in the iron foundry, Bill McDonald, had been seen coming out of a pub in Accrington, some 30 miles north of Ashurst, with the sister of his wife Gloria. They were laughing and joking, looked quite inebriated and were very smartly turned out. The person who had seen them was Ken Walker who worked in the machine shop and was driving home after watching his son play football for St Helens Town at Nelson.

Ken mentioned it to his wife when he got home an hour later. She mentioned it to her next door neighbour, who told it to her husband as he was eating his tea. The word got carried a bit further when he told the lad he shared an allotment with on the Sunday morning and by Monday it was all over the factory: "Billy Mac's having an affair with his wife's sister."

Well, she was younger, more attractive, under 12 stone and better looking than their Gloria, who was a little bit overweight to put it tactfully.

The reality was quite different. Billy and Gloria, along with Mavis and Frank, had just been to Burnley to say goodbye to some friends who were emigrating to New Zealand the following day. At the precise time that Billy and Mavis had been observed laughing and joking, apparently together on their own, Gloria was in a telephone box on the other side of the road ringing home to make sure the kids were all right and Frank was spending five minutes in a bookies in the next street.

Around this time rumours were rife in the town. There were some about what further slum clearances were planned, which buildings in the middle of the town were coming down, when the plans for a new swimming pool were going to be announced and what was going to happen to the wasteland on Eastfield Street. The last one would almost certainly be nothing, for it had been like that since 1969, when a long row of Victorian shops had been pulled down for no apparent good reason.

One rumour concerned the future of the Eagle and Child. It was the favourite watering hole for many of those who had worked at Wilkinson's over the years. The reason was threefold, first its proximity. For a long time it had once shared a wall with the wages office. But when the company had been split into two those who worked at Wilkinson's PLC (1982), anyone who wanted to get to it had to go through Wilco-Allison Products, which was a practice that was greatly frowned upon.

When Wilco-Allison closed down, most of the land it stood on had been cleared, so now the pub stood on its own in the middle of an industrial wasteland. It was no longer possible to sneak into the place unobserved for a quick half. Finally, word began to get round that the pub was going to close and on its last day the price of the beer would be the same as it had been in 1937, when it had first opened. It was a miserable day, but that didn't deter many who decided to relive a few memories and go there. Needless to say it attracted such a large number of people that it had sold out by 1pm, much to the regulars' dismay.

The closure of the pub was another nail in the coffin of the town's character. Over the last few years many of the oldest and best loved pubs in the town had either been demolished or turned into wine bars or trendy night clubs. These had included The Red House, The Neck with Two Swans, The Besum, Lady Ellen and The Old Dog.

These closures led to a reduction in the number of bowling greens in the town. Once, the Ashurst Bowls League had included four divisions each with 10 clubs. Most were either linked to a pub or a park, although the best team for years had always been Ashurst Congregational Church, something of an anomaly because the church had been one of the first buildings to be demolished to make way for the new link road to Warrington

Fortunately, The Crimea was still standing, along with The Wigan Arms and The Hyde Bank Arms. That was until the council decided to widen Billinge Road. So, as 1993 proceeded, the whole nature and character of the town began to change beyond all recognition. Some described it as progress, while others were consoled with the knowledge that you can't live in the past. But despite all the changes, it was now quicker for many people to walk into the town than either use the infrequent bus service or drive the car and then find that you couldn't park it anywhere.

Even someone like Thelma, who had only seen the town for the first time in 1962, could easily get upset at what many called the senseless vandalism by people in authority. For Alan, it was

108

much worse, being able to remember what the town was like as far back as the last year of the war when he was five years old.

Then right out of the blue a different sort of rumour began to circulate. Another blast from the past, the former draughtsman Sam Holroyd – or Yorky as he was always known – was back in town, or so it appeared. He and his wife Joyce had spent the first half of the year living with their daughter in Devon. But now he had been seen signing on at Nelson Street Labour Exchange, in a betting shop at Hyde Bank, and at a bus stop at Collins Green heading towards Widnes.

Alan did not believe any of these so-called sightings. There was no way Sam would be back in town and not have made contact, if not with him, then certainly with Charlie. He decided that there was only one way to find out what Sam was up to. He would go up to his house in Hemsley. One of Sam's grandchildren had been living in it while Sam and Joyce had been away. He asked Alan to come in, made him a drink and told him that both Sam and Joyce were definitely still in Devon, although by this time next week they would be back home. So whoever had been seen around town, and looked like their favourite Yorkshireman, was obviously not their favourite Yorkshireman.

A week later Charlie received a phone call from Sam, inviting him and Alan to come round and hear his news; and for him to catch up with what had been happening in Wilkinson's, as Sam still called it. It looked like being a long night, all three had plenty to talk about and as Joyce decided to join them, they decided to listen to Sam's West Country tales rather than talk about what life was like working for Koen Koevermanns. That could be done later.

Joyce and Sam had gone down to Plymouth a week before their daughter Tracey was due to give birth. When she did, it was triplets. Sadly one died fairly soon, but the other two were in excellent health. They had not intended to stay too long, but because of the slightly changed circumstances decided to. Then, just as they were getting ready to return north, Sam had been rushed into hospital to have his appendix removed. Slight complications had meant he had to stay there, and so finally their period of stay in Plymouth was almost three months.

"So what are you two going to do now with all the free time on your hands?" asked Charlie.

"We'll have a couple of months practising doing next to nothing, and then we are going travelling," said Sam.

"Does that surprise you?"

"That depends where you are going travelling to?"

"All over?"

"Like Southport, Blackpool and New Brighton?"

"No. Like both sides of the Equator, like Europe and South East Asia and maybe even America."

"Have you won the pools while you were down there?"

"No. Last month, Joyce's uncle died. She was his last known relative and so she got the house. We are going to sell it, which will pay for the holiday and enable us to give the kids something. Also, we are going to rent this house out while we are away. So I suppose the holiday won't really cost that much anyway."

Then Joyce chipped in: "We each chose three places that we wanted to go to and then we put them all together to see if we could make a grand trip of it."

"So where did you choose?"

"The first place I want to go is to Aravaca. It's a small place just outside Madrid. You see my brother Alex is buried there. He was killed in the Spanish Civil War fighting for the Republic. He was only 19 years old."

She paused for a moment, remembering someone who had obviously been dear and close to her a long time ago.

"The second place I want to go is Robben Island to see the prison where Nelson Mandela was kept for so long. I have always admired him and what he did."

"I didn't know you were such a progressive person. However did you finish up with such a reactionary old dinosaur as Sam?" laughed Alan. "And where is the third place?"

"Vietnam and particularly Hanoi. I have the greatest regard for the Vietnamese people too. I want to see what the place that I have heard and read so much about in the past. You see Alan, I come from a very political family. My dad was involved in the National Minority Movement in the 1920s. He was put in prison for his activities during the General Strike. My mother was similar. She was in the Young Communist League in Manchester when she was a teenager, but that stopped when she had all us kids. There were six of us, but there's only me left now."

"And where are Sam's three places?"

Joyce jumped in before he could answer the question: "Egypt would be the first port of call. That's Egypt near Queensbury on the edge of Bradford where he was born. Then it would be Bailiff

Bridge near Brighouse, where he had his first kiss. It was from a girl called Mona who used to wear strong glasses and then we would be off to Todmorden to a second hand book shop where they sell old comics like the *Beano* and *Dandy*."

She obviously had a good sense of humour and an interesting political background too but then Sam had always spoken well of her. Not surprising either.

"Thank you for that, my dear. Would you now like to leave the room and see if the servants need any more pig swill?"

As he spoke the door bell rang. He went to answer it, came back, told Joyce it was his friend Jimmy, and said: "I'll be back in 10 minutes."

"Have you noticed much of a difference in him?" was the first thing Joyce asked once he was out of hearing. They both replied in the negative. Sam seemed little different than how they had known him for what was now nearly 40 years. He had lost most of his hair, but then so had Charlie.

"I have. I certainly did while we were living at our Tracey's. I don't think he's enjoying being retired. You see, he loved working with you lot, all the humour and backchat, being a bit important because he was a good draughtsman and, of course, he enjoyed drawing things and then seeing them made and all that. I think he also liked being the only Yorkshireman among a bunch of Lancashire folk."

"So what was he like while you were down in Plymouth? Did he not like it down there?"

"One day he said to me 'if laughter is like a medicine, then I haven't any medicine since I've been here'. There was nobody down there he could relate to. There was nobody he could even talk to. He met the odd holidaymaker from up north now and again, but there was never anybody else."

"What does he do with all his time when he's at home?"

"He fiddles about in the shed. He used to go and play bowls with one of the neighbours, but that lad is housebound now. He'll walk down to the library a couple of times a week and read the papers. I just think he's missing being at work."

"He had all sorts of plans for what he was going to do in the last few months before we finished work" said Charlie.

"He's tried different things" Joyce continued, "cooking, fishing, learning a foreign language."

"Which one? English?" laughed Alan.

111

"That's what he misses, someone to have a laugh with all day everyday."

"Can't you make him laugh?"

"It's not the same. Don't get me wrong, he's still good company for me, he always has been, it's just that he needs people around him who are like him."

"Maybe this grand foreign holiday you are going on is what he needs."

"It probably is. He'll be fine being in different countries, maybe having to understand another language. But I know as soon as he gets back, he'll not be happy. I don't suppose there's much he can do about it. It's just old age, I suppose."

"Does he ever do any gardening?" asked Charlie. "That's one thing I do. I've got an allotment and I usually go there two or three mornings a week. Mind you sometimes it's just to have a brew and talk to some of the other gardeners, old timers like me."

"There you are, it's as much a social thing, if you've got other people doing the same thing as you. It's a bit like being in the drawing office, people to talk to, people to get help or advice from, people to share things with and all people like yourself. If Sam does any gardening, he has to do it on his own. There's never anybody in next door's garden. They're a young couple and are out all day at work."

"He was never much interested in sport was he?" she continued. "You could talk about the Saints until kingdom come, you've been watching them for years and you know all about their history. Sam doesn't have that. He might watch the odd match on *Grandstand* but that's it."

"Do you think he'd like to come up to Thatto Heath for a game of bowls now and again? He could meet a few of my pals there, they are all very friendly."

But before she could reply, Sam had returned. As he sat down, Alan looked at the books in the book case behind him. Two books immediately caught his eye: *The Draughtsman's Tale* and *The Actress goes to Heaven.*

"Have you read those two books that Les wrote yet, Sam?" he asked, pointing to them.

Reading them was something Sam had said he would do once he had the time, and being retired meant he had the time.

"I've read the first one. I took it to Plymouth with me."

"Did you enjoy it?"

112

"Oh, aye. I thought it was brilliant. Now that you've reminded me, I think I'll start on the second one."

"How do you fancy doing the same, writing a novel about being a poor, under-nourished, semi-literate Yorkshireman who finds romance, friends and purpose in life in war-torn Britain?"

"I'll get back to you on that one" he replied, using a phrase frequently heard from the mouth of their old section leader Alan Groves, now resident in Malaga in Spain.

"You've got a computer, haven't you? You wouldn't be the first Wilkinson's draffie to take up a career in writing. Les has done, Len Turner did it, Roy Hall has had a couple of articles in *Lancashire Life* and even Alan is at it now."

"Are you" asked Sam.

"Yes, he is" continued Charlie. "Everyday he writes out a shopping list. I mean how much material have you got from your war time experiences in the Merchant Navy for example. Has anybody ever written a novel set in the Arctic Ocean? And just think of all the real people you have known who you could create your characters out of. There's me, there's Greeno, Joan, Mick, Anne, the slowest tracer in the west, John Battersby and all his tales about being in a submarine, Ronnie Garner and that woman from Lees in Oldham who he thought lived in Leigh, Lurch, that tea girl Hazel. It would be a bestseller."

Sam looked at his wife. She nodded encouragingly: "Why not? It would keep you off the streets. You could go to Ashurst Library once a week to do your research. You could even start your novel in Mytholmroyd so you could go over there and look for ideas from your childhood days. You could put the word around the British Legion club; there are a few old-timers there who might help. It might give them something new to do. When it's finished you could get Les to put a word in for you with David Frost. Who knows, in 18 months time you could be a household name."

"Like Harpic or Daz or Omo" laughed Alan

"You could even come and see me and I'll tell you a few stories about living on Elephant Lane that you could twist to your kidney's delight."

"There you are Sam. That's something to get your false teeth into. You could do what Les did when he created his fictional town of Garsdale somewhere between Ashurst and Wigan. You could do the same and maybe call it Darsgale or a place in Yorkshire and call it Huddlesfax or even Mytholmhurst."

113

"Eh, you've made my day."

Then turning to his wife he asked: "Have we got any blank paper and a pencil?"

Had the old Sam returned? But before their conversation could continue any further, there was another knock on the door. It was Sam's friend Jimmy again wanting a bit more help with mending something in his shed.

"I'll let you know how he gets on with it" said Joyce. "I won't push him; I'll just leave him to it."

Then she surprised them both when she went on to say that she had always fancied writing a novel based around the life story of her father. This was something that would be greatly helped by the fact that up in the attic she had found an old suitcase in which were dozens of sheets of paper that he had written during his last two years on earth before he had died in 1960. As someone who had been a veteran of the First World War and was then in the ARP in the Second World War as well as twice having been involved in life-threatening situations as a miner in the bowels of the earth and being put in prison during the General Strike in 1926, there was much to tell.

"I'll go out and buy a couple of pencils and two exercise books this afternoon in ASDA. I'd better get a rubber as well, I'm sure he'll make a couple of mistakes" she jokingly said.

"Eh, thanks for coming lads, you don't know just what you've just what you've done for the pair of us."

"I'll tell you something else you could do Joyce so you don't put all your eggs in one basket. Start playing chess–- that will keep another part of the grey matter working and maybe start on a foreign language as well. You could even sign on at night school."

"Alan, you are an absolute star. I don't know why I didn't think of all that before. I suppose we have just slunk into being old age pensioners when really we are just mature people with time on our hands to be more creative and inspirational."

"Look, you have even started using big words already."

Joyce smiled. "Next time you come up you had better ring for an appointment first because we won't want to be interrupted in our intellectual pursuits."

"Before long you know what you'll be saying" said Charlie.

"What?"

"I don't know how I ever found the time to go to work."

16. Thin Lizzie

"What are you laughing at?"

"You'll never believe this."

"I won't if you don't tell us."

"It's your friend Mr Mortimer."

"What's he done this time?"

It was Pete Mulholland, who had just walked into their office with a story to tell them that would most certainly liven up their lunch time break. Pete's total lack of interest in sport would mean that it wouldn't include any reference to what had been the main subject of discussion all that week. He pulled up a chair, sat down and went on: "Late last night he flew back from that meeting in Brussels he had been to and came straight into work. He must have been hungry, so he went into the coffee room, found some bread and John's new toaster. What the clever bugger didn't know was that while he had been away, they had installed a fire detector in there. The bread must have burned a bit, because it set the alarms off and five minutes later half a dozen firemen came storming into the place."

"It couldn't have happened to a more arrogant, self-opinionated, miserable species of Neanderthal man."

"What had he been doing in Brussels?"

"I think that he was trying to get some money from the Common Market to fund the research on the new leveller device the research lab is working on."

"More likely he has been trying to get some money to fund his expenses. That must be the fourth time this month he's been abroad."

"How does he get away with it?"

"I wish I knew."

"Mind you he has got the necessary qualifications for his job."

"What?"

"A first class degree in failure studies."

"He certainly doesn't have qualifications in man management."

"He has in mad management."

They carried on eating their sandwiches.

"We had a bloke like him at Cross Gates. I never knew anyone who got away with doing so little and be paid so much."

It was Shaun, ready as always to tell them about another of the characters who he had known when he had worked at an engineering company in Leeds.

"Was that your mate Norman?"

They all knew about Norman Butterworth. Shaun had told many a tale about his run-ins with his one time boss, so they knew what to expect.

Shaun nodded and went on: "He always used to stay late two nights a week, although nobody ever seemed to know why. It was always on Monday and Tuesday night and then suddenly it changed to Wednesday and Thursday.

"Then we found out why. You see the wife of one of the lads in the office was friendly with one of the cleaners. Around this time she had told Adam's wife that she was going to change her nights cleaning there to Thursday and Friday because she'd just got another job working Mondays and Tuesdays at a shop in town. So when Norman changed his late nights as well, it seemed a bit more than a coincidence. We began to suspect that him and her were having a bit of a fling. Anyway, the following week the shop foreman Frank decided he would look into the matter.

"He knew that the last place she cleaned was the drawing office and that she usually went in there about half seven. He was another one for always working late, so he sneaked in through the back door and found the pair of them at it in the print room. Now he would have made a great detective because he took with him a balaclava and a camera. So when he saw what was going on, he pulled the balaclava over his face so Norman wouldn't know who he was if he saw him, took some photographs and left. But he told nobody what he had done.

"A week later he announced that he would be selling raffle tickets in aid of an appeal to repair the roof on his local church and one of the prizes would be a collection of some saucy photographs. He also put the word round that they showed somebody on the council, which was partly true, though not in the way everyone suspected. Well he sold over a hundred quid's worth. It was all for a good cause and without knowing much about it, the vicar of the church was very pleased.

"So you can imagine what happened when the photographs went on public display just before they made the draw. The first one was one of the Lord Mayor of Leeds holding a bottle of HP sauce in each hand and sitting in front of a huge mound of chips.

It turned out he was Frank's cousin, but the rest were of Norman and Thin Lizzie.

"The following day when Norman heard about how he had been photographed he went ballistic. He stormed down to Frank's place, started shouting and bawling at him, threw a couple of punches at him in the presence of at least three witnesses and was subsequently sacked. Of course nobody was quite sure whether it was for making war on somebody at work or for making love to somebody at work."

"Why was she called Thin Lizzie?"

"Because her name was Elizabeth and she was pretty thin, although very sexy with it."

"And what happened to her?"

"She got sacked as well, but she wasn't too bothered because a week later she got offered a job as a stripper at a club in Hunslet."

"And what about Norman?"

"Nobody knows, he just disappeared and then a few weeks later the redundancies started and I was one of the first to be shown the door so I never found out."

Then he made a comment that he often made: "You wouldn't believe some of the things that used to go on there."

"Was it as good as this place?"

"Hard to say. I've heard you lot tell me about what things used to be like here in the past. All I know is that that place was unbelievable when I first went there. Well it seemed to be and yet at the same time, the bosses made a lot of money and we were always busy. Mind you the pay was crap, but we made up for it on the social side, particularly when ever they sent us out on site."

"A bit like here. We were never the best paid in Ashurst."

"And we still aren't."

Before any more could be said, there was a very loud explosion. It was the fourth they had heard that morning. As they looked through the windows, they could see a huge pall of smoke rising. One thing that they could no longer see was the old copper refinery. Eckersley's Demolition had just demolished it. Another bit of Wilkinson's history and one of Ashurst's landmarks had just disappeared. If Bold Power Station had still been standing they would now be able to look across the town to see it about four miles away, but a few weeks earlier that had also been raised to the ground. In fact, the whole landscape, not only of Ashurst, but of the whole of the industrial north was slowly being destroyed in order to make space to have houses built upon it for people who didn't have employment, or at least any meaningful employment.

This prompted Cliff to say that the new estate on what had once been known as Mount Everest was now finished and ready for occupation. But before any further could be said, they were interrupted by the arrival of Mr Johnson.

He had now come out of his shell. For his first few months he had rarely ventured out of his office and whenever he did walk round the factory, he never seemed to acknowledge anybody whose path he crossed; even the very most simple of things, like smiling back at someone who had smiled, or nodded, or said good morning to him. Not even saying thank you if a person had held a door open for him. Wherever he had been brought up, they had certainly never been taught any manners.

One of the rare examples of his other side had been with Alan when he had returned from Porto. Then he had been quite charming, but then he did have the surname Johnson, just like Alan's wife Thelma had once had. This, of course, had led to Charlie declaring one day that he thought he must be one of her relatives: "Maybe he's Greeno's father-in-law."

But nothing could be further from the truth. In fact the only person in Ashurst that Mr Johnson was anything like was Councillor Moore, one of the town's least popular residents.

Maurice Moore was well known around the town for the devious and self-rewarding way he carried on. Most councillors were usually elected to serve their constituents. In Maurice's case it appeared as though he had been elected to serve himself. He was a self-made man, a man in love with his creator and was frequently out of town on council business with all expenses paid, as well as his salary for his job as a quality control inspector at Hiltons. Whenever anyone commented about the amount of time that he spent away from work, he would complain bitterly to them about not being able to lead a normal life, having to travel to conferences and exhibitions at such awful places as London, Brighton, Edinburgh and on one occasion Paris for a whole week.

Eighteen months earlier and a month before polling day, Maurice began to realise that he would not get re-elected, unless he did something that won him a lot of public support. As a result and with the full support of the vicar of Ashurst Parish Church and the priest at St Theresa's Church, he launched his election

118

campaign around the need to keep Sunday as the Lord's Day. In his view this meant stopping the playing of organised games on council-owned property, which basically meant the town's public parks. With the full agreement of the Council's Ways and Means committee, this proposal was voted on and passed by council. A full report was carried on the front page of both local papers on the following Friday. Going well over the top, the *Ashurst Reporter* had also included a statement that police would be on hand to deal with any trouble from teenagers who might feel aggrieved by this decision.

Of course, none of the people who were going to be affected by this decision actually had the vote. They were the young lads who played in the Ashurst Junior Under-17s League, an organisation that had its own set of rules. This was because the two teams could decide on the night whether to play seven-a-side rugby or seven-a-side soccer. The regular teams in the league were Gillarsfield Giants, Mather's Apprentices, Hilton's Social, Nook End Park Rovers, Queens Park Rangers, Ashurst Spartak and Ashurst Dynamo, with the last two only ever wanting to play soccer.

The Giants played at the back of Gillarsfield Labour Club, the apprentices at Mathers' Social club, Hilton's Social on wasteland at the top of Bell Lane, and Ashurst Dynamo and Ashurst Spartak both used fields at Lowton Bank. Thus, only Rovers and Rangers would be directly affected by this anti-social act by the Council.

One person who was greatly annoyed by this decision was Joe Stephens, whose son Tony played scrum-half for Queens. Joe had been scheming for a long time to expose Councillor Moore for something he had done in the past. Joe had once been the secretary of Ashurst Trades and Labour Council and was particularly skilled at fighting campaigns on issues about social injustice. This latest act by the council provided him with an ideal opportunity. The following day he went to see Councillor Moore and politely asked him if the park was going to be out of bounds to the public every Sunday evening, or would it still be permitted for ratepayers like himself to walk dogs on the grass. Not realising that he was being set up, Councillor Moore said that the park would still be open to the public. In his words, Britain was a free country and there was nothing to stop any member of the public using a public park as long as it wasn't for organised team games.

This was just what Joe wanted to hear. He worked out his plan with Tony and a couple of his teammates. They then visited members of the other team to tell them how they could beat the killjoys on the council, but they had to keep quiet about it.

On Sunday evening around a dozen members from each team, plus a few apprentices headed towards Boundary Lane Park, although few knew exactly what was going to happen. Tony told the members of his team to stand on the grass in a line about two yards apart. They were followed by members from Hilton's Social, who stood behind them followed by lads from Ashurst Dynamo, some of whom had brought their girlfriends and parents. Behind them lined up members of the other teams, their girlfriends, more parents or brothers and sisters along with four nurses from Victoria Hospital, who had never seen some many eligible young men in one place at the same time. Within minutes there were at least 200 people all stood on the grass in a very long line.

People walking by, some going to church, others visiting relatives and friends, and stopped in amazement to ask what was happening which, of course, was absolutely nothing. Then a photographer and a journalist from the *Lancashire Evening Post* appeared. They had been promised a scoop by Joe and got it. Not long after, a police car had appeared to find out what was going on just as the photographer was about to take his first photograph. To cap it all, in the next day's paper, splashed right across the front page was a photograph that focussed on a young draughtsman from Mather's Foundry holding a poster that declared "Vote for Maurice Moore and he'll let you stand on the grass for nothing".

Never had there been so much laughing and joking about such a ridiculous form of a protest. In the end around 500 people must have joined in. And the funniest thing to come out of this was when the owner of the Wigan Lane Photography shop decided to stand in the forthcoming elections as an independent and proceeded to defeat Councillor Moore handsomely. At the same time he got a huge amount of free publicity for his new business with his slogan "Vote for me and I'll not be negative about sport".

Rather ironically, a few weeks later the league fell into terminal decline. A week after the 'party in the park', Gillarsfield's ground was sold to a property developer who immediately fenced it all off and then proceeded to build flats on it. The tip that Hilton's used and had once been part of Gillarsfield Colliery was designated as the site for a memorial for all those Ashurst miners who had been killed in various mining disasters and shortly after became the entrance to the Mayfield Business Park.

Around this time, three members of the Ashurst Spartak team signed on for St Helens Town, while their goalkeeper went for a trial at Ashurst Magistrates Office and was subsequently sent down for the remainder of the season. As all this was going on, the other members of the team decided to change codes and signed for the Astley Rovers Rugby League club. And so the league fell apart, but not Councillor Moore's ambitions.

Before long he had wormed his way back onto the council for North Ward, the previous holder having suffered a heart attack on hearing that he had won the pools. Soon Maurice was on the planning committee, where he acted in an anti-social way, in the name of cost effectiveness and open governance. But it ended in grief when he upset the town hall caretaker and odd job man.

Neil was one of the nicest people you could ever hope to meet. Some of the managers and a couple of the busiest or laziest councillors would often get him to do things that were not his responsibility. But his actions helped the running of various departments. The bonus for Neil was that he managed to get plenty of overtime, plus trips out. All this was done without him filling out a timesheet. But once Maurice learned that Neil drank every Friday in The Lamb with Joe Stephens and a few of his mates, he decided to have a go at him and his lax way of working.

Just about everybody else who worked in the ways and means department had to have a job number for any work they did. Getting Neil to do many bits of jobs at no cost to anybody's budget helped the smooth running of the department. But as soon as every minute of Neil's week had to be recorded, many of the staff could no longer use his services for free. So Neil soon discovered that he was stuck in his store room in the town hall basement all day long. Maurice said that "ratepayers' money had been saved".

A few weeks later, Neil was told to work late one Thursday evening for an important meeting of the ways and means committee which was to be held in the committee room at the end of the corridor on the third floor. One of his tasks was to arrange for a buffet to be delivered along with the usual liquid refreshment. As soon as all the members of the committee had arrived, Maurice told Neil to go back to his store room in the basement and come back at nine to lock up.

It was clear what was going to happen. There would be a short meeting, where the decision on which local builder had been given the contract to put up a block of flats on the site of the old Newton Road School was made. Then there would be a long break for the buffet to be eaten and the fine wines tasted, all which would end about 8.45pm. This was nothing new on the Ways and Means committee, its members were well known for wasting much of the ratepayers' money by working out ways to save the local ratepayers money.

As Neil left the room, in a most patronising way, Maurice said: "Don't forget to lock all the offices. We don't want people going where they shouldn't go."

As a result and as he always did, Neil walked along the corridor and locked all the office doors. But he also saw fit to lock the door to the toilets. He repeated this on the second, first and ground floors, went into the basement and opened the door of the lift.

Maurice was quite well built, but had a weak bladder. Within a few minutes after having drunk two glasses of wine, he said to no-one in particular: "I'm just nipping to the office".

But, of course, he found the toilet door was locked. So he shuffled down the stairs and discovered that the second floor toilet was also locked. Then down he went to the first floor, ground floor and then to the basement to find Neil who was nowhere to be found. This was because he was hiding. Now somewhat desperate, Maurice pushed the fire doors open and went out to relieve himself albeit in the drizzling rain into a little grid in the town hall car park. Quick as a flash, Neil pulled the fire doors to, leaving Maurice to go all round the car park in a vain attempt to get back round to the front of the building. But on the night in question, there in the rain, Maurice was somewhat relieved, but then not pleased to discover that the staff gate to the car park yard had also been locked.

Not surprisingly, the story went round the town the following day and amused no end of people, none more so than Joe, who then put the knife in, so to speak, by deciding to stand in the next local elections in Maurice's ward, beating him handsomely on a programme that including limiting any councillor's annual expenses to a maximum of £1,000.

17. Rugby disunion

"We've got a new man starting on Monday. He's from the Amsterdam office, though by the sound of his name he must be a true blue Englishman."

"What is it?"

Alan looked at the paper he had on his desk and replied: "Nigel Huntringham de' langelo Carruthers"

"You are joking."

"That's right, it's John Davies."

"Well if he's good enough to work here, he must be good. What's on his CV?"

Alan looked at the papers again and replied: "It looks like tomato sauce, but then it might just be red wine."

"You are in a good mood today. What did you have for your breakfast?"

"Egg and bacon with tomato sauce and all washed down with red wine."

"Have you won the pools or come into some money?"

"No, I've just come into work and met you."

"So you must want to borrow some money off me?"

"Why, have you got some to spare?"

"I will have when I've won the pools."

"And when will that be?"

"This week I hope, I've just had the gas bill."

They then switched to the more serious subject of work and the current job they were both engaged on; the design of a new metering system for Aberthaw power station in South Wales.

"It'll be a bit of a coincidence if this new bloke is from Wales. He could be with a name like Davies."

"I wonder if he is a rugby man. That might liven things up a bit in here especially if he's a rah rah."

"What has he been working on in Amsterdam?"

"Haven't a clue. This bit of paper doesn't tell me much about his background, other than he's 32 years old, married with three wives and 14 children."

"Sounds like a productive sort of a guy. I don't think he'll fit in here. Where are you going to put him?"

"I was thinking of sacking Colin and let this new bloke use his computer, but I suppose that will only have him moaning again."

"Too right it will; blatant discrimination against the younger members of the office if you try and sack me."

"Young, you? There's nobody young in here. We are all old men sailing off into the industrial sunset. When did you last see a young draughtsman?"

It was a comment made in jest, but it was true. The only young draughtsmen ever seen in the drawing office now were the apprentices spending three or six months there. If Scott had been in, he would have been able to remind them that he was still young, but every Thursday he went to Ashurst Technical College.

On the following Monday morning the new man arrived. Alice brought him up from reception. If he did play rugby or rather if he had once played rugby, he would probably have been a half-back. He may not have been a big man, but he had a strong grip as Alan discovered as they shook hands. They went into Alan's office, sat down and started to exchange useful information. After a while the new man looked at a photograph on Alan's desk and asked who it was? It was a photograph of Thelma, all decked out in a typical Welsh outfit and with a tall pointed hat on her head.

"It's our Maud."

Then he went on to say that was a local way of referring to one's wife.

"Her name is Thelma."

"Is she Welsh?"

"Yes."

"Where from?"

So then Alan explained how she had been born in Tonyrefail and lived there until her mother had died when she was a baby and been put in a home in Cardiff where she had lived for the next 16 years of her life.

"Tonyrefail, eh. I know that place well."

He went on to say that it wasn't that far from where he had grown up, which was just outside Swansea, and had two aunties who lived there and who he had always visited in the summer. One used to live about five minutes walk from Thelma's mother's house in Beechmount Terrace. He was aiming to go to Swansea once he had got some transport sorted out and was planning to call in and see her in the old people's home where she now lived.

That had certainly helped get him off to a good start, not that he needed it. He was dead easy to get on with and chatty too, although a bit unsure about the Ashurst idea of humour that was all around him.

Much of his first day was spent on the shop floor. On Tuesday he went to Blyth power station in the north east with a senior engineer and didn't return until early Friday afternoon; not a bad time to wind down and chat with his new workmates.

He told them that he had been working in Holland for five years and had lived with a woman from Thailand until they had recently split up; she wanted to return to her family in Bangkok.

"So what brought you from Amsterdam to Ashurst?" asked Colin. "Most folk I know would have preferred to go the other way."

"This is a bit of an unbelievable story but I had to leave Amsterdam for my own safety. I could easily have been murdered or beaten up and for something I hadn't done."

They waited with interest for his explanation.

"About two months ago one of Amsterdam's underworld was released from prison. He'd been in there seven years for various crimes he'd committed. He'd come straight back onto the local scene to settle a few old scores and get involved in drugs, thieving, robbery and crime involving young children. The main problem was that he is the spitting image of me, although he was three or four years younger. I heard about him from a policeman who lived in the same block as I did.

"I didn't think much of it at first, but a week later I got roughed up by two young lads on my way home late one night for no reason at all. This guy's reappearance really messed everything up for me. I couldn't safely go out at night, people would have had a drink and emotions could run high, because of what he had done. So I told the boss and he said there was work for me if I wanted it either in a new office they are opening in Saudi or here. Well I'd already worked in Dubai and didn't fancy going back there so I came here. He said there was three months guaranteed work here so I took it. Strange, eh."

It was, but then Colin could also easily appreciate the man's predicament. Going home one night to Haydock, he had been attacked by two drunken men who had obviously mistaken him for somebody else for with every punch and kick, they had kept calling him 'you dirty Scottish bastard'.

"You are here for three months at least then?"

125

"Yes, so I'll need to know where a 30-something can get his kicks in this town."

So Alan chipped in with some suggestions on how John could spend time and money and be well entertained: "You have plenty choice of things to do here over a weekend. Take Sunday for starters. There are at least seven churches where I am sure you will be made welcome on Sunday morning and again on Sunday night if you want a repeat performance. On Sunday afternoon, you could catch a bus into St Helens and go and walk round Carr Mill Dam, plenty of fishermen will be there to watch or whisper to.

"On Saturday morning Ashurst library has a poetry reading session that usually attracts quite a crowd and this Saturday afternoon the animal rights people are having a stall on the market. That should be quite good for a punch up if the Cat's Protection League people are prowling about and on Saturday evening, the Gillarsfield Light Sympathy Orchestra is performing in Ashurst Theatre."

John smiled to himself. This was his introduction to Ashurst humour and he was enjoying it.

"The best bit of entertainment though over the whole weekend will be at Knowsley Road tonight. The Saints are playing Halifax. That's where me and Cliff are going. Come with us if you want."

"I suppose that must be rugby league."

"Indeed my friend. Have you ever seen a live game before?"

It turned out he hadn't. He had watched the Challenge Cup Final at Wembley on the television and the odd game on *Grandstand* on a Saturday afternoon. He had played rugby union to a reasonable level and seemed fairly open-minded about the other code. So he decided to take up Alan's offer and go and watch his first live match.

On the way there Alan explained the main differences between the two codes. As he read the programme after having picked their spot near the halfway line, he showed John the team and pointed out that the numbering system in League was with the numbers one to seven being the backs and eight to 13 the forwards. He told John to look out for the Saints number six. It was Jonathan Griffiths a Welshman who had been signed from Llanelli rugby union four years earlier.

John watched the game with interest. Saints were on form and in the end won 34–25. But the Halifax team had contributed to an entertaining evening; one that John had thoroughly enjoyed judging by the way he talked about what he had just seen on the way back in the car to the Hemsley Hilton where he was staying.

"When I played union and lived at home, we used to think that rugby league was all start-stop with that play-the-ball. I think we must have been allowing ourselves to be brainwashed. I'm surprised just how quickly play continues after a player has been tackled. I think some of my old teammates would have quite enjoyed that game tonight."

"Are you still in touch with any of them?"

"I will be next week. I'm going down there on Friday night, unless of course Saints are playing," he laughed.

"There's only one game on next week. It's the Challenge Cup Final at Wembley on Saturday. Wigan and Widnes are playing. It should be a cracker too. Get all your mates to watch it on BBC."

Just like Hugo, who was now working in Hong Kong, John was a dab hand at using the computer. He could rattle off drawings with great skill and accuracy and then sit back and chat. And for much of his time, he liked to talk about the Dutch way of life. But at the start of his third week he had a new topic of conversation, the result of his visit home to Swansea.

He had been very busy going visiting all his relatives, some in hospital, some in old peoples' homes and one, a former miner, in a caravan, living there because his house had been repossessed by an uncaring building society. He had watched the Challenge Cup Final in a mate's house and was interested that many of the old negative attitudes to rugby league had gone. In addition on the way down he had called in at Tonyrefail to see his two aunties. Sadly both had died quite recently, so he walked round to Beechmount Terrace and took a couple of photographs to give to Alan's wife Thelma.

On his return he went in to see Alan with the news that he was not now intending to stay too long. Something of the inevitable had happened. Going back home had convinced him that he wanted to return there. He had spent over eight years away, had worked in at least seven different countries and made a lot of money, some of which he had spent foolishly, but the most of which he had saved. He had also met an old flame in Swansea, taken her out on the Saturday evening and realised he still held a candle for her. She wasn't quite like he had first known her – when she was just 17 – now she was almost twice as old, a widow, mother of two children and lived in a damp council house.

127

He stayed another three weeks in Ashurst, long enough to return to Knowsley Road to watch the Saints beat Leeds 15–2 in the Premiership semi-final. He also spent a small fortune in the club shop buying stuff both for himself and kids and baby stuff for two people that he was going to have a hand in helping make sure that they were brought up properly.

In order to ensure that the work he had started on at Blyth Power Station would be finished on time, an agency man on a short term contract was employed. He was quite different to John both in his attitude to work and to those he was working with. He arrived late on his first day, only five minutes but still late, inexcusable really since he only lived in Egypt Street which was little more than a quarter of an hour's walk away. By 9.30 he was in trouble with the office rules, when he tried to light up, only to be told that no smoking was allowed in the office. Anyone wanting to smoke had to go outside, which clearly upset him.

At 10am he asked if anybody could change a five pound note in order for him to get a drink out of the vending machine and before he had drunk it, he had managed to place the cup on a print on his reference table, leaving a coffee stain on it. Just before lunch he used the phone twice for personal calls, one to tell someone the office number where he could be contacted and one to a dentist to arrange an appointment on Friday afternoon. During all this time he had hardly said a word to anyone in the office, neither did it appear that he had added much information to a block cable diagram he had been given to modify.

Where he went for his lunch nobody knew or cared, though they were all amazed when he walked back into the office 10 minutes late. The general view was that he wouldn't last long. On Tuesday he was a bit better both in respect of his timekeeping and his appearance in that he had had a shave. He only went out twice for a smoke and even chatted to Scott. On Wednesday and Thursday he appeared to be quite active on his computer and then at 4pm on Thursday, he asked Alan if he could stay late as he wanted to leave at lunch time the following day to go to the dentist. All this in his first week. Needless to say he was not invited to join the party for the following week.

His short stay reminded Colin of a situation he had once experienced when he had worked in London a few years earlier. One Monday a new draughtsman had started. He was very chatty, friendly and highly skilled. By Thursday morning everyone who he

128

had dealt with or spoken to was impressed by him. At lunch time he told the draughtsman on the drawing board next to him that he was going up to Oxford Street, about 10 minutes walk away, to do some shopping. He never returned. He left all his equipment in his drawer and any letters sent to the address he had given were never answered. Strange, but true.

Colin then told the embarrassing tale of his first job in London when he had worked in a drawing office in the BMA building near to Euston station. On his first Friday lunchtime, he went to Heal's, a large department store just off Tottenham Court Road. It was only five minutes walk away.

He spent about 20 minutes in there and then set off to return to the drawing office and after a few minutes discovered that he was heading in the opposite direction towards Oxford Street. He asked about half a dozen people the way back to Tavistock Place and of course no one knew and in the end finished up returning in a taxi to make sure he was back on time. What he had done without realising it, was to enter the store at the north side and leave by the exit on the south side. But it was his first time in London so was understandable.

However, as he got out of the taxi, four of his new workmates were just about to enter the building. One of them a right chirpy Cockney made some comment that Colin didn't quite catch, but guessed it had been directed at him rolling up in a taxi. So in order to make them laugh or just make an impression he replied: "That's not the only thing I've ridden in or on this lunch hour."

With the end of the rugby season nigh and the arrival of summer, the other most popular sport began to take up the time of those who had it to spare. No it wasn't cricket or yachting or eventing or polo, but crown green bowls. At one time around 30 draughtsmen would play in the office league. At least once a week you played against an opponent, two games of 21 up during the lunch break. At the end of each day the league table would be updated. In late September there would be the office bowling outing to Blackpool. The game was an important part of the culture of the whole area. But with the decline in the number of draughtsmen and then the decision to build on the bowling green, the league had come to an end. However, it was still easy enough to play in the local park, something that Alan did every week with his neighbour Phil and a couple of old timers from Clyde Street.

129

Playing bowls in Boundary Lane Park was always a good way to spend a couple of hours, especially with Donald and Arthur. There was the enjoyment of bowling off the jack and then remembering the line it had taken and conscious of the difference in the bias between your bowl and the jack, aiming to get a toucher, or a noddy as they liked to call it in Ashurst. Then observing the way your opponent with a bowl with a different bias to you, attempted the same. The game could be so engrossing you often saw grown men running after a bowl muttering: go on, go on, go on, go on.

Another good thing about Donald and Arthur was just listening to them chat and back chat. It might be one of a great number of different topics, politics, local council business, the Saints, the youth of today, mother in law jokes, old pals they had seen or who had recently died. No matter what it was, it was always entertaining to listen to them.

Another plus about playing there was that people would be walking past all the time, some you knew, some you didn't. Some would want to chat and hold up the game, others just shouted their news right across the green for every man and his dog to hear. Now and again somebody famous would walk past, a footballer or a rugby league international, a boxer or maybe someone who had had his name in the local paper recently.

Another thing about bowls was that it was so absorbing and relaxing. Sometimes there may be four or five groups of two or four players on the same green. At those times not only did you have to pay attention to how you could get as near to your jack as possible; you also had to time your go so as not to miss a bowl going across the crown from some other game. Perhaps the reason for the great interest in the game was to be found in the school playground. As children, everybody had spent much of their free time both in the dinner hour in the playground or in the evening in the street playing stonies.

Not many children could do that now. They would risk life and limb in many streets just trying to cross to the other side. Another place to play stonies used to be on Mount Everest. That was no longer possible with the new housing estate that had been built on It. But, in the new houses there, young children would invariably be seen watching television, playing on their computers or pestering one of their parents to drive them to the house of one of their friends who might live less than a mile away.

130

18. Ashurst women's group

As he walked into the house, Alan heard the sound of snoring. He entered the living room and saw his wife Thelma fast asleep on the settee and two empty wine bottles on the table.

"Well, it looks as though you have had a very busy day. Has your wine tasting circle been round again?"

"Make us a drink of coffee will you Alan" she replied as she struggled to get up, then, knocked one of the bottles on to the floor, staggered across the room and went upstairs.

Five minutes later, she told him that there had been a visitor to the house that afternoon. It was Joyce Holroyd, Sam's wife.

"She came about two o'clock. She left about half an hour ago and we never stopped talking."

"What about?"

"All sorts of things. It would appear that Charlie's suggestion to Sam to start writing a book has worked. He's already written three chapters, Joyce has read them and somehow it's given her the idea that she wants to do something different with her life. I think that they were both in a bit of a rut. Well they aren't now."

"So is she going to write a book as well?"

"No, but she's come up with a few interesting ideas and I'm going to get involved in something with her as well. A women's readers group or maybe some sort of a discussion group. She knows a lot of women up Hemsley who would be interested just to get together and have a chat now and again. It seems a good idea and she's full of them, so I'm going up there next Monday to have another chat about it."

"And drink their wine as well!"

"Discussing matters of importance is very thirsty work, Alan."

"Well, there are two things you could get involved with?"

"What?"

"I heard today the council is considering closing Bell Lane library and there are also rumours that there are going to be big changes at Victoria Hospital. Dave Ainsworth told me about it today. It came from his daughter, she works for the health authority and saw some so-called confidential papers that her boss had left in the photocopier."

"I could get involved in either of those. All these cost-cutting measures by the council have to be opposed. It's about time somebody did something about them."

"So Sam must be all right, by the sound of it."

"He is. They've put off going on that world trip for a bit so he can have this book he's writing finished in time for Christmas."

"He won't find it that easy to get it published. And what's going to happen to the family that were going to live there while they were away?"

"I don't know, she never mentioned anything about it. You know she's really nice. I know she's older than me, but she's right down to earth and friendly too, well for an English woman."

"Does she want me to go up and see him?"

"I'll ask her next week. I think Sam is too busy to see anybody at the moment. He went to Liverpool today to look at some records in the Maritime Museum and she said he's going to the library in Manchester next week. "

"Good for him, but let's just turn our attention now to one other extremely important matter. What's for tea?"

"We've got quite a wide range of options. It could be fish and chips, or fish, chips and peas, or fish, chips, scallops and peas or fish, chips, scallops, peas, curry sauce and gravy."

"I'll go and get them. You lay the table and after tea, maybe I'll lay you."

"Oo, promises, promises; and what are you going to do after seven o' clock?"

He walked out of the house, went up Silkstone Street as far as the ginnel that ran between numbers 40 and 42 and went through into Dalton Street. He crossed Fairclough Street only to discover that Edith's Chip Shop was not open on a Thursday. He walked back down Dalton Street, turned right up Tyrer Street and was pleased to see that Frank's was. There was a long queue so he had to wait. He looked at the people stood in front of him, they were nearly all women, all about his age or older. They looked as though they would not be out of place in Lowry painting. Somehow, he couldn't imagine any of them being involved in a women's group run by Joyce. Not that there was anything wrong with them or with Joyce. Far from it.

He had recently read a book about Ashurst in the 1930s and the way that a group of Oxford University academics had portrayed the women who lived there in a series of photographs and interviews. It was clear that those women and those who had interviewed them lived in two separate worlds. Looking at the

132

couple in front of him, they gave the appearance that they still were living in the 1930s. But then Frank's Chip Shop had altered little since it had been opened by Frank's dad in 1945. Being in there was like going back in time, like being part of history that had gone, and been forgotten about by those with power, influence and wealth.

"What do you want lad, octopus, shark, walrus or cod?"

It was Frank himself, waking up Alan who was miles away.

"Fish, chips, peas and scallops twice to take out."

What a daft thing to say. There was no room in the place to eat anyway. In fact, Frank once had a notice up declaring "No food to be consumed on the premises".

After they had eaten, Alan suggested she could do with some fresh air so they went out with the aim of walking round Boundary Lane Park. As they approached the bandstand, they saw a large crowd stood round the bowling green. Alan remembered that it would be the Ashurst League semi-final between Hemsley Victoria and Ashurst Congs for the right to meet Carlton Lane Conservative Club in the final in a fortnight's time.

They found a space to stand and, after asking who was winning, proceeded to watch for a while. The Vic were in Division Three whereas the Congs as always were near the top of Division One. The Vic had unearthed a new star in the form of one Guptar Singh, a patternmaker at Mathers' foundry and whose family ran the mini-market in Dob Lane.

He was clearly able to perform at a higher level than Division Three, something that was being noticed around the town. As they watched, an old guy stood next to Thelma said to his mate: "I didn't know they played bowls in India. He's a bloody good bowler, that lad."

"Well, he did used to play for Little Lever when he lived in Bolton."

It didn't take long for the Congs to win their way through to the final though, despite Guptar's valiant efforts.

As the players shook hands, the man stood next to Alan and said: "Well there'll be some fireworks in the final now."

"Why?"

"There always is when them two meet. Last time they did, one of the Congs players got sent off. How can you get sent off playing bowls?"

"It's all the fault of the Conservative Club. Whenever you play

133

there, there's always a dog roaming round. I reckon when they are losing, they let it loose."

"How do you mean?"

"Nook End Labour Club played them last week. My mate was bowling for them and winning 19–4. Then this dog appears from nowhere, pisses all over the jack and bites my mate on his ankle."

"Look out, here comes the rain. I'm off for a pint."

"I don't suppose you fancy a pint do you, Thelma?"

"Alan, I couldn't drink a pint if you paid me. Let's go home. Watching that game has put me right in the mood."

"For what?"

"Staying up late to watch that horror film on Channel Four."

The following Monday afternoon Thelma went up to see Joyce. They had the house to themselves, Sam was out again. He had unearthed a lot of information about that period of the war which saw British ships sailing to Murmansk to take supplies to the Soviet Union. He had also found the names and addresses of three people who had written about the subject. One lived in the Shetland Islands and another near Dover and so Sam had written to them both. The third lived at Heptinstall, just over the border in West Yorkshire, close to his old house in Mytholmroyd and fairly near to that bookshop in Todmorden, the one that sold comics like *Dandy* and *Beano* along with *Rover, Hotspur, Adventure, Wizard* and *Radio Fun*.

Thelma and Joyce both agreed it would be a good idea to set up a writers' group. Neither had ever tried any serious writing before although having seen the change for the better in her husband, Joyce had begun thinking about doing something similar. She wasn't sure whether to base it on the life of her father or on herself. At first she thought that she hadn't led such an interesting life, but as ideas floated round in her head she realised that she had plenty material to choose from. For a start, there was her link with Sam. This went back to when he had come unexpectedly into her life when visiting Ashurst for the first time to attend the wedding of an old shipmate in 1947 and how he had come to adjust to life in Lancashire.

Then there had been her first husband, Mick. He had worked at the Southport Edge, Old Benton and Montagu pits, the last one being where he had been killed in a horrific explosion of methane gas. There had also been Mick's father, an old soldier who had managed to survive four years in the trenches in the Great War

134

and had a wide range of stories to tell. There had also been her own father, whose experiences in the way he and thousands of others were treated on their return to 'a land fit for heroes' had led to him joining the Communist Party.

In the 1930s he had become involved in the fight against the Mosleyites and had been beaten up by the police after a big anti-fascist demonstration in Manchester. He had left her not only a fascinating amount of papers and documents, but also an outlook that had dominated her through life, until she had brought her young son Paul into the world. Marriage with Mick, his sad death and then getting together with Sam followed. Not long after that they had taken in her young niece after Joyce's sister and her husband had been killed in a motorbike accident at Burtonwood.

As she grew older, she began to think more about her childhood days and contrasted it with what was now going on in the world. She wanted to do more than just sit back and complain about what the government, the council and big business were doing. In Thelma she had found a soul mate, Thelma who had lead such a different life, although she likewise could equally see through all the gloss, glitter and drivel of early 1990s Britain.

On that very morning, it had been announced that Bell Lane Library was to be closed. It was only open three afternoons a week and all day Saturday and few new books ever seemed to arrive on its shelves. Once upon a time it had a reading room, but that had been closed as part of a previous cost-cutting exercise by the council. It was a place where people bumped into neighbours and friends and had a chat. Of course you shouldn't talk in a library, but the place did fulfil a useful function, although not one that most of the local council's members thought important.

"They can buy their *Sun* at Wainwright's newsagents when they are buying their cigs" said one 'Independent' councillor.

"Half of them round there can't read anyway," said another "so why should we be bothered?"

In the past, Councillor Franshaw, for whom economics and good governance were the be-all and end-all, had suggested that a 20p entrance fee to the library might separate out those who were worthy of using the place from those who went there to save having the heating on at home. These were men of little imagination, typical of other councillors. They were soon to meet the wrath of Thelma and Joyce who that afternoon decided they were going to organise a campaign against the decision.

135

They decided to do three things. They each agreed to talk to six friends and neighbours and encourage them to join the library. Within a week, 32 people had followed their lead. Secondly they decided to invite a few sympathetic neighbours to a meeting to discuss the matter. Thirdly they decided to organise a public meeting and where better to hold it than in the library itself.

Alan designed a poster on his computer at work, Thelma took it into the library and asked Mrs Large if it could be put on the notice board. She was more than pleased to say 'yes'. For the next few days Thelma looked in each day to make sure it was still there and chat with Mrs Large who told her what a positive reaction she was getting from the regulars. Then on Friday she called round, almost in tears, to tell Thelma that the notice had been removed.

It had been done on the instructions of Councillor Franshaw on the grounds that the leaflet and the issue were political. Thelma went up to see Joyce, she brought a couple of her neighbours round, a 'committee meeting' was held and it was agreed to get a couple more neighbours together and go to see Councillor Franshaw the following morning in his house on Carlton Lane.

He was rather surprised to see a group of seven women as it was only 10am, quite early for an important person like him and with more pressing things to do with his time.

"What can I do for you ladies?" he asked rather pompously.

"Councillor Franshaw. There is something on the notice board in the library that should not be there."

"What is it, Mrs Holroyd?"

"It's a notice about you holding a ward surgery next Thursday night at Nook End Constitutional Club."

"What's wrong with that? I hold one every month."

"Yes, but it's political."

"Not really, it's just to tell those who are interested about the closing of Pasture Lane for a month while MANWEB are digging up the road, altering the 207 bus route and changing the way the bin men work. It's just local stuff. You can all come if you want."

"Is closing Bell Lane library was just local stuff as well?"

"That's different, not the same ... erm".

He was clearly struggling. He hadn't realised that his action had upset some pretty clever people.

"Why did you take our notice down?"

"Well you didn't have permission for a start."

136

"Mrs Large said it was all right. She even pinned it up for us."

"Well, she shouldn't have done. Everything that goes on a library notice board has to come before the committee."

"Councillor Franshaw, there's a notice about Astley Bird Watchers on the board. Has that come before your committee?"

Mrs Eckersley knew it hadn't. She had pinned it up herself with the full agreement of Mrs Large.

"Well, things like that don't have to."

"What do you mean things like that?"

"Non-political things."

"Has your notice come before the committee?"

"No, that doesn't have to."

"Why?"

"Because that's my meeting."

"If it's your meeting, why can you have it on council property? You should have it in your house, it's big enough."

A couple of the women were getting rather annoyed, so Joyce suggested that to make some progress, Councillor Franshaw had this issue discussed on his committee, but in the meantime the notice goes back up or his notice comes down. Also all the other notices should be discussed at an emergency meeting of the committee to which members of the public would be invited.

"Nobody is going to tell me how to run my ward, least of all you lot. You women don't know anything about all the rules and regulations for the council."

It was just starting to rain lightly and storm clouds could be seen in the distance over Earlestown. Joyce held her hand up; the others went quiet as she said: "We'll be talking to our solicitor on Monday about this, Councillor Franshaw. In the meantime we'll put another leaflet up, with or without your permission and we'll see you in Hull."

"If you put that leaflet up, I'll inform the police."

"If you inform the police, you'll get charged with wasting police time. And that is in section three, paragraph four of the 1984 Local Police Act."

And with that they marched down his drive and back onto Carlton Lane and as they walked back towards town, the sun came out and it stopped raining.

"Thelma, get Alan to do another leaflet and go and put it up again, after you've told Mrs Large that it's all right and then this afternoon come to our house and we'll discuss what to do next."

Four of those present asked if they could come as well. Mrs Stevenson was really enthusiastic, she absolutely hated Councillor Franshaw for reasons which at the time were unclear. Mrs Hunter though was just not quite sure what she was getting herself into.

"Joyce, why are we going to meet him in Hull?"

"Just a play on words, Joan. It was instead of saying we'll meet him in Hell."

"And how did you know all the details of that Police Act? You sounded very knowledgeable."

"I don't. I just made it all up, but I think it frightened him a bit."

"And do we actually have a solicitor? That will be expensive won't it?"

Joyce laughed.

"You mean you told him a pack of lies."

"I wouldn't put it like that. We just said what had to be said to put some pressure on him. The newspapers do it all the time and they get away with it."

"Will we be in the paper?"

"We might just get into the *Ashurst Reporter*. Their deadline is Wednesday at two o'clock. A lot might happen before then. Anyway it's all good publicity for us."

"It certainly is" said Thelma "because the only bad publicity is no publicity."

Mrs Hunter looked a little bemused at what she had involved herself with that morning. She also felt that she was with some very clever people and she liked them. They made her feel important and a member of the group. She decided she would come again, if they asked her to.

And over the next few weeks people who had known Mrs Hunter a long time and had seen how much she had changed began wondering if she was taking some magic pills. And if she was, they wondered how they could get hold of some as well.

19. The little bar steward

As a result of their altercation with Councillor Franshaw, the campaign began to gain support among people who lived in the area. The notice about the meeting on the following Wednesday evening stayed up on the library notice board and three local shops put a notice in their window as well. As a result more than 50 people turned up, for what was probably the first public meeting to be held in the district for over 20 years. On the top table was Joyce Holroyd who was going to act as chair, Mrs Large and Frances from Ashurst Comprehensive whose interest in the issue had resulted in the attendance of more than 12 of her friends from school.

Joyce began with a brief explanation of what the issue was all about. Basically it was to say 'no' to the closure of the library and to urge the council to reconsider the issue after they had met with representatives of the community. Most of those present had probably never been to a meeting like this before. If the truth were known, many of them had probably never been in the library or used its services before. But the way Joyce kept calling it our library, our town and how it should be run for our benefit, seemed to strike a chord with all those there, except for one young man who no one had ever seen before and who had been stood outside before the meeting had started, selling a newspaper.

She spoke briefly, then asked for comments or suggestions from those present. A few people spoke though none said anything very profound and then Mrs Hunter stood up. She was clearly nervous, maybe this was the first time she had ever spoken in public before. She said she was so disgusted by the way Councillor Franshaw had spoken to them that she was going to complain about him. She had now started coming to the library again and discovered how nice it was to read a good book. The more she spoke, the more relaxed she became as she went on to say that she was an old age pensioner and couldn't afford to buy books at Smiths or Waterstone's. For her, the library was a fine place to spend time and she thought that they should have a petition to keep it open.

There was then a lull in the proceedings, so Alan decided to speak to keep the momentum going. He began by congratulating the women who had started the campaign and visiting Councillor

Franshaw in his large Georgian mansion, a comment that made everybody laugh. He noted that his wife was one of those involved and although she had done it without his permission, he had forgiven her. He made a brief reference to the petition that had helped keep Ashurst railway station open and indicated his support for Mrs Hunter's suggestion for a similar petition.

It was short and to the point. He was followed by a woman who worked in Jaundrill's newsagents and who agreed with everything he had just said. She was followed by a bus driver, still wearing his uniform, who said that a petition might be a good idea as long as the words were chosen carefully.

Then the unknown man amongst them rose to speak. It was clear he was accustomed to speaking in public. The way he spoke made some think that he was somebody important. On the other hand it was possible that he had come to the wrong meeting, for in a long rambling speech, he attacked the TUC for not supporting the miners during their long and bitter dispute. He may have had a point, he may not, but at the first meeting of a campaign to stop the council closing a small branch library, it hardly seemed to be the main thing to talk about. Then he turned on Mrs Hunter's suggestion for a petition and said that that was worse than useless and petitions were a total cop out.

In his view, mass action was needed, as was the need to link this struggle with other struggles going on against the government and particularly one in South London where a group of building workers had been on strike for a month and had one of their leaders put in jail. When he started drawing parallels with the situation in Paris in 1968, Joyce stopped him.

Although he had already spoken, but in the absence of anybody else wanting to speak after the stranger, Alan decided to counter the man's comments and get the meeting back on track: "I just want to say something about Mrs Hunter's suggestion for a petition. I don't think a petition against Doctor Beeching in 1962 was a waste of time. It got us loads of publicity and it was what stopped British Railways in their tracks, didn't it."

He could have gone on much more but didn't want to be seen to be hogging the meeting so he sat down.

Another young man was now with the newspaper seller. He jumped up and said that the petition had been a waste of time because the station had now closed anyway? What was required was mass action to tackle the government on a whole range of issues and not just deal with such a relatively small issue.

Who were these guys and why had they come to this meeting? Maybe they were from of one of the groups that had been formed after the recent split among the Dob Lane Anarchists.

Alan was soon back on his feet: "The reason the station was closed in 1986, was to do with the subsidence above the old Southport Edge pit. Even if it wasn't, the station still kept running for well over 20 more years. I also know about a similar campaign that kept St Helens Shaw Street station open as well. That line is still running and Bryn, Garswood, Thatto Heath, Eccleston Park and Prescot stations are all still open so you can't say that petition was a failure either, can you? To suggest it was is a bit dishonest to say the least."

Conscious that he had a very interested audience, that many of those in the room knew him and to those who didn't know him, he was speaking in a way they could identify with, he went on: "The lad who spoke earlier about the TUC and their support or lack of support for the miners might have a valid point. But that is a different issue. Closing the pits and trying to smash the National Union of Mineworkers was very important to the government and particularly for Maggie Thatcher. That's why the full force of the state was used and why most of the newspapers printed what in my opinion was a load of lies about the whole issue anyway. Is the decision to close this library the same? I hardly think so. Mrs Hunter made a good suggestion to get a petition going. It won't be the only thing we have to do but it's a start so I will be voting for it, and so will my wife. I've told her to."

He made the final point to add a bit of humour; most of those present were probably at their first meeting and he didn't want anybody getting bored or leaving before the end.

Then Joyce banged on the table, achieved the necessary attention and proposed that they decide whether to start a petition or not. She asked for a show of hands and it got overwhelming support. She said she would circulate a sheet of paper and asked those who wanted to get involved in the campaign, or know about the next meeting, to sign it.

At this point, the bus driver came to the front of the room, wrote his name and address down and apologised for having to leave. At the same time, the two strangers left while Joyce was thanking everyone for attending. Then she finished with some provocative words of her own.

"This decision, or maybe we should now call it this proposal, to close this library has been taken by a handful of councillors to save money. Well they should stop some of their representatives going on jaunts all over the place. They should look at how much they are paying this new chief executive and why some of the people in the council's maintenance department are on short time and work is being farmed out to that firm in Manchester who are making a fat profit over it."

As she sat down there was a round of applause, and then a youngish woman asked if she could just say something: "I just want to give a vote of thanks to the chairwoman for running this meeting. I teach English literature at Ashurst Comprehensive and I always encourage my students to read widely and regularly. If that meant having to buy books, I know many of my flock come from families who could not afford to. But having a library here means I can encourage them to use it even more.

"Can I also say how pleased I am to see women running the show, especially after how those two loudmouth lads tried to take over. Last night I was watching a programme on the television about how the Americans sent Lance Armstrong to the moon. I thought to myself now that we've sent one man there, why can't we send the rest of them, except of course for that bus driver who's just left and your husband, Thelma."

As she spoke Alan looked at her. He recognised the voice, but who was it? He was soon to find out. On that humorous note Joyce closed the meeting. As everybody walked out a few minutes later, Mrs Large was stood by the door along with the caretaker with a big bunch of keys in his hand, ready to lock up. She said thank you to everybody who walked past, shook hands with a few and gave one old woman a big hug. It was somebody who she hadn't seen for years, somebody who said she might start coming to the library again as long as they had a large print section. Next to her was the woman who had spoken at the end. She looked well dressed, neatly though not out of place and stood with Frances and a couple of her school friends.

"Hello, Alan. Are you still working in the funny farm?" It was Hazel Hutton who years ago had been the tea girl at work.

"Hello, Thelma. Still caring for the old, infirm and decrepit?"

Hazel was now a teacher, something she had wanted to do when she had spent her days serving tea and coffee every morning and afternoon and doling the chips out at lunch time. But she was well remembered and well liked for much more than that.

She turned to Alan and told him she had put her name and address on the paper and to get involved in the campaign: "So now you know where to get hold of me, but not before midnight."

Then it was down to the pub for a drink, Thelma, Joyce, a couple of nurses who had come in late and a few others including a woman who was clearly a Glaswegian. Soon they were joined by Joyce's husband. Sam had been to Selby to meet an old shipmate, somebody he had got in contact with through his research for the book that was now taking up so much of his time.

The lady was sat between Joyce and Thelma. She hadn't spoken during the meeting but now made up for it. In her view it had been a very good meeting, most of those present were locals and all, except for the two lads, enthusiastically supported the vote for the petition: "That vote was a sort of a defensive position. What you are doing is defending something, in this case, that is defending the library as it is. What it might be a good thing to do is go on to an offensive position; in other words put forward ideas on what new things the library could be used for."

"What do you mean, Anita?" Joyce asked.

"You could suggest getting a readers' group set up that can meet there once a month or even a writers' group. Why not a Saturday morning group for kids to have stories read to them? And since that was such a good meeting tonight, why not organise a public meeting now and again and get famous speakers to talk about literature and what they have written?"

"I don't think we know anybody famous" said Mrs Hunter. "I don't, although I did stand next to Harold Wilson once in Prescot."

"I know somebody famous." It was Thelma with an idea. "Well Alan does, he used to work Les Earnshaw who wrote two books."

Turning to her husband, she went on: "He'd come wouldn't he Alan. Maybe he could bring David Frost or Sandie Shaw with him."

Everybody seemed quite taken with this idea and with Alan's suggestion for a poster to be put in the library window: "All welcome except Councillor Franshaw and his partners in crime."

Then Sam chipped in with a suggestion connected with his new found hobby. It was to get local people to talk about their war-time experiences. Although he was not a true born Ashurster, having been brought up in Yorkshire and only having come to Ashurst to get married, he could talk about what it had been like sailing up to Murmansk in the depths of an Arctic winter.

143

Mrs Hunter said they could have a talk about old Lancashire recipes and Anita suggested getting someone from the small Asian community who lived at Hyde Bank to talk about Indian cookery.

"One other thing we could have is people talking about sport. I could get my mate to ask Ray French to come and talk about when he played for the Saints and Widnes," Alan added.

"My brother once played cricket for Lancashire" said Mrs Hunter "but I don't think he'd want to come."

"Why not?

"He lives in Australia."

By the time they left the pub, they were all full of good intentions. What had started off as a relatively small issue was escalating into something much bigger. It was odd really. If Councillor Franshaw had not tried to shut the library down, in a couple of years it could easily have lingered on to a slow death, but now it had been given a great kiss of life. Then Mrs Hunter, who seemed to be rapidly coming out of a shell that she had been in for years, had suggested that they could also have a meeting for youngsters about the dangers of drugs, smoking and alcohol.

The following night, the *Lancashire Evening Post* carried a large article about the meeting. All the main points were well covered, highlighting that the majority of those in attendance had been women and that various ideas about the extended use of the place had been raised to counter any plans about closure. It was a good article and gave a bit more impetus to the campaign. But who had written it? Alan thought it might be Hazel.

A week later Councillor Franshaw went to see Mrs Large. He was not his usual bombastic self. He told her that he knew there would be opposition to any threat of closure and knew that it would almost certainly have got a lot of local people annoyed and interested. So, although it didn't seem like it at the time, really he had been on their side all the time, but had acted as a sort of 'agent provocateur'. He would now urge the council to set money aside to make big changes to the layout of the place and provide a room where the readers' and writers' groups could meet. Mrs Large thanked him politely and told him she would pass the news on to the newly formed committee.

Later that evening she told Joyce what he had said. But she also finished with some words that were quite strong for a librarian: "Devious little bar steward. I wouldn't trust him as far as I could throw him. I can read him like a book. A horror story."

20. Finnegan's awake

That night Joyce and Sam talked about what Councillor Franshaw had told Mrs Large, after which Sam made a suggestion. Since there was so much support for the library staying open, they ought to organise a celebration. Why not do it as a meeting to which they would invite Les Earnshaw to be the speaker?

Les had recently been on the radio again and was becoming quite famous. His price for a visit would probably be a Ramsbottom meat and potato pie before the meeting, a couple of pints of mild after it and somebody to drive him to his sister's house in Hemsley, where he would no doubt stay the night.

Mrs Large had to clear it with the town hall, but that was no problem and she was over the moon. "Maybe we could have another one later in the year" she suggested more in hope than anything, "maybe with someone like Catherine Cookson", her second favourite author.

Posters went up all over town, but most people heard about it by word of mouth. It was a long time since anyone famous had been to Ashurst and it was Les, who many people knew.

Everything was a bit rushed but it didn't matter. Les was keen, Thelma, Joyce, Mrs Hunter and Mrs Large were keen and Hazel was doing her bit to make sure there was going to be a good turn out from her friends at school. The event was due to start at 7.30pm. Les planned to come from London early in order to see a friend in Peasley Cross Hospital in St Helens and have his tea with Sam and Joyce. But then he rang to say he was going to catch a later train and come straight to the library, a pressing engagement with Channel Four had to be dealt with that morning.

By 7pm everything was ready. Thelma had made some butties for Les in case he hadn't eaten. The ever cool as a cucumber Joyce was a little edgy and Mrs Large kept walking out onto the street to see if he was coming and to be the first one to greet him.

By 7.15pm the first three rows were occupied, by twenty past the room was half-full at which time photographers from both the *Star* and the *Reporter* arrived as did a girl from Radio Merseyside. Where was Les, but then just like Alan, punctuality had never been one of his virtues. A minute later the caretaker came out to tell Joyce she was wanted on the phone. She was the first to hear the bad news. She spoke to the others who had put so much

145

effort into the planning and then she stood up and spoke: "I am very sorry to disappoint you all. Unfortunately Les can not be with us this evening. There has been a train derailment just outside Crewe which means no trains will be arriving at Bank Quay station in Warrington before nine o'clock at the earliest."

There was the usual noise associated with disappointment, but it was nobody's fault. "However it is not all gloom and doom. We have Plan B as we have an alternative speaker for you. Many of you will know Hazel Hutton. She grew up at Hyde Bank and worked for three years at Wilkinson's until she decided that she wanted to become a teacher. Four years later after she had qualified, she went travelling for a year. She spent six months teaching English to Japanese students in Tokyo, and then went to Sydney where she stayed for three months with her cousin and returned home via South America.

"She travelled through Peru, visited the ancient city of Cuscus, the home of the Inca civilisation, a subject she probably knows more about than anybody in Ashurst. Based on what she has seen and done while she has been travelling, Hazel tells me that she is now thinking of writing a novel based on this period of her life. As some of you may have heard, a few of us are setting up a writers' group here in the library, so this might be a good time to start."

And with that introduction, the former tea girl, Hazel, walked to the front of the room and proved to be an excellent speaker, certainly for a stand in at such short notice. She enthralled her audience with her knowledge of Inca civilisation and denounced its destruction by the Spanish conquistadores. She explained how she was going to turn her experiences into a novel and that she was looking forward to becoming a member of the library writers' group. Her speech had been delivered with passion, without notes, and received a well-earned round of applause.

Joyce proved that she was also a skilled performer and organiser when she said it would be difficult for anyone to follow that, but there were another three people in the room who had a tale to tell. It looked like being an interesting evening.

"Our next speaker will be someone many of you know, if you had ever worked at Wilkinson's. I also know him very well, in fact I have the pleasure to know him better than anybody in this town. It's my husband Sam. He is writing a novel based on his experiences in the Second World War as a Merchant Navy seaman sailing up to the edge of the Arctic Circle to take supplies to

Murmansk. Without anymore from me, I give you Sam Holroyd, will somebody please take him away?"

If you had worked with Sam, you would know full well what he was going to talk about. But many people who lived in Ashurst and knew him might still have little idea about what he had done in the war. He talked for much less time than Hazel and not quite as comfortably as her, but linked well his research and his novel.

"Thank you Sam, you can now go home and do the washing up," Joyce said to the amusement of everybody in the room.

"Our next speaker also has a story to tell us, not so much about her war but about the First World War. Frances Whiteley is one of my pupils at Ashurst Comprehensive. While recently working on her family tree she became very interested in the life of her great grandfather, who had fought on the Somme in 1916 and later won the Victoria Cross. Sometime during the Second World War he disappeared and was never heard of again, Frances is using this as a background for a novel she is going to write."

For someone so young, she spoke well, although nervously. She spoke more about fiction and how she had begun by asking relatives about the subject. She stood in front of her audience for less than five minutes and finished by saying she and some of her school friends thought a writers' group was a great idea.

Then Joyce announced the next speaker, it was John Rivington who worked in ASDA. He was soon to go to Australia to watch the Great Britain Rugby League team play in three test matches. He talked first about his previous trip Down Under four years earlier and about some of the things that other members of the group he was with had been involved in. This included a wedding, a night in a police cell, a big win on a slot machine and the consumption of an enormous amount of alcohol. Four years older and a lot wiser, this time he was intending to remain sober for most of the time. He also intended to make notes about what he saw and did because he was now thinking of writing a book about his time on the Australian eastern coast.

By the time he had finished, it was approaching 9pm. Joyce asked if anybody had any questions or whether they thought something like this should be repeated. For this idea there was overwhelming support and again, a sheet of paper went round the room asking for names and addresses. As people filed out almost everybody thanked a beaming Mrs Large who was stood at the door shaking everybody's hand as they left.

Over 20 people from the meeting went to the pub. Alan and Thelma were sat with Joyce and Sam, along with Mrs Large, Mrs Hunter, Hazel with another teacher who might well have been her boyfriend, along with a couple of Sam's neighbours and the library caretaker, who insisted on buying everyone a drink.

"Joyce, that meeting couldn't have run better if you had actually planned it. Did you?"

"You might laugh at this Alan, but you see the first thing I look at in the paper every morning is the stars. On Monday they said 'someone you are waiting for may not appear'. It got me thinking as to what we would do if Les was late or was taken ill. So I rang Hazel and asked her if she could she give a talk about her travels if that happened. She said 'yes' and said she would also have a word with Frances. That's how I got those two. Sam was quite happy to talk about his book, it's all he talks about now anyway. John's mother is a friend of mine, so that's how I knew that he might speak. I thought that he did very well too, although I don't think he included any of the saucy bits that happened over there."

Hazel was sat there looking pretty pleased with herself. Alan remembered when she had first gone to Bradford College and had become interested in geology, not that it had anything to do with her course. Had she now given that up for her new found interest in Inca civilisation or was she one of those people who have a wide range of interests? She had started life as what she would often refer to as a simple Lancashire tea girl and she had clearly moved onward and upward with now being a teacher. But she had lost nothing in the process, she still looked, talked and behaved like a girl who was brought up in a prefab at Hyde Bank.

"It looks as though you are going to be famous now, Hazel" Thelma said as Alan and Sam returned with the second round.

"You look like getting your picture in the paper too, that photographer was taking shots of you. I think that he was trying to chat you up as well."

"Thelma, did you know that your husband is famous in Brazil?"

"No, I didn't. I mean he's not even famous in his own house, except when he's in there on his own."

"Did he ever tell you about when he was working on that power station job on the border between Brazil and Bogotá at Colombo?"

"Corumba." said Alan.

It had been a job in which everything that could go wrong did

148

go wrong. Strangely, it seemed not one draughtsman could be found to be at fault. It was ultimately all blamed on Joan, the tea lady, who it was rumoured used to check Alan's drawings.

"I travelled into Brazil from Bogotá on a coach. There was an overnight stop and we stayed in a small hotel nearby. That evening a few of us went for a walk up to where this power station was. The bloke who ran the hotel worked there and said he would take us round for a few pesos. It looked very impressive. When we approached the main building there was a crossroads, one road had a sign saying Estrada Henderson on one side and Estrada Eccleston on the other and the road into the building was Estrada Holroyd."

She looked at Joyce, nodded and said it was true. Alan knew she was joking; it was just ridiculous. She went on: "We went into the place where all the generators were and on the right hand side there was a large sign with an arrow pointing down a corridor and do you know what it said: "Los Alan Greenall senhoras."

"And what's that in English?"

"The Alan Greenall ladies toilet."

"Hazel, you haven't changed a bit. You've got worse or better, depending on how you judge matters of a useless nature."

Then Joyce turned to Mrs Hunter who looked as if it was a long time since she had been with such an interesting group of people.

"Did you enjoy yourself to night, Mrs Hunter?"

"I did, I really did. I have never been with so many famous people before. I feel quite honoured."

"Are you going to join our readers group then "

"Yes, if you'll have me, but I'll have to start reading. What do you think I should start with?"

"Well, how about James Joyce. What do you think, Joyce? How about *Finnegan's Wake*?"

Before Joyce could say anything, Mrs Hunter replied in a way that surprised them all, but indicated that she was now feeling quite comfortable with her new friends.

"I didn't even know he'd been asleep." Then she turned to Hazel and said: "I was very impressed with young Frances. Is she one of your pupils?"

"Yes, I teach the girls who were at the back. They're a good bunch."

"No lads, I notice"

"They would probably be all out chasing girls."

149

"Pity they didn't chase them into the library."

"I think there must have been a football match on. I was expecting a few to be there."

"It was a good idea getting that man to talk about the rugby in Australia. I suppose sport is one way to get lads interested."

"You are going to ask Ray French to come; aren't you, Alan."

"Yes, I'll have to go round to see that mate of mine who knows him. I'll do it on Saturday. He's working away during the week."

"So how did you like Australia, Hazel?"

"I loved it, but what made it so good was staying with relatives. My cousin lived in Widnes until she was seven when her family emigrated and she had a friend whose mother had once lived at Hyde Bank, where I used to live. I met quite a few English people there and they all seemed to be enjoying it. But they all still had fond memories of such idyllic places as Gillarsfield, Standish Lower Ground, Pocket Nook and Fingerpost to mention less than five.

She then went on to tell them about Jason, a lecturer in English Literature, who she had got to know rather well out there: "I introduced him to our subtle misuse of the English language, punning and what passes for humour in Lancashire, something which he found fascinating as well as incomprehensible. I even gave a few talks about it to some of his students. I might even have settled there until I found out that not only was he married with two kids, he was also the father of three other children all with different women. So I kicked him into touch and decided to come back to Ashurst by the scenic route, you might say. That's how I visited Sacsayhuaman and the rest you've heard about."

Then she looked directly at Thelma and continued: "I'm seriously thinking of going back there next year in the summer holidays. I'm also thinking of taking Alan with me, just to make sure I don't get into any sort of mischief, you understand."

Then Mrs Hunter spoke. In the short time that they had known her, she seemed to have taken on a whole new personality.

"I was enthralled with your talk, Hazel. Would you let me know if you are going to give another one? I'd love to come and listen to it, that's if it would be all right."

"There you are Hazel. Mrs Hunter your number two fan," laughed Alan.

"Who's the first? Don't tell me, it's you."

"Yes, but don't let Thelma know."

21. The Grim Reaper appears

The only absolute certainty in life is death. In a town the size of Ashurst, it is probably true to say that at least one resident proves that point every day. The manner of the death and its significance may vary enormously. Sometimes a death may go completely unnoticed; at other times it may have an impact far and wide and be remembered for years to come. That was particularly true of Mrs Stott, who had lived in Hamer Street all her life. The day she had been born in 1893 had coincided with the Ashurst Green rail disaster when five people, including her uncle, had been killed. At 99, she had been the oldest living person in the town. Now she was gone, although many future residents of the town would know all about her since her grandson had written her life story.

Another former resident of the town had also died on the same day. It was John Warner, killed in a car crash while heading back to Aldershot Army Barracks shortly before he was due to set sail for Iraq. An even younger person to die was a three hour old baby in Victoria Hospital. Luckily, if that word can be employed in such sad circumstances, she was a twin and her sister came into the world full of vitality as she was to demonstrate fully in later life.

Sometimes a death may be totally unexpected, at other times it was just a long time coming. It was as though the Grim Reaper would appear and then decide not to act or come back the next day, the next week, or maybe 20 or 30 years later. It was said of him that he had a plan for every living soul in Ashurst and was the only person in the town who would never be made redundant.

One person who was quite thankful for death was the editor of the *Ashurst Reporter*. Every week at least one full page would be devoted to the announcement of the death and subsequent funeral details of various local people. It was a page that many would cast an eye over, for often it was a way of finding out what had happened to someone you may have known in the past. It was a page that Alan always read with interest and the previous week's edition had been most informative.

The first funeral he had read about was that of Mrs Chadwick. She used to live opposite him in Chisnall Avenue when he was at Lane Head School. Her husband had been a fireman and Alan had been friends with her two sons Pete and Ronnie. She had died in Billinge Hospital after a long illness. The list of mourners numbered well over 50 as she had been well liked in the area, having worked on the counter at Bell Lane Post Office for years. There was no mention of her husband being present, maybe he had already died, but the two lads were both listed along with their wives and what could well have been their children. There was also a floral tribute from what was almost certainly their young sister Janet, now called Hale and living in New Zealand. Among the mourners, he also recognised a few other names from around Chisnall Avenue, still living there no doubt.

The second name he saw was Samuel Kershaw. His report was much briefer, only four people at the funeral, not surprising as he never had many friends, when he worked at Davis Pumps. The third came as a big shock. It was Johnny Shufflebottom, a week younger than Alan and with whom he used to play in a skiffle band in the 1950s. A nice lad, big Saints fan, always good for a laugh particularly when talking about when he worked at TT Vicars in Earlestown, but a 20 cigs a day man, something that probably killed him in the end. The chief mourner at this funeral was his widow Margaret, who Alan also knew many years ago.

The following Monday, Cliff told Alan that his wife was going into hospital on Thursday, so Alan made no reference to what he had read in the paper. Fortunately it was nothing too serious, just the removal of gallstones that had been troubling her for a long time. But the day after her return home, other news about the hospital emerged. The local health authority had decided to downgrade its function.

The maternity ward was to close and expectant mothers would now have to go to Warrington, a town that was no longer in Lancashire, having been relocated to Cheshire by some Government diktat. Some operations would no longer be available and two wards closed pending a public discussion about the whole future of the hospital which probably meant that it would close.

This issue stirred up many people in the town. Ashurst had been hit hard by the miners' strike, had lost its railway station and if nobody had done anything about it, they would have lost Bell Lane branch library as well. Four firms had recently closed down and another two were on short time. The council had sold off green land for housing development, in what many saw as a dodgy deal with a property developer from North Wales. It all happened bit-by-bit and maybe the threat of the closure of the hospital was going to be the last straw. In the pub on Friday lunch time, Dave Ainsworth told Alan that there was going to be a meeting the following week to start a campaign against this closure. This and the fact that it had been splashed all across Friday's *Ashurst Reporter* gave some indication of the strength of feeling. Various trade union activists and others who had fallen into inactivity turned up to the meeting which elected a committee and decided on a course of action.

At the beginning of the following week it leaked out that some expensive medical equipment was being moved to a private hospital in Essex. It was considered essential to stop this and so it was decided to mount a week long 24 hour picket as the actual time was not known. It was easy to find volunteers for the night shift. Many who volunteered had been shift workers and for them it was like being at work again, something some had not done for years. During the course of the week their secret mole inside the hospital kept feeding scraps of news to the committee. It appeared that the powers that be were highly annoyed and that the issue had even been discussed in London.

Then Marion, a staff nurse in the hospital, suggested a good idea for publicity. It was two slogans: "We are all nurses because we are nursing a grudge." along with "It's bedpan time for Mr Young", Mr Young was the highest paid consultant at the hospital. He was also the most arrogant and vociferous in his attacks on all who worked under him.

She also suggested that Ashurst housewives should organise a day of action with the Friday picket appealing to women all over South Lancashire to join in. Needless to say it found widespread support and not surprisingly from Thelma and Joyce.

On the day in question around 100 women turned up, some with children in prams, some with older children in tow and one old lady who had been brought from Dob Lane Old Peoples' Home in a car and was stood there leaning on her Zimmer frame. Turned 80, she hadn't intended to stay long, just long enough for a photographer to take some shots of her.

A young lady from Radio Merseyside appeared who was clearly sympathetic and an older reporter from the *Daily Telegraph* who clearly wasn't. Cars and lorries driving past pipped their horns and waved in support. Suddenly the mood turned nasty by the action of a well-heeled woman in a four-by-four, driving through the picket line. It was Mr Young's wife, Celia, coming for a meeting of one of the many committees that she sat on and for which she only claimed nominal expenses, but always had a slap-up meal at the taxpayers' expense. She was in a bad mood, the traffic had been held up along Wigan Lane and she was late. She screeched to a halt to within six inches of Mrs Delaney's Zimmer frame. Mrs Delaney might have trouble walking, but she certainly had all her wits about her. She screamed and fell to the ground, totally unharmed, but aware that it would provide some good publicity.

Showing no concern for what she might have just done, not even getting out of the car to see if the old lady was all right, Lady Muck accelerated backwards and ploughed into two other women and a pram. Straightaway one of the policeman who was on duty, but who had had nothing to do so far, radioed for an ambulance. The pram was badly damaged although the baby was uninjured and still fast asleep but there was blood everywhere, one of the women was lay on the floor grasping her leg while the one who appeared the worst injured, lay motionless.

News travels fast, it certainly did that day and the carrier of the news into Wilkinson's was a lorry driver from Preston delivering some cable drums. He told the gateman and soon the news was all round the factory, but it was Cliff who brought it into the drawing office.

Almost at the same time, Alan received a call from Alice in reception to come down straightaway as there was a young woman to see him. It was Marion, who had rushed down to tell Alan the bad news. Thelma had been knocked over, was covered in blood and been rushed into the Accident and Emergency department. Cliff drove him there. It was only a 10 minute drive but it was the longest 10 minutes Alan had ever known.

He rushed into the hospital and was soon met by a large nurse with a very sad face.

"Are you Mr Greenall? Well I have to tell you that your wife was knocked unconscious at the scene of the accident. As far as we know, she has broken her ankle and a couple of ribs, and has general bruising. If you wait for a bit, you can go and see her when we've found out which ward she has been put in."

All the way down from work, he had feared the worse, it was Marion's reference to all the blood that made him think that way, but then the nurse had just described it as broken bones and general bruising. He had to wait nearly an hour before he could see her. A young nurse, who sounded as though she came from South Wales, took him to the ward. Thelma was fast asleep, under sedation the nurse told him. There were bandages on her cheek and neck and the lower half of her right leg was in plaster.

"Don't worry, it's not life threatening." the nurse said, "Come back tonight, she should be awake by then. I'll tell her you came."

Highly relieved, Alan smiled at her, clearly relieved and said: "Where are you from?"

"Merthyr Tydfil. It's in South Wales."

"Well she's from Tonyrefail, so you'll look after her won't you."

"Don't worry. She'll be fine."

"On y croeso Cymru". It was the only bit of Welsh he could think of, but the nurse knew what he meant.

He went back to work, and arrived there around 3pm. Before leaving the hospital he had rung Cliff with the news and then left a message for his daughter Rebecca at her office in London and for his son Robert at his flat in Birmingham where he was a student at the University.

Back in the office, it was clear he was in no frame of mind to do any work. Slowly he began to unwind as he told various people who had passed through the office how she was. Then Pete Mulholland arrived with the same questions. After telling him what he had told everyone else, Alan then showed that he was getting back to normal: "I'm annoyed about this, today especially."

"Why's that Alan?" asked Colin.

"It was her turn to make the tea tonight."

"Don't bother about your tea Alan," said Pete. "Go home and get changed and come round to our house. Our Maud always makes a big stew on a Thursday, so there'll be plenty and then you can go straight off to the hospital."

Mates, isn't it great to have mates who have just said something like that. That was just typical of Pete, though for Alan remembered how he had looked after Hazel Hutton, a friend of his daughter Clare, when she was being dragged up in a prefab in Hyde Bank by a mother who didn't deserve to have such a nice girl for a daughter.

He walked into ward seven and saw the great love of his life in the first bed. She looked pale, almost as white as the bandage around her head. It made the freckles on her face stand out even more. As he kissed her, she drew away from him, the bruising on her face made any contact painful. She told him that she had broken her ankle, bruised her ribs and had cuts to her face, shoulder and leg. He told her what Marion had said about her

155

being covered in blood, which had made it seem so much worse.

"It wasn't blood Alan. I had a tin of red paint in my shopping bag. The lid must have come off and it had spilled all over me."

She asked if he had seen the *Lancashire Evening Post*. He hadn't, but a man stood at the next bed had one sticking out of his pocket. There was no mention of Thelma in it or the little baby in the pram or the baby's mother. But there was a fine shot of Mrs Delaney on the ground surrounded by a group of angry women.

"Have you told Rebecca and Robert?"

"Rebecca is coming tomorrow. She was in a meeting in Croydon and can't get away today, but she'll be on the first train in the morning. I left a message with one of Robert's friends. He will come on Friday night because he's got an exam tomorrow."

He told her that he had had his tea at Pete Mulholland's house and his wife Rachael sent her best wishes, as did everybody he had spoken to that afternoon.

Then Thelma told him that one of the nurses was from Merthyr Tydfil, which Alan knew and that she spoke Welsh fluently and was encouraging Thelma to learn a bit while she was in her care.

"Well, it'll keep you off the streets," Alan jokingly replied.

He left her an hour later and decided to finish the evening off with a pint in his local. By this time, the news was all round Ashurst and despite attempting to buy a pint himself, he couldn't as various neighbours insisted buying one for him.

It was approaching midnight before he finally arrived home, absolutely knackered. It was not surprising that he was late into work the following day. But nobody was bothered. It was just good that Thelma, the former print room girl, was alive and well.

The extent of her injuries was still unknown. Tests would be done and her leg would be in plaster for at least six weeks. Despite the shock to her system, she seemed little different to how she normally was and how she had been with him ever since Christmas Eve in 1962 when they had first got together.

It seemed such a long time ago, but then it was, over 30 years; not gone in a flash, but just gone. He remembered many of the people he had known over that period of time, relatives, school mates, colleagues from work, neighbours and then there were those who he only ever saw when he went to the match.

So many people and so many he was glad to have known, but none so much as his wife now happily recovering in ward seven in Ashurst Victoria Hospital.

22. Sergeant Pepper's lot

Rebecca was on the first train out of Euston the following morning and arrived at the hospital just after lunch, carrying the obligatory bunch of flowers and bottle of orange juice. Thelma told her what had happened, why she had been there and why the Government couldn't be allowed to get away with closing the hospital. Rebecca listened quietly. Since she had got the job with the bank and moved to London, she had begun to develop some fairly right wing views and attitudes. If this issue had been about saving a hospital in Gateshead or Kilmarnock or Wrexham and the injured person had been somebody else's mother, she might have just said tough or ignored the issue. But the reality of this could not be any closer to her.

Thelma made references to 'your' government for she knew her daughter was an admirer of both Margaret Thatcher and John Major. In political terms, she was totally different to her brother Robert, who she often referred to as 'that crazy lefty brother of mine'. Then after being introduced to the nurse who also had the same name as her, Rebecca said: "Mum, what are going to do with all your time while you are in here?"

It was clear now that Thelma was going to be all right. It wasn't clear how long she would stay in hospital or the long-term effect on her leg; but at least what might have happened, hadn't.

Thelma took a handful of grapes from the bowl, smiled at her daughter and said: "You know all those books your dad has got in the front room. Well I'm going to read one of them."

Rebecca laughed. She knew her dad well. The number of times he had come home having bought a book in town, put it in the bookcase in the front room and when asked why he had bought it, had declared that he would read it when he had a bit of time.

"Which one will it be?"

"Probably the *Great power station cooling towers of the western world* one or maybe that *101 memorable walks along the Sankey Canal in 1892.*"

Rebecca knew that her dad was always full of good ideas of things to do in the future, but which never seemed to get done or even started. Still she thought if that was his only fault, both her and her brother Robert had been lucky to have him as one of the two most important people in their lives.

They talked for a long time and then Rebecca said: "Mum, there's something I've never asked you before. How did you get that scar on your face?"

"You want to know all about me, don't you."

"I want to know what sort of a person I have got for a mother."

"Why, are you thinking of swapping me for some one better?"

Rebecca smiled and said what many children have said to those who have brought them into the world and then given them a good start in life.

"No, you are the best mum in the world, but I still want to know all about you."

Thelma stroked the side of her face and carried on: "I got this when I was living in the hostel in Cardiff, when I was 17. There were always lads hanging about there, they were not very nice lads and always making rude comments about us when we walked past them. One evening I was coming home a bit late from somewhere, it was going dark and one of them was sat there on the wall.

"He told me to come to him but I didn't, he frightened me so I walked away quickly across some wasteland, then I saw him get off the wall and start to follow me. I started to run away from him and then he started running. I knew he was catching me up; there was nobody around and I was sure that something awful was going to happen. Then I tripped and fell to the ground. He grabbed me, tried to turn me onto my back and then he said something like 'Christ almighty' and ran off. I struggled to my feet, put my hand to my cheek and it was covered in blood. I had fallen on some broken glass, you see.

"I was in a real daze, the blood was pouring out. Nearby there were some cottages and a man who lived there saw me. He took me into his house and wiped the blood off it. Somebody must have rung for an ambulance, because in no my time I was being driven to the hospital and they kept me in there for a few days. I was very lucky not to lose my eye."

There were tears in Rebecca's eyes as she put her arms round her mother.

"Aw, poor mum, poor mum."

"After that things seemed to get better in the hostel. I made a few friends there and then four of us decided to go to work in Butlin's holiday camp at Rhyl. That's where I met Beryl. We were

158

a bit of an unlikely pair but we seemed to hit it off straightaway and it was through her that I finally came to live here in Ashurst."

"And are you going to stay here?"

"This is my home Rebecca. I know it isn't the prettiest of places, I know there's a lot of things that would make it better, but its home and its where I know a lot of very nice friendly people and despite what your Mrs Thatcher says, there is such a thing as society and we are all in this together. So as your dad would say, put that in your pipe and smoke it."

"It's a different world down there, mum. Everybody is out for number one. Most people there think everybody from north of Watford is either an imbecile or a plain or common loser."

"Is your dad an imbecile or a plain or common loser? Are all his work mates imbeciles? What was the first thing Pete Mulholland did when he heard about me?"

"Thanks for all that mum. I've learned a lot today. Thanks for putting up with me since I've been working down there."

"Don't worry none of us are perfect. Well except for your dad."

"And you are as well."

They kept Thelma in hospital for a week and then discharged her with strict instructions to rest. But after a few days spent in the house, she decided she would like to go out for a drink. It was not that she had not seen anybody since she had come out of hospital. There had been an endless procession of neighbours, friends, former work mates and others who had called round to see her. Most said they were just popping in for five minutes, but stayed for more like an hour. Some she had not seen for ages, but they were often people who had heard on the grapevine what had happened and made that the excuse to go and see an old friend.

They decided to spend the evening in the Colliers' Arms. It was over a mile from Silkstone Street, but that was not a problem because their next door neighbour Phil drove them there. There was one thing that Alan never did and that was drink and drive, even for such a short distance. It was risky and it was wrong. It was also because he would never forget what had happened to little Hayley across the street a few weeks earlier. Phil had the same attitude, so each helped the other on occasions like this.

There were not many people in the best room as they walked in. It was a Wednesday night, and the place was fairly quiet, ideal really for a relaxing chat and for Thelma to rest her leg on a bar stool. They sat by the large window that looked out onto Ashton

Street. After a while a group of young people walked in and sat near to them. A short while later, another young man joined them, carrying a tray of drinks. Thelma thought he had a familiar face. He left the room to taken the tray back and when he returned he came over to where they were sat and said: "Hello Mrs Greenall. Do you remember me?"

"I do. You were one of Robert's school friends. Is it Dave?"

It was. It was Dave Crompton, who had been in Robert's class at Ashurst Comprehensive.

Like Robert, he was also at university, in his case though it was Oxford where he was reading philosophy, but then he had always been a clever one. He introduced her and Alan to his friends. There was Hamish, Mary, Miles, Charlemaine, Ben and Penelope. They were also at Oxford as well except for Mary who was studying medicine at Liverpool University.

"So what are you all doing in Ashurst? Have you come to observe what life was like in the 19th century?"

"No, we are here for the nuptials."

It was Mary with a very distinctive upper class way of speaking.

Robert translated into more everyday English: "We are going to a wedding on the Wirral on Saturday so we are staying at our house while mum and dad are away."

Dave's parents lived in a large house on Carlton Lane, that being the area where the hoi polloi of Ashurst resided.

"Where are you all from, not round here by the sound of it?"

Except for Hamish, who came from Peterhead, a few miles north of Aberdeen, they were all from the south; Stratford on Avon, Chelsea, Bournemouth, Chipping Sudbury and Guildford.

"You don't sound very Scottish," Alan continued to the lad who looked like tossing the caber was his sport.

"I did until I went to boarding school" Hamish replied.

It turned out that except for Dave, the others all had similar backgrounds, having parents who were rich enough to send their children away at an early age to start their education. Why, didn't they really love them?

"What do you think of our twee little village? Have you observed its distinctive architectural features, its quaint Byzantine ginnels and sniggets and its wide array of tiny back to backs?"

They all smiled politely. Whatever was Dave doing with such a group of individuals, Alan thought. He was sure that Robert did not have such a characterless set of mates at his university.

"I met your son Robert a couple of weeks ago after a rugger match at uni."

It was Mary, the red haired fashion queen, wearing a distinctive three piece suit and totally out of place in the Colliers Arms, particularly in the way she had pronounced the word match to sound more like metch.

"A rugger match eh. Was that league or union?"

It was a simple question but one that she couldn't answer. She almost certainly did not know that there were two codes of rugby and it was hardly worth Alan giving his usual account about what had happened at the George Hotel in Huddersfield in 1895, much as though he would have liked to. Then she went on to say that they all found him in company to be so funny, but it was rather humorous to hear her pronounce the word funny more like fanny.

Despite the irritating way they used the English language, they were a friendly and pleasant enough set of people, but before Alan could say much more they were interrupted by the arrival of one of his neighbours. It was Tony who used to work at Sutton Manor Colliery before being finished there, when the Government did away with the National Coal Board presence in Lancashire.

"You wouldn't think he used to be a banker, would you" Alan said to some amazement from them all after Tony had left the room. Locally, or in any mining area, a banker, sometimes called a banksman, had an important function to perform at a colliery. But how could any of them know that?

"So what's the latest news from the world of philosophy? Has anybody come up with a good reason why we are all here then?"

The statement by Alan led on to various views on the meaning of life being aired. It soon became clear that their views on the world were not based on the same world in which the Greenall household and most of Ashurst lived. In the case of Ben, Alan didn't think his views were based on the same world that anybody else lived in; maybe he was on cannabis or some other mind bending drug.

Mary and Charlemaine were clearly strong supporters of Bill Clinton, while Miles, who had a long pony tail and had a large cross around his neck, kept referring to Christian liberation theology as providing his *raison d'etre*. It was probably the first time that the best room had ever heard so many big words strung together. Or were they just trying to be clever. On the other hand,

161

when they had first entered the room it looked as though this wasn't the first pub they had been in that evening. Or maybe Dave had found where father kept his malt whiskey hidden.

Alan listened to them for a while and then decided to join in.

"You might be pleased to hear that I find philosophy a fascinating subject. It is something that I have studied in some depth over the years, although I haven't read all of them, just the main ones, Pluto and Harry Stottle, Weber and Durkheim, Marx and Spencer, St Augustine and St Helen."

Not a bad opening gambit, although by this time he was well into his second pint in a company that was providing him with a challenge.

None of the others made any comment. Were they being polite, were they not able to identify or appreciate his Ashurst humour or could they just not understand his Lancashire accent which he usually laid on in situations like this?

Hamish then made the comment that it was Karl Marx with his theory about the relationship between theory and practice that had truly advanced the world of philosophy. It was his pet subject, one he was writing a 30,000 word dissertation on at uni.

"I suppose you'll be familiar with the work of Mr Hegel then."

Hamish nodded approvingly while all the other looked on with some amazement that Robert's dad was familiar with this early 19th century German philosopher.

"I can understand what he was trying to say, but I always found him a bit of a handful. The one thing I do remember about him though was when he was sat in that coffee bar in Stuttgart and watched Napoleon and his army march past on the way to Moscow and later he wrote that he had just seen the spirit of the 19th century pass by."

That was a totally accurate description, something that Hamish was quite familiar with from his knowledge of the man.

"For me it was a statement that summed up the whole development of ideology in the early part of that century."

The others were impressed. Robert had never mentioned anything about his father being an intellectual. He had always said that he was just an electrical draughtsman.

"I bet you don't know that six months later Hegel was still living in Stuttgart and saw Napoleon and the remnants of his army struggling back to Paris after failing to take Moscow. And I bet you don't know what Hegel had said to his wife that night."

None of them did, it was only on Boney's outward journey that Hegel's comment had become fixed in time and none of them were absolutely sure that there was a Mrs Hegel.

"'Look, he hasn't even changed his shirt."

They all smiled; anyone who knew Robert could now tell where he had got his sense of humour from.

"Do you know what I think was the most important bit of philosophy ever written?"

They all expected another long drawn out bit of nonsense.

"It was Ludwig Feuerbach when he wrote 'Nothing exists outside nature and man, and the higher beings created by our religious fantasies are only the fantastic reflection of our own essence'."

And then with a wave of his hand and imitating a typical university lecturer he said: "Discuss."

No one quite knew how to respond to Alan's comment so nobody did. Just at that moment, another of Alan's neighbours walked in with his wife. It was Harold Potter from the assembly shop. He looked at Alan, then looked at the group he was sat with and said in a most disturbed voice: "Are you all right Alan?"

"Yes, thanks Harold, I'm champion. We are just about to discuss some of the ideas of Frederick Engels. You can join us if you like."

"No thanks, we've just come for a game of darts."

And with that he quickly left the room. No doubt he would be calling in the drawing office tomorrow to find out what Alan had been doing sat with a group of people who looked like members of Sergeant Pepper's Lonely Heart's Club Band.

At this point Dave and his little entourage decided to move on. He wanted to take them up to the Wigan Arms at Hyde Bank.

"Have you got your travel insurance?" Alan asked "because if you haven't, I'd be a bit wary of going up there."

By now the room was beginning to fill up. Many of them were the regulars, most of whom Alan and Thelma knew. Now sat next to them was Arthur Turner, who worked as a printer at the *Ashurst Star* and his wife Alice, a nurse at Peasley Cross Hospital.

She smiled at Thelma and said: "How are you?"

"It's still really painful."

"What's that, Thelma, your leg or having to live with him?"

Then Arthur asked who all his new found friends were and where had they gone. On hearing that they were heading for the

163

Wigan Arms, he went on: "They won't feel very comfortable sat in there tonight."

"Why?"

"The brewery closed it down last week."

The pub had been going downhill for a while. Some people believed that it had once been voted pub of the year and given an award by Queen Victoria, before she had ascended the throne. Others just said that it was not so, it was just that the last time the place had been decorated was before she had ascended the throne. Still if it was shut, no one would ever die of thirst up at the top end of Billinge Road. There was The Shepherd, The Besum, The Railway Arms, The George and finally The Hyde Bank Arms and that was just on the left hand side walking north.

The people now in the best room were a totally different collection of good souls. One man in there had once told Alan that he had never read a book in his life, another said that his son always bought him a book at Christmas and he usually aimed to finish it before the works shutdown. At the other extreme was Mrs Wainwright who lived next door to the pub. No need to ask what time it was when she walked into the room. *Coronation Street* would have just finished five minutes ago, although clearly it must have over run tonight because it was now turned half past eight. Every Tuesday morning, without fail, she would also be seen taking a carrier bag to the main library in town. There she would hand in the three books she had taken home the previous Tuesday and find another three to keep her going for the next seven days.

Back in work the following day Alan talked about Dave and his student friends. And, hardly surprisingly, not long after, Harold Potter appeared with the reason for his visit being 'mistake' on one of Alan's drawings. But that was only an excuse to find out who he had been drinking with the previous night.

He didn't stay long and as he walked out of the office, Alan bawled out: "Are you all right for 240 volt DZZ relays?"

Harold laughed. That was his usual excuse to go and be entertained in the drawing office.

That night there were two visitors to 15 Silkstone Street. It was Joyce and Sam, maybe come to find out about the students in town or maybe tell them about an incident in a pub on Billinge Road, if there had been one. But it wasn't, it was just a social call.

"We're not staying long" said Joyce. "Just come to see how

164

your leg is."

"Oh, that's good" said Alan. "That must mean you'll be leaving before midnight."

"Can I ask you a question, Sam?"

It was Thelma.

"How do you disperse a group of Yorkshiremen?"

"Tell them there's some washing up to do," growled Joyce.

Alan then gave her the correct answer which was to start a collection and then went on to talk about their drinking partners in the pub on the previous night.

"When our Margaret was at university in London, there were some strange people in her class" said Joyce. "One is an MP now."

"Sounds about right."

"I never used to believe her until I went down to see her one time in her flat and met a couple of them. I just thought she was having me on."

"Anyway talking about intellectual pursuits, how are you getting on with your book, Sam?"

Joyce smiled very proudly in an exaggerated sort of a way: "He's just had his first rejection. "

"Well don't get put off. Ernest Hemingway had over 50 rejections before he could find someone to publish his first book and you've only had one."

"Well that's really cheered me up Alan. Now I only feel like one beer instead of two. Have you got anything in?"

Alan always had beer in and so it was well turned midnight before their welcome visitors finally left.

23. Given away at birth

It was now the middle of May and approaching the end of the season, one that was to be crowned with the Premiership Final at Old Trafford between St Helens and Wigan. As thousands of fans who lived within a 10 mile radius of Billinge Lump began to prepare for the event many would recall what had happened on the last encounter between the two teams. It was five weeks earlier on Good Friday in front of nearly 30,000 fans packed in Central Park. The game had finished as an 8–8 draw but as exciting as the game had been, it was for another reason that many would remember it.

Anybody who has ever played such a high contact physical game would know about the risk of getting injured. A broken nose, or arm or leg could easily occur and require at least six weeks in plaster, although clearly not for a nose, although that didn't make it any less painful to endure. Ligaments could get torn, teeth lost, muscle damaged, concussion could always carry the possibility of brain damage immediately or maybe later in life.

All this was brought to the fore with what happened when Mick Cassidy had tackled the Saints front row man Kevin Ward. It was the last time the Yorkshireman ever played, for he suffered a horrific broken leg. Some people stood many yards away reckoned they heard the crack as he buckled and fell to the ground. It was a sobering end to a career. At first there was the possibility that he might never walk again but thankfully things were not that bad although it was a long time before he could do. But he could have had to spend the rest of his life in a wheelchair.

That was something that had happened to the brother of one of Alan's friends. It had only been a friendly between Ashurst Social Club and Gillarsfield Labour Club. John had been drafted in to make up the numbers. It was played on waste land on the site of the old Montague Colliery. It was by no means a dirty game. In fact the crowd of around 100 had had to wait for over 10 minutes before the referee had given the first penalty. Just on half-time a scrum had formed, there had been the usual tussle for the ball between the two opposing hookers and whoever else who could get his foot or hand anywhere near it.

Finally it was in the hands of Gillarsfield's stand-off who saw a gap in the Social Club's defence and had raced through it and scored under the posts. The scrum had broken up, but left John lying on the pitch in agony. What had happened nobody really knew. Before long an ambulance arrived and taken him to Victoria Hospital where he was kept for the next six months with permanent damage to the base of his spine that meant he was never again any more than five yards from his wheelchair.

Other injuries often occurred at the match, not on the pitch, but on the terraces. On one occasion at Fartown, Alan had been stood with a group of Saints fans next to a couple of old age pensioners from Brighouse. They both were the life-and-soul of the party and stood in that particular spot because they had both stood there for every game since the time that Joe Platt had first been elected as secretary of the old Northern Union. Or so they said. Rather surprisingly, the home team were in front by nine points and seemingly heading for victory. Then Saints had pulled a try back, Paul Loughlin had tacked on the goal, the home team had kicked off again with a minute to go and the Saints forward John Harrison had knocked on. Everybody had seen this happen except the referee. Nobody was more annoyed than the older of these two Fartowners because the ball went through a dozen pairs of hands with the winger Barry Ledger scoring in the corner to win the match for the Saints in thrilling circumstances.

Alan and his mates were jumping up and down, throwing their clenched fists in the air and hugging each other. What excitement, what drama, what a way to end the game. Too much for the pensioner though who had 10 seconds earlier been screaming at the referee. He now lay dead on the floor, from a massive heart attack. Not a nice way to finish one's life.

Injuries, some life-threatening, but of a different nature also occurred at the match, sometimes on the terraces, sometimes on the way to the match and sometimes going home from the match. These were the ones caused by troublemakers, usually young men whose reason for being involved or in attendance was to cause trouble, vicious trouble often involving knives which they would use without any shred of concern.

Although the situation at rugby league games was never as bad as it had been at soccer in the 1970s, there were often outbursts of trouble. Sometimes they might break out near the Black Bull, the nearest pub to the Saints ground. Other times in Wigan they could kick off in pubs on Wallgate or Standishgate, both quite close to Wigan's Central Park stadium.

On odd occasions a group of lads would wait for a solitary fan or maybe a group of younger fans of the away team. Sometimes those who had started the fighting did not have any intention of even going to the game; they just wanted to fight.

Back at work, the weeks rolled by. Soon it would be time for the works shutdown, two weeks in which essential maintenance work would be carried. Normally it would be a time when the power to the copper refinery would be turned off and a thorough investigation of its lining made. No need for that this year. This once essential part of the factory had been knocked down six months earlier. Still there were many other pieces of equipment that only ever stopped running during a fortnight in the summer.

In its heyday there had been 50 men employed in the works maintenance shop: electricians, plumbers, motor rewinders, fitters, turners, welders, bricklayers, joiners, labourers. That had been in the days when the department had been run by Jock Walsh, an absolute law unto himself, but a fine organiser, a man who could do everything that any of his men could do and better. He was an essential part of the successful running of the whole factory. The management had always known that and Jock also knew that they knew that. As a result he always got what he wanted. That is why he had his own machine shop, drawing office, two draughtsmen and a tracer, his own wages department and his own buyer.

He had also been prepared to stand up to Basil Wilkinson when he was in charge and had even said 'no' to a request from Basil's father, Joshua Albert George Wilkinson. Now Jock was just one of many employees who were no longer alive. Too much whisky in the pub on his last day in work had led to him stumbling into the kerb outside and being run over by a reversing lorry.

After that and with all the changes that had gone on since, works maintenance was now down to 10 people, two of whom were on long-term sick and one on jury service. In the past the works maintenance would have started on the Saturday morning, but not this year. They started at eight on Monday morning and would not even be required to work overtime, something that had never been known before.

Modern technology is so good; it doesn't need the same degree of maintenance for machines that was needed in the past – that was one explanation given. The company was saving money by not doing as much as they should do was the other.

The unspoken explanation and one that was feared by many, was the place would be closed by the time they all returned a fortnight later. On Friday evening in ASDA, Alan had bumped into Jim, one of the labourers. In Jim's words: "I've been all over the place fitting new fluorescents, cleaning windows, carting rubbish to the incinerator and helping the fitters. I've been in the new rolling mill and nobody has been in there which is highly unusual, because there's always been plenty of maintenance there. I can honestly say that there has been nothing hammered, welded, soldered, rewired or painted. In fact the only thing that's been screwed was Lillian, who works for Stan Wright and that was all over in five minutes in the library."

Jim never missed a trick, though what Lillian was doing there when she was supposed to be at Blackpool on holiday was anybody's guess.

But when everybody returned a fortnight later, no major announcement was forthcoming. It looked like business as usual. In the past draughtsmen would have been found during the works shutdown on holiday all over the world. But this year there was the thought in many people's minds that the factory could easily go the way of many of the other factories in the town and get closed down. And if it did close there would be little alternative employment for all those who were now aged over 40.

For their holiday, Alan and Thelma decided to stay at home and have days out riding around on the bus or the train to places, they hadn't been to for ages: the Wirral, where Alan had had his first sight of the sea, something which had frightened him enormously when he was five years old, Southport where you had to walk a long way before you could actually see the sea, Billinge Lump, Rivington Pike and Bury on a Wednesday to walk round its famous market and sample the local delicacy, black pudding.

Back at work after this little 'holiday', the big thing to look forward to was the start of the 1993–94 rugby season. Saints' first three games were Widnes in a friendly at Naughton Park followed by Hull Kingston Rovers away and then Salford at home, the second league match being on a Wednesday night.

There was now something to look forward to each Monday morning. That was when Alan, Cliff and Colin met to discuss how the work for the coming week had to be organised. It would also include planning longer term for any necessary site visits. Usually it would finish with an analysis of what had happened at the

169

match on the previous day, what had happened in town on the Saturday night and any scandal or gossip doing the rounds.

Since his second visit to Portugal, Alan had hardly been out of the office. In Shaun's words, "Greeno can't be much of a manager, if he can't manage to get out on site anymore". So it came as a pleasant surprise when Mr Johnson told him on Friday morning that he wanted Alan to go to London on Tuesday for a few days. This was necessary because of a number of problems had arisen at three electricity sub stations where the outside contracts division had recently installed some Swedish electronic equipment.

As a result, the following Monday meeting had to arrange how things would be dealt with in his absence. When Alan told them that he had been booked into a hotel in Finsbury Park, Cliff's immediate suggestion was that he should go and visit Les Earnshaw, something that Alan had already arranged. As a result it looked like being an interesting week. During the day he would be spending time with a National Grid engineer that he knew well, meeting Les would take up one evening and if he couldn't find other things to do in London, well it would be a poor show.

All the technical business associated with his visit went smoothly enough. The fault lay with the equipment that had been installed, not with its installation and a couple of orders for new work were promised. However, his visit to see Les in his flat in Islington was not quite what he had expected. When Les was an apprentice, he had generally behaved as though he was still at school. Until he was about 30, he had behaved as though he was still an apprentice. From then on he behaved as though he was 10 years younger than what his birth certificate indicated. Now he was turned 70 and was behaving like it. Alan thought later that it was as if he had spent the evening with Les's father, not that Alan had seen Les's father, but then neither had Les. This Alan had discovered during the course of the evening in his flat when Les had started talking about his background.

Les had been born in Ashurst Victoria hospital on Christmas Day 1921. His mother had also given birth to a child on Christmas Day 1921 in the same ward of the same hospital. Telling that to most people would make them say that that was obvious, but sometimes fact can be stranger than fiction. The baby that had been born to Les's 'mother' had died within the hour. The person who had given birth to Les, did not want him. It was because she

170

was a rich woman who had better things to do with her life and when she heard what had happened to Mrs Earnshaw, she said that she could have her baby. In this way Les had acquired his parents, something that he had discovered much later in life.

He had grown up in Gillarsfield as an only child, although in a family that included half a dozen uncles and aunties and a score of cousins. His childhood had been no different than most other children in his street, in Gillarsfield and in Ashurst. He had spent most of his early life playing football, rugby, cricket and stonies, trainspotting and as he had grown into his teenage years being interested in girls and having the usual scrapes and brushes with the law. After spending six years in the Army from 1940 and 1945, he had come home and started working as a draughtsman.

When Alan had first met him in the drawing office, he was a pretty fit sort of a bloke and quite tough as well. Now, 30 years later, he looked his age. The meal he had prepared was a very basic one, scouse made with corned beef, potatoes, carrots and onions followed by golden syrup pudding with custard. That was probably a typical meal for Les, except when he was invited to dine at Claridge's or the Ritz when meeting a film mogul wanting Les to sign a multi-million pound contract that would enable Hollywood or Elstree studios to turn his latest novel into a film.

It was hard to discover whether Les was enjoying his time living in London. Being there made it easier for him to be a grandfather for both his daughter and his son lived fairly near and each had children, none of whom could understand much of what Les said to them because of his broad Ashurst accent. His wife had died a few months earlier and so Stanley and Mavis and their children were all that were left of his family.

Les talked about some of the famous people who he had once met. It all stemmed from his appearance on television with David Frost. Somehow and for some time he claimed that he had been in a circle of people that included Sandie Shaw, Marianne Faithful, Tom Jones, Dusty Springfield and Gerry Marsden, who used to be a draughtsman at the Automatic in Edge Lane in Liverpool, he always hastened to add.

Les had now developed that annoying habit of talking about things that he had already told the person he was with, before. But the way he told them could still make those in his company laugh again.

He spoke again about the big party that had once been held in

171

the Manor Arms to celebrate the return of Alan's daughter Rebecca after she had gone missing on Mount Everest.

"Eh, do you remember that bit about the Scottish football results that I made up, it was a belter, wasn't it" and then repeating what he had said some 20 years earlier, he carried on:
"Forfar Four, Stenhousemuir More
Cowdenbeath Two, Bullenbeath Three
Ayr One, Wind and Water None
Hearts Two, Livers Two
Alloa Two, Goodbyea Two
East Fife One, West Fife One
North Fife One, South Fife One
Third Lanark Three, Fourth Lanark Four
Academicals Two, Dumbarton School of Hard Knocks Seven
Stirling Albion Three, Stirling Moss Nil"

As he was talking, Alan looked behind him. Les hadn't remembered all he had just said, it was written up and in a picture frame on the wall. Les had just been reading it out loud. Then, obviously from memory, he carried on:

"There was one cricket match today and it finished up Lancashire 987 for one declared, Yorkshire 12 all out and 26 for nine. Rain stopped play match drawn. Two points each."

"Well that brought back a few memories, Les."

"How is Rebecca now, I take it she didn't run away again."

"She's fine, in fact she is living here as well, with her boyfriend at New Cross, so I'm going there for my tea tomorrow."

"And how's Thelma?"

So then Alan told him about the accident outside the hospital, the small bottle of red paint that had been mistaken for blood and how she was recovering nicely and sent her regards. He then asked Les if he was doing much writing. He was, it was material for *Brookside* and *The Bill*.

"I've got a good contact at ITV, so I've got a few ideas I'm working on."

Then Alan asked him if he had many mates in London. Les shook his head: "Not really. It's not like it used to be at Wilkinson's or in Ashurst. Most folk down here seem to be only concerned with making money, looking after number one and rushing around. I sometimes wonder if I'd be better off going back to where I was brought up."

"Well you can't go back to your old house. That got knocked down as part of the Ashurst Rejuvenation Plan a month ago."

Then Alan went on to say that things were not like how they used to be in Ashurst either: "At work everything is rush, rush, rush, there's little time for any humour, there's no tea lady, no tea breaks and no canteen either, well not a proper one. Another thing that has changed as well is the distance folk travel to work. It's not too bad in our section, but among the mechanical lads, one comes from Rochdale, another from Blackpool and two share a car from Port Sunlight. And my next door neighbour who used to work at Pilks has just got a job in Stockport for three months."

Then he went on tell Les about their former tea girl Hazel, her time in Japan and Australia, travelling back through South America and now a teacher at Ashurst Comprehensive. He also told him of her talk in the library about the Inca civilisation, her command of English and how she had never lost her Ashurst accent.

"She hasn't got a proper Ashurst accent. She's from Hyde Bank, they've got their own language up there. They always did have, not like me."

And for the next half hour or so Les used as many old fashioned phrases and sayings that he could think off to someone who had some appreciation of what he was talking about. And for the rest of the evening it was just like the old Les again, the one who had also once entertained the whole country for an hour when he had been on the television with David Frost

Alan didn't stay much longer. It had been a pleasant couple of hours with an old mate, but it clearly wasn't the Les he had once known. As he travelled on the tube to his hotel, he also decided that old age was something else he didn't agree with.

He travelled back home on the Saturday morning enabling him to go to the match on the Sunday afternoon It was the first match of the new season, Hull Kingston Rovers away. Not too good a start though as Saints lost by 14–10.

Not too good a journey home either, an accident on the M62 meant a long diversion which took them through Halifax and over the top of the Pennines and down through Lees, Oldham and Chadderton. But then in the good old days that was how everybody used to travel into Yorkshire and according to Charlie whenever he had done it, through six foot of snow, even in the months of September and October.

173

24. A ride on a donkey

"Sandra."

"Thelma."

A week earlier, Thelma had been watching a programme on television about apartheid in South Africa. As she watched the credits while waiting for the start of the 10 o'clock news she saw the name of one of those who had put the programme together. It was a familiar name, Sandra J. Beasley.

When Thelma had been living in the home in Cardiff, her best friend had been a girl called Sandra Beasley. Could it be the same person? Thelma often wondered what had happened to her. Sandra was older than her and was in a different class at school, but they had still been close at a time in life when, without loving parents to look after them, a good friend in life was so important. Then one fateful day Thelma had come home from school and discovered that Sandra had left. Where had she gone? Why had she not said goodbye? Why was the world so cruel?

Thelma rang the enquiries desk at the BBC in London, been given a number in Manchester to ring and left a message. And when asked who was calling, she had for the first time for a long time used her maiden name, the one by which Sandra would know her, Thelma Johnson. She had left her telephone number and her address, but had heard nothing. Perhaps Sandra now lived in South Africa, perhaps she hadn't received the message, perhaps it was a different Sandra and worst of all perhaps she didn't want to renew a friendship. Then suddenly she was here stood on her doorstep, a woman who looked as though she had done well for herself, with style, well dressed and attractive.

It looked as though Sandra had been drinking, but that didn't matter. She was here and if she was a little bit inebriated, it didn't matter. Thelma brought her into the living room and asked her if she wanted a cup of tea or a glass of wine. Sandra indicated the latter, she almost seemed a little nervous. As soon as they were sat down and had exchanged a few pleasantries, Thelma started off by telling Sandra what had happened after Sandra had left the home, and how she had come finally come to live in Ashurst.

Then it was Sandra's turn. She began by saying how she had always felt bad about the way she had had to leave the home. Unlike Thelma, Sandra had one parent, her father who was in the

Army. One day he had appeared in his uniform and taken her with him, first to London where she lived with his parents and then they had emigrated to Brisbane where her new mother came from. By the time she was 20, she had got married, moved to Sydney and started working in the media.

It was something that had taken her all over the world and when her marriage broke down, Sandra had returned to London and for the last 12 months had been working in Manchester for the BBC.

They talked at length about what it had been like in that sad period in their lives, about some of the other girls who had lived there, the old battle axe who had been in charge for so long and Mrs Morgan, who had taken over, and how much things had become better virtually overnight.

At this point Alan walked in from work, was introduced and Sandra was invited to stay for a meal. Their discussion moved on to Sandra's current situation. She was now living in Worsley with her partner, who seemed a bit of a shady character with interests in property. Thelma told her about Rebecca and Robert and then asked her friend if she had any children.

"No, being a mother was not something that I really fancied, certainly not with my first husband. He was not someone who would have been any help to with children. And now it's too late."

"I bet you would have made a good mother. You certainly looked after me, didn't you?"

Sandra smiled then turned to Alan and went on: "She must have been the smallest one there. She always seemed to get pushed out of the way and some of the others used to bully her or make fun of her because of her freckles. I remember one day there was a big fat one there, Joanna I think she was called. She was being her usual obnoxious self and making some nasty comments about Thelma's face. Thelma said to her that 'her freckles were where God had kissed her' and this Joanna had said 'no, it's where God had shit on you'."

Thelma nodded. She remembered it and why it was that Joanna always trying to make her life a misery. Then Sandra referred to another incident from the past: "I remember one summer day we were all taken down to the beach. We were each given a shilling to spend. Most of us spent it on ice cream or buying a bucket and spade, but you didn't. All you wanted to do was have a ride on a donkey. I remember watching you do it. You

175

sat on this donkey and the man walked you right up to the end of the beach, farther than anybody else and when you came back, I'll never forget that look on your face. You looked so happy, so content as though you didn't have a care in the world. It almost brought tears to my eyes seeing you like that. I still remember that day out. I remember you telling me on the bus back to Cardiff that when you were grown up you were going to buy a donkey. It must have made a big impression on you."

Thelma smiled sadly, she did remember those brief moments of complete happiness in her early years. Then she asked her long-lost friend when she had come back to England.

"It was in 1984. I remember because the miners' strike had only just started. England was nothing like what I thought it would be. Everyday in the papers I kept reading about how they were trying to take over the country, bring down the government, roaming round everywhere with their flying pickets and stopping decent people going to work.

"It was just as bad on television, I didn't feel safe. I think I might have gone back to Sydney if I had had the money. I'm glad Mrs Thatcher stood firm. How any decent person could have agreed with what the miners did must have been mad. Don't you think so? I was living at Watford, so it wasn't too bad there, but it must have been bad up here. Were you frightened of them?"

"Well, actually Sandra, we were in a miners' support group. We helped collect money to help feed them and their families. The papers always put one side of the story. They were all told what to print by the government. The actual reality was quite different."

And for the next hour or so Sandra heard a different side to what had been one of the most dramatic period in Britain's post war history, one that had seen the planned decimation of the country's mining industry, unemployment rising to well over two million and the closure of many factories in and around Ashurst.

Perhaps one thing that made the biggest impression on her was when Thelma told her about the husband of her friend from Astley. When the strike started he was a well-built 15 stone man, big enough to prop for Hemsley Hornets. By the time the strike was over he had lost his job and was down to 11 stone due to not eating enough combined with the financial worry and stress.

In the end Sandra stayed the night. She only had to be back in Manchester at midday and her partner was away at the moment in London, no doubt doing some big property deal. Whatever he did no longer seemed to bother her that much.

"As long as I feed his tropical fish when he's away and he has his leather once a week, he is happy enough. What he does when he's away, and who he does it with, I'm no longer bothered. We've got a big house in Worsley, he pays the bills and when he's away I sometimes stay out all night as well, but then what the eye doesn't see, the heart doesn't grieve over, does it?"

They promised to keep in touch, although they couldn't meet up again for a while because Sandra's next BBC assignment was in Alaska where she would be living for the next three months.

As they were eating their meal the following evening, and after Alan had told her what had happened at work that day, he asked what Sandra had said about her riding on that donkey.

"We were all given a shilling to spend and the donkey ride was three pence. I gave the man sixpence and asked if I could have two rides. 'You can have a long ride for three pence', he told me. 'How about that?' And so he took me much further than he normally went. Maybe he felt sorry for me, but I know I felt so happy sat on that donkey. All my cares seemed to disappear. It wasn't that bad in the home, it just wasn't very nice and I all I wanted was to have a mum and a dad like nearly everybody else at school. But at least I had Sandra as a friend and then a few weeks later she left without even saying goodbye."

At this point there was a knock on the door. It was Howard, who had come to borrow an electric drill. He hadn't met Thelma before so was introduced and easily convinced to have a cup of tea and a couple of scones that she had baked that afternoon.

As they talked he looked around the room at the photographs on the wall and then surprised them both when he pointed at one and said: "That's my great grandfather."

It was a photograph of the Jarrow Marchers on the road to London in the 1930s protesting about the high unemployment in the town and trying to get something done about it. The man that Howard had pointed to was at the front of the march, playing a mouth organ. They waited for him to continue.

"I don't know much about him, other than he was a welder and had worked in the ship yard at Wallsend. He went with them as far as Leicester and then he fell ill. Luckily there was a couple there who let him lodge with them for a while. They must have had some good connections as well as a good heart because they even helped him find a job when he got better."

177

"I didn't know you were a Geordie, Howard."

"I'm not. My granddad was in the RAF during the war and after he was demobbed he got a job with Hawker Siddeley and they moved to Manchester and stayed there until he retired. So that's how I came to be brought up in Eccles."

"Have you still got any relatives up there?"

"I don't think so. My granddad told me that most of our family died, got killed in the war or emigrated after the war. I know that a cousin went to Australia although I've lost touch with him, unfortunately."

"You've never mentioned any of this at work, have you? You would have had a very interested audience."

"Maybe I would have, but I couldn't afford to risk it. The last two places I'd worked at, I'd been sacked for being too active in the union. I was the office committee chairman at one place and at the other I just spoke out of turn. I decided to keep my trap shut here. I was too much in debt when I first started."

Then he continued: "Do you know those lads on that march, all they wanted to do was raise some awareness about their plight and try and talk to Stanley Baldwin and do you know what, he didn't even have the common decency to meet them after they had walked all that way.

"Mind you even if he had seen them he wouldn't have done anything for them. I know one thing a few weeks later, the Ministry of Labour decided to merge the Jarrow Labour Exchange with the Hebburn Labour Exchange. The unemployment in Jarrow was over 70 percent but Hebburn was fairly prosperous in comparison. The result was that the unemployment figure fell to 40 percent. So that was how the government dealt with the problem. Talk about massaging the figures. They did it even more than this lot now."

He then went on tell them about the family that he had married into. His surname was Smith and by a strange coincidence that was his wife's maiden name as well. So not only had that not changed for her on getting married, the pair of them were now living in the house that Sally had been brought up in Winwick Avenue in Astley. The Smith family had been involved in mining for generations. Her father had worked at Old Benton and then Beswick, her eldest brother had been at Bold and her second brother at Sutton Manor. In addition, her younger sister had worked in the NCB offices at Gillarsfield. Sally had been the odd one out, she had been a nurse first at Peasley Cross Hospital and then at Victoria Hospital, two places though that often had to look after miners who had been injured at work.

"She'll be going into hospital herself soon. She's expecting our second child. One thing is for sure, if he's a lad he'll never get the opportunity to dig coal, will he. In fact I don't think there will be one bit of evidence around here to show that there once was such a thing as a mining industry."

He stayed at least an hour. Sally would be all right, it was the night her mother called round and as he and her never saw eye-to- eye on most matters, it was better if he was out of the way.

Shortly after he had left, Thelma made a comment that Alan knew she would make: "I suppose the next thing you will pick up and read the first chapter of will be a book about the Jarrow March."

His ability to start reading with good intentions something that was in his environment was well known in the Greenall household.

"Probably, I've just finished reading *War and Piece Work*, so I might just start tomorrow in the dinner hour."

Then he went on to make the obvious point that history and particularly labour movement history was much more interesting when you had relatives involved in it or knew of people who had taken part, just like Howard's great grandfather. He had coincidentally recently read a book about the Jarrow March and knew a bit about its background and significance.

"I'll tell you a couple of things that I read in that book about things that happened on that march. One of the marchers hadn't eaten meat for ages, neither had any of his family back home in Jarrow. One day he took some off his plate, put it into an envelope and posted it to them.

"When they were going through Harrogate, another young one lad was stopped by what looked like a right toff. She forced open his hand and put half a crown in it. When they went through Barnsley where the unemployment was almost as bad, the local people came out and did what they could for them, a case of those who had little helping those who had even less. And Stanley Baldwin wouldn't even agree to meet them.

"No doubt if they had come through Ashurst they would have had a similar response. I remember my granny telling me what it was like here at that time. She told me that my dad was out of work for over two years. It was a good job my granddad and uncle Eric managed to hold onto their jobs, I'm sure that's how all our family must have managed to survive."

"And no doubt some well heeled politician in London would have said that it was still a price worth paying. You know the more things change, the more they remain the same. There's still us and them."

"Do you think it'll ever change, Alan?"

"I'd like to think it will, but I sometimes wonder."

Then he went on to ask his wife a question, one that indicated that even if the powers that be were firmly in control, they couldn't prevent people in places like Ashurst continuing the tradition in times of adversity of bringing humour into much of what they said and did.

"By the way, have you been tidying up in the attic?"

"Not recently, why?"

"I can't find my machine gun. Have you seen it anywhere?"

25. Scott's last day

It was Scott's last day in the drawing office. He came into work wearing his oldest clothes because he knew that some trickery would have been organised to send him off in style. He had already taken home most of his personal stuff just in case somebody used araldite to prevent the drawers in his desk being opened. At 10am he went to see the apprentice training officer and when he returned there was a large sheet of paper taped over his monitor:

Four things Scott never understood
The difference between first angle and third angle.
Scales
Ohm's Law
Electricity

Four things Scott never did
Buy a round in the Eagle
Get a drawing right first time
Overthrow the government.
Go out with Clare

Scott looked at the sheet, and said: "Wrong, wrong, wrong, wrong, wrong, wrong, right, wrong."
"When did you go out with Clare?"
"About a month ago, but I never told any of you."
"Why not?"
"Because I had just started going out with a girl from Astley and I didn't want her to find out."
"How did you manage it? Where did you take her?"
"I took her to bed."
"He was a dreamer when he came here, he's been a dreamer all the time he's been here and he's still a dreamer on his last day."
"Well at least he's been consistent."
"Do you want to hear about it or not?"
"Go on then and don't forget this is how we'll remember you because it won't be for any of your drawings."
"That bucket he drew for the oil handling plant at Eggborough

was quite good."

"Oh aye, but it was only a NTS drawing."

"NTS?"

"Not to scale."

"Go on then, tell us."

Over the last few weeks Scott had begun to get himself involved in the political life of the nation. It was a mainly as a result of what the government was doing, his dad having been made redundant and his uncle going on short time. It was at the same time that he came under the influence of Red Roy, the leader of the Gillarsfield Revolutionary United Brigade, otherwise known as GRUB. As a result Scott was now seen every Saturday morning outside Ashurst Library selling the magazine, *The Spark*, which was a good name for an organisation that included four unemployed electricians among its members.

On his first day there Clare, who used to work in the wages department had walked past. It was the first time he had seen her since she had left the firm in January. While she had been there getting a date with her had become his main reason for living, even though she was three years older than him.

She bought a copy of *The Spark* and chatted to him for a while. Then to his complete surprise and amazement, she had invited him to a party she was having that night. For the next six hours he could not believe his good fortune, but finally 7.30 arrived and found him walking down Carlton Lane to what he assumed was her parent's house. However, it didn't look as if it would be for much longer because there was a 'For Sale' board in the front garden.

She took him into the living room where most of the furniture was covered with large white sheets. She poured him a glass of beer and asked him about what GRUB stood for and whether they believed that women should be treated with respect and as equal partners in the grand scheme of things.

Of course, Scott didn't know much about all that GRUB really stood for, but that didn't really seem to matter for she just rambled on as he did also. Finally and now more than a little inebriated she told him she was going to ask him one final question. Was this strange party now coming to the end?

Actually the party wasn't ending. In fact it was only just beginning. And it wasn't one final question it was two final questions.

"Would you like me to show you round the house?" and with that she took him first into the cellar, full of bottles of wine he noted, then into an enormous kitchen and two other large downstairs rooms.

By now holding hands, they went upstairs, where she showed him three bedrooms, all with furniture covered with white sheets and then took him into what must have been her parent's bedroom, at the centre of which was a large four poster bed with curtains around it. Then came her second question and what a memorable one it was: "Will your mum be worried if you stay out all night?

It was here where the strangest party he had ever been to really begin. It also was one that had a bizarre end to it two days later. After they had eaten breakfast, she had told him she was going to Chester to see her cousin and would be staying there overnight.

"Come back on Monday after work if you want to. My parents won't be back for a while, but please keep this a secret. I daren't let my fiancée hear about what happened last night."

On Monday evening he walked back to the house. The 'For Sale' board was gone, but then she had told him that her parents were returning to Guildford and she was going to rent a flat in Warrington. But when he looked in the front room window all the furniture had gone too and so had Clare.

"So why didn't you tell us about it?" asked Alan.

It turned out that he had just started going out with another blonde, Ruth, the sister of one of his mates and didn't want her to find out about his little fling with Clare. But now it didn't matter as Ruth had decided Scott was not really a suitable companion for a young and enthusiastic Sunday school teacher.

As he was trying to convince them that all he had told them about Clare was true, Charlie walked into the office, looking very unhappy.

"I've got some bad news for you all. I've just been finished."

He went on to tell them what Mr Johnson had just said to him about a reallocation of company resources and no money in the budget for the work he was doing.

"So it looks like curtains for me."

"Aye and it was curtains for young Scott here all round the bed he was in with that magician Clare."

"I thought she was a wages clerk."

"No, she's a magician. She's just disappeared."

Shortly afterwards, Alan walked into the Eagle and Child. Benny was at the bar buying the ale for everybody. This was because on arriving home the previous night there was a cheque from Littlewood's waiting for him. It was obvious he hadn't heard the news about Charlie, who had gone straight into town.

Around their table the topic of conversation had been nuclear power, because Shaun had visited the Sellafield nuclear power plant on West Cumbrian coast the previous Friday.

"I wouldn't say that the people up there are worried, but most of them have still got Anderson shelters in the back garden."

"Maybe they don't know the war is over."

"We used to have an Anderson shelter. I wished we'd never knocked it down, I could have lived in it whenever the mother-in-law was due for a visit."

"Benny, did you know that Charlie has just been finished?" He didn't and to this bit of news, he also had something to add: "Johnson told me this morning not to send the van in for its annual service. It makes me wonder whether there are more things going on behind the scenes."

"There's always been things going on behind the scenes, ever since I've been here" said Alan.

"Johnson's going to Amsterdam next Monday" replied Benny, "and he's going to be there all week."

"I wouldn't be surprised if this is the end of the road for us" said Cliff.

"We'll have to join GRUB and fight the buggers. What do you think Scott?"

Back in work, they told Scott how much they would miss him. It was true and if he was going to become part of any new revolutionary government, it would be a good idea to keep in with him. As he finally left, he reminded them that if ever they wanted to see him again they would find him outside Ashurst Library on a Saturday morning.

"Unless there's some overtime going in the machine shop" laughed Alan

"Well I reckon all that will be going in the machine shop will be the machines and they'll only be going to a scrapyard."

Never was a statement made in jest by Cliff proved so right. The following Friday Mr Johnson returned from Amsterdam and spent most of the day on the phone. It was clear that something was afoot, but before anything could be learned from him, something of much greater significance occurred.

It began somewhat innocuously. Colin had made himself a cup of tea, left it on his reference table while he went to the print room and when he returned there was a bit of plaster floating in it. He thought little of it and said nothing. A few minutes a couple more bits of plaster dropped to the floor. This was followed by the appearance of a small crack in the outside wall of the ladies toilet late on Friday afternoon. Nobody thought much about it, as most attention was focussed on Mr Johnson and why he had hardly spoken to a soul since his return to Ashurst.

On Monday morning the crack in the wall of the ladies toilet was wide enough to peep through, more plaster had fallen from the ceiling, and the door into Alan's office wouldn't close. And by now reference to the old Southport Edge colliery, and what had happened in Smart Street when all the houses had had to be demolished, was crossing the minds of many of the staff.

Were some of those old miners who had once worked below in the bowels of the earth and then been killed and lay buried there, waking from their long sleep or just turning in their graves?

"This place was never as good as what it was cracked up to be" joked Cliff during the lunch hour. Famous last words because by the end of the day as he switched off his computer, the picture he had pinned to the wall behind it began to tear revealing another bit of evidence that the drawing office was now a dangerous place to work.

Everybody began to fear the worst. Most took their personal possessions home with them. It was a good job they did because when they arrived the following morning, it was considered no longer safe to enter the building.

"I'm really annoyed" said Colin. "I'd booked half a day's holiday this afternoon."

"I think I'll go home and crack open a bottle or two to celebrate" laughed Shaun.

"Well this place was never what it was cracked up to be." chipped in a rather disconsolate Howard, clearly fearing that he might soon be out of work again.

"Cliff cracked that one yesterday" said Scott. As he spoke Mr Johnson arrived on the scene and took Alan on one side.

"I've arranged for your men to work in the computer lab in Ashurst Technical College. Can you go down there now and see

Mr Mercer? We'll try and get a few of your computers down there this afternoon. We've got all the latest drawings backed up."

This had been perhaps one of the only decisions their former boss, Mr Taylor, had made, ensuring that every day's work was now stored on a hard drive at a disaster recovery company.

And so Alan found himself returning to the same room he had sat in 30 years earlier for the exam for his Higher National Certificate in Electrical Engineering. Soon, the top brass in Amsterdam made their long term plans known. They wished to keep a manufacturing presence in Ashurst, but one that was much smaller than had previously been the case. There would be a machine shop, assembly shop, wiring shop and the drawing office; along with the Outside Contracts Division which would continue to send engineers all over the world installing and commissioning machinery and equipment for the power generation industry.

As a result the work force was again reduced in number from its peak in the mid-1960s of around 8,000 people. Quite a few of those who were finished never worked again, some never worked again in engineering, some found work miles from Ashurst, some emigrated and a couple began earning their living in the most unexpected of ways.

Warrington Road, Aspinall Street and Mersey Street remained as before. The former was still the main road from Ashurst to Warrington, but the other two became roads to nowhere. It was a great shock for local people. Coal had helped make the town what it was, but it was the digging of the 'black gold' that had contributed to the demise of its largest place of work. Despite all this, life in Ashurst carried on. People were born, got married and died. Some worked each day and some didn't.

A few councillors got caught fiddling their expenses and others got away with it. Indeed, the goings on in the town hall caused increased attention and amusement.

The suspicions of corruption which had been around for a long time finally came to light a few weeks later. It happened when a chambermaid at the Hemsley Hotel walked into one of the upstairs rooms in order to clean it and had seen the chairman of the transport sub-committee in bed with the wife of the owner of the Hop Along Transport Company.

What a scoop for the soon-to-retire editor of the *Ashurst Reporter* to go out on: "Never a dull moment in Ashurst" his headline thundered "Not even at bed time".